THE MYSTERY DOWN UNDER

Two private detectives have a busman's holiday

Book #3 in the Quentin Cadbury Investigations

Christine McHaines

Published by The Book Folks

London, 2024

ISBN 978-1-80462-145-5

www.thebookfolks.com

THE MYSTERY DOWN UNDER is the third standalone cozy mystery novel in this series by Christine McHaines. Details about the other books can be found at the back.

Chapter One

November 2006

Quentin Cadbury's decision to visit Australia wasn't entirely influenced by the fact that someone had threatened to kill him.

Of course it wasn't, he told himself as the stewardess lingered, checking to see that his seat belt was fastened. He had been promising his parents he would go to see them since they'd emigrated two years before, and anyway he was due a holiday.

He looked across the aisle at Wanda, wishing they could have been seated together. Sadly, late bookings didn't come with that option. Wanda Merrydrew, his widowed travelling companion and partner in the detective agency they ran together in London, was blonde-haired and seductively attractive, with a stunning figure that belied her mature years. She had agreed to accompany him to Sydney, not least because, as Quentin had pointed out, his adversary could attempt to get to him through her.

He sat back in his seat, anticipation of the warm days ahead evoking excitement tinged with apprehension. The few days stopover in Hong Kong had been pleasant, but now he looked forward to seeing his sister, Shelagh, her Australian-born husband, Howard, and the nephew he had never seen. He longed to see his mother, with whom he had a close bond, but his father – his father was a different matter. Quentin could almost hear the gruff greeting, the frequent put-downs, though since learning of his recent success as a detective his father had at least stopped telling him to get a "proper job".

A disembodied voice told the cabin crew to prepare the aircraft for landing. He caught Wanda's eye and she smiled.

'Nearly there,' she called. 'Don't look so worried. We can relax now.'

Quentin released his grip on the armrest. 'I'm not worried.'

Through the window a panoramic view of Sydney came into sight and he gasped. The wide expanse of the harbour gleamed in the sunlight, its turquoise waters punctured by myriad boats. The black and grey steel arch of the harbour bridge contrasted against the azure of the sky, and the shell-like lines of the Opera House showed white at the edge of the city. Sydney was a cluster of buildings, a mixture of old and new, big and small, set like a pearl in its green and brown surroundings.

Yes, they were nearly there. Excitement rose in Quentin. At twenty-five he'd done a fair amount of travelling but he'd never been out of Europe, and as the Boeing 737 started its descent into Sydney airport he drew a deep breath. Australia at last. He'd heard so much about it and now he was here, Wanda with him, no detective agency, no case to work on, no danger. Bliss.

* * *

After his first colourful impression of the city the last thing Quentin expected to see in Hibiscus Crescent, the quiet suburban street in Roseville where his parents lived, was the flashing red and blue light of a police car; but there it was, outside a house a few yards from the corner. Since the emotional welcome from his mother, a short 'So you made it, my boy' from his father and then the drive from the airport, he had almost forgotten the reason for their hasty departure from the UK. The sight of the police car brought an unwelcome jolt of remembrance.

'What's going on?' his father barked, putting his foot on the brake.

Two policemen, peak-capped and short-sleeved, emerged from the house followed by a woman, distress showing on her face.

'It's Janet,' Quentin's mother said. 'Stop, Herbert.'

The car came to a halt and she got out. Feeling a rush of affection for her, Quentin's gaze followed her slight figure as she walked through the long front garden and approached the woman.

His father switched off the engine and went to join her. Quentin wound the window down but couldn't hear what was being said.

'This is a good start,' he said, turning to Wanda. Then, seeing how tired she looked, he asked, 'Did you get any sleep on the plane?'

Wanda shook her head. 'I can't sleep on planes.' She nodded towards the garden, where Quentin's mother seemed to be comforting the woman she'd called Janet. 'I hope nothing awful's happened. Nice houses, though, aren't they?'

'Yeah.' Quentin looked along the crescent. Most had front gardens planted with shrubs and bushes rather than bedding plants, presumably to withstand the heat and dry climate. It was a pleasant vista. Quentin could see why his parents had chosen to settle here.

A man appeared from the house. Quentin saw his father speak briefly to him, then he and his mother came back to the car, his father frowning and his mother looking upset.

'They've been burgled,' his mother told them. 'They've just got back from visiting their daughter. Someone broke in while they were away.'

'Another bloomin' break-in,' his father growled. 'It's getting bad, isn't it, Rosemary?'

Quentin noticed his mother's pale face as she nodded.

'Have there been others, then?' Wanda asked.

'Not in this road, but one round the corner and one near where Shelagh lives,' Quentin's father answered. 'Only good stuff taken, small things usually, money, jewellery, miniature paintings, anything worth a bob or two.'

Quentin struggled to recall how much a bob was worth, but gave it up. His father still refused to modify the language he'd grown up with.

His mother's quiet voice stopped his thoughts. 'They always target houses when people are away. It's as if they know exactly when they're going. The police can't seem to work out how.'

Quentin felt Wanda's purposeful look. He turned to meet her eyes. *Don't even think about it*, they warned. *We're on holiday, remember?*

'Anyway,' Rosemary went on, 'their son's on his way over. Let's get home, Herbert. Quentin and Wanda must be dying for a cup of tea.'

Tea, thought Quentin, wondering when he should produce the bottle of duty-free whisky he'd bought on the plane. Not yet. Tea first.

And tea it was.

Chapter Two

Within two days of their arrival, Quentin had recovered from his jet lag, explored the local area, enjoyed a reunion with his sister, Shelagh, been introduced to neighbours and become reacquainted with his mother's cooking. She'd obviously taken great pains to make what she recalled were his favourite dishes, and although his tastes had changed somewhat, he showed his appreciation by clearing his plate and praising her efforts.

On the third day, Sunday, he and Wanda were in Shelagh's garden looking forward to a lunchtime barbecue. Shelagh sat with them while her husband, Howard, busied himself with preparations. His brother-in-law was as easy going and good natured as Quentin remembered from when they'd met in England. A big, muscular man with brown eyes and close-cropped dark hair, he was the type of person everyone got on with, even, Quentin was surprised to see, the domineering, bullish man Quentin called "Father".

Shelagh, older than Quentin by five years and clearly superior to him in their father's eyes, had apparently been forgiven for not marrying into the higher echelons of British society and settling for a commoner from the colonies. The fact that Howard was well set up in the real-estate business and that his grandfather had served in the war probably helped.

'Play again, Auntie Wanda.' Michael, Shelagh and Howard's four-year-old son, plonked a ball on Wanda's lap. Wanda stood and obligingly threw the ball across the garden, then pretended to lose the race to retrieve it.

'Do you mind him calling you auntie?' Shelagh asked when Michael had tired of playing ball and gone to dig in the sandpit. 'It seems easier for you two to be Uncle Quentin and Auntie Wanda.'

'Of course I don't mind,' Wanda said. 'I've got two nieces, so I'm used to being an auntie.'

Quentin gazed at Wanda, her fair hair ruffled by the breeze and her face pink from running. After the excitement of their last case and the threats they'd received, he hadn't had time to dwell on how lovely she was.

'I wouldn't mind being an auntie,' Shelagh admitted, and for a moment Quentin thought she was hinting that it was time he provided her with a niece or nephew. She had known, without being told, that he and Wanda were more

than just business partners, but surely she didn't think…
He stiffened, then relaxed when she continued, 'It's got to
be easier than being a mother.'

'Bit late for that now, with number two on the way.'
Quentin indicated her swollen belly. She looked different
from how Quentin remembered her. Of course he'd never
seen her pregnant, but he'd forgotten how tall she was, and
with her brown hair bleached by the sun she didn't look
much like the sister who'd left England four years before.
Her eyes were the same, though, long eyelashes
surrounding her caramel-coloured eyes, inherited from
their mother like his own. Apart from that, Quentin, with
his lean good looks and the heart-shaped mole by his right
ear, looked nothing like her.

'Oh, I wouldn't be without Michael or this bump,'
Shelagh said. 'It's just, you know, it's tricky with the salon
as well.'

'You don't have to run the salon,' Howard called as he
emerged from the house with a tray of sausages and steaks.
'You can get a manager in. You'll have to let Dina take
over when the baby comes anyway.'

Shelagh sighed. 'I know, but you have to keep your
finger on the pulse. Still, I expect Mum will do her bit, but
looking after two isn't the same as looking after one.
Michael will be in kindergarten next year, so that will help.'

Quentin tried to imagine his mild-mannered, delicate-
looking mother heating bottles and changing nappies, or
worse, dealing with childhood tantrums. It didn't fit with the
image she presented, yet he knew, better than anyone, that
she was much stronger and more resilient than she seemed.

'You've got a lovely house, Shelagh,' Wanda said.

Quentin followed her gaze. One of the more modern
houses in Sydney, Shelagh's was bigger than his parents'
but built on similar lines, double-storeyed with four
bedrooms, two bathrooms, a huge lounge and a kitchen-
diner as well as a basement recreation room. The patio at
the back gave out onto the lawn, currently more brown

than green due to the lack of rainfall, and it also sported a pool, which his parents' property lacked.

'It makes our houses seem tiny, doesn't it, Quentin?' Wanda said.

'Yes,' Quentin agreed, thinking of his two-up-two-down terraced house in Greenwich. 'I like my house, though. Warm, convenient and low maintenance.'

'There's something to be said for that,' Shelagh told him. 'Something always needs doing here. Still, it's nice here, or at least it was until recently.'

'You mean the break-ins?' Wanda asked.

'Yes. We've never had any problems before, but two people we know have been burgled, and now there's the people near Mum and Dad. We're thinking of getting an alarm. Not that we've got anything really valuable, only my pearls. They came from Howard's grandmother. They're worth quite a bit. I'm frightened to wear them in case I lose them, family heirloom and all that.'

Wanda curled a lock of fair hair round her finger. 'Oh, it's a shame. We know what it's like to be burgled. Perhaps it's just a spate. With any luck whoever's doing it will be caught soon.'

'Let's hope so,' Shelagh said, 'or we might be putting you to work.'

Despite his longing for a complete break, Quentin felt his detective instinct rising.

'So how long are Mum and Dad going to be, did they say, Quentin?' Shelagh asked.

'Apparently Father had to go somewhere after they dropped us off. He said they'd be here by two.'

'Oh, *Father* did, did he?' Shelagh mocked. 'For goodness' sake, Quentin, can't you call him Dad?'

Quentin felt Wanda's enquiring gaze and shifted on his chair. 'I've never called him Dad, you know that. He told me to call him Father when I was a kid and he's never told me not to.'

'Stubborn as ever, then, eh? You're as bad as each other.'

'That's not fair! You know what it was like when we were kids. You stood up for me then.'

'I still do, but you're grown up now and he's better than he used to be, so get over it.'

Quentin bridled. It's all right for you, you were Miss Goody Two-Shoes, he wanted to say, but didn't. Because she was right. Especially now. Especially since he had established his own business and helped to solve two high profile crimes and put members of two international criminal rings in prison. The man behind both these organisations had escaped capture, but his father didn't know that. As far as Herbert Cadbury knew, the Metropolitan Police Force could not have made their arrests without him, and he had risen somewhat in his father's estimation.

'Why don't you try calling him Dad?' Wanda suggested. 'It wouldn't hurt. I'm sure he'd be pleased.'

I don't care if he's pleased or not, Quentin thought, his mouth set in a tight line. But, as ever, he thought of his mother. She had always borne the brunt of his father's anger when Quentin had crossed him.

'All right, I'll try.' After all, he reasoned silently, what did it matter what he called him?

Wanda leaned over and squeezed his arm, as though realizing that the decision had been hard to make.

'Good,' Shelagh said, 'and just in time.' She peeled away as the side gate opened and their parents arrived.

Oh, bloody hell, Quentin thought, I'll have to stick to it now I've said it.

Standing up he said, 'Sit here, Mum, next to Wanda.' Turning to his father he swallowed hard. 'I'll get you a chair… Dad,' he offered.

His father's reaction was lost in the confusion that followed. As Quentin started to move away, his foot caught in the leather strap of Wanda's handbag and he stumbled forward, knocking into a trolley supporting a jug of iced water. The jug slid off the trolley, sloshing water and ice cubes everywhere before thudding onto the ground. Little Michael immediately ran forward, grabbed one of the ice cubes, slipped on another, fell over and howled.

Shelagh sprang to swoop him up. 'Oh, Michael!'

'God, I'm sorry,' Quentin said when he'd regained his balance. He retrieved the jug, which miraculously hadn't shattered, though a spider's web of cracks had appeared.

When Michael had stopped crying and Shelagh was satisfied he wasn't hurt, she took the jug from Quentin.

'Never mind. I've got plenty of jugs. Are you all right?'

Quentin gave her a rueful grin. 'Wet, but that's all.'

'Sorry, Quentin,' Wanda said. 'I shouldn't have put my bag there. That strap is always getting in the way.'

'Are you sure you're all right, Quentin dear?' his mother asked, concern showing on her face.

Howard just laughed and Quentin's father frowned as Quentin brought him a fold-up chair and opened it.

Grunting his thanks, his father sat down, his heavy eyebrows showing dark in his red face. His bulk filled the chair, though Quentin could see that a diet of barbecued food and his mother's cooking hadn't increased his weight.

'Herbert, we've left the wine in the car.'

'I thought you picked it up, Rosemary,' Herbert growled. His whole demeanour reminded Quentin of a bear.

'I'll get it… Dad,' Quentin said, holding his hand out for the car keys. He saw the meaningful glance that passed between Wanda and Shelagh as he strode away. They couldn't say he wasn't trying.

When he returned, Howard was tending the barbecue and Shelagh had gone into the house to put some music on, while his mother was making sandcastles with Michael. His father was in conversation with Wanda. Quentin hovered a few yards off, listening.

'Shelagh's done well for herself,' Herbert was saying. 'She's got a first-class degree, you know, in mathematics. Could have been an analyst, a lecturer, anything. Still, she seems happy enough doing what she's doing, and she's making a good job of it.'

Honestly, Quentin thought, it's like he's apologising for Shelagh being a hairdresser and beauty therapist, never mind that she owns the damn place. Still, as well as marrying an Australian, it looks like she's been forgiven for doing something she enjoys, too.

'Quentin's done well, Mr Cadbury.' Wanda's voice was all honey. 'He's been invaluable in the business. Well, he is the business really. A really good detective.'

'Yes, yes, he seems to have found his forte at last. I expect you've had something to do with it, being his business partner – a woman of the world and all that, eh?'

Quentin's eyes widened when his father's hand patted Wanda's knee a little longer than was necessary. It seemed even a bigoted, ex-army officer like his father wasn't impervious to Wanda's charms.

Wanda's voice didn't falter and her expression didn't change.

'Let's just say we make a good team.' She swivelled round as though sensing Quentin behind them. 'Ah, Quentin, you've got the wine. Can you open it? I could do with a glass.'

After clearing his throat noisily, Herbert said, 'Yes, my boy, I'll have one too. Your mother will drive.'

Does she get a choice? Quentin wondered.

'I could drive while I'm here if you put me on your insurance,' he suggested.

His father looked at him doubtfully, as though considering whether he could entrust his precious Audi to someone as ham-fisted as Quentin.

'That's a good idea,' Wanda said. 'It would give you a break sometimes, Mr Cadbury, and Quentin's a good driver.'

'All right, my dear, I'll get that sorted,' Herbert conceded.

Feeling a beat of victory, Quentin went in search of a corkscrew. He rummaged in the kitchen drawer until he found one, and met Wanda on her way to the bathroom.

'Thanks for sticking up for me,' he whispered, aware that Shelagh was in the next room. 'You can twist him round your finger. So can Shelagh. I should have been a girl – we might have got on better.'

'You take it to heart too much,' Wanda replied, not bothering to whisper. 'Do you think he knows about us? That we're not just business partners, I mean.'

'Mum does, but either she hasn't told him or he's just being bloody-minded, giving us separate rooms.'

Wanda gave him a cool look. 'It doesn't matter. After all, we live next door to each other but we don't actually live together. How is he supposed to know if no one's told him? We don't exactly act like young lovers, do we?'

'No, but we could, you could–'

Wanda raised her hands. 'Don't start that again. I've told you, it's no good you shackling yourself to me. I'm nearly fifteen years older than you, and one day you'll meet someone your own age. That's how it should be.'

'No, it isn't. I don't want anyone else. I want you. I– I love you.'

'We can't always have what we want in life, Quentin. As for love, you'll love someone else more than me one day. You had enough girlfriends before you met me.'

That was true, Quentin realized, and he still had an eye for a pretty face, but no one he'd met was like Wanda.

'So... you don't love me at all, then?'

Her face softening, Wanda moved towards him and kissed him on the mouth. 'Of course I do. I love being with you, working with you, but what we've got won't last forever. Let's just enjoy it while we can.'

Quentin was about to protest, to offer a reason, any reason, why she should commit to a permanent relationship, when he heard a movement behind him. Swirling round, he saw Shelagh in the doorway holding a stack of CDs.

'She's right, you know,' she said, offering no apology for listening. 'But you should tell Dad. I mean, I'm sure he'll work it out sooner or later if he hasn't already, but you're staying in his house so it's only fair that he knows. I'll tell him. Get everything out in the open.'

'I can tell him myself. Like you said, sis, I'm grown up now, though I'm not sure about him being much better. What if he throws us out? You know how old fashioned he is. I don't want to upset Mum.'

Shelagh shook her head. 'He won't. Leave him to me.'

With that she walked back into the lounge and soon Scissor Sisters' *I Don't Feel Like Dancing* was booming through the house and into the garden.

'She's got her head screwed on, your sister,' Wanda observed, raising her voice over the music. 'She's got the measure of your father, and you, too.'

Quentin pulled a face. 'Yeah, she always was the sensible one. Brainy as well.'

'You've got brains. You don't always use them, but they're there, under that thick skull of yours.'

'Thanks a bunch.'

'Don't sulk. Are we having this wine or not?'

'Could do with a scotch.'

'No, Quentin. Too early. Wine or nothing.'

'Good,' said Shelagh, reappearing in the doorway. 'I'll get some glasses.'

Chapter Three

Whether Shelagh had said anything to his father or not Quentin couldn't determine, but when they were back at his parents' house he detected a subtle change in his father's attitude towards him. Several times he caught him staring at Wanda and then shifting his gaze to him, as if asking himself what this mature, sophisticated woman could possibly see in someone as inept as Quentin.

'Inept' was a word he'd often used to describe Quentin, along with 'unreliable' and 'bone idle'. As Quentin had pointed out equally as often, dropping out of university halfway through a law degree and only working when he actually needed the money didn't make him unreliable or idle. He couldn't argue with 'inept', though. 'Accident-prone', his mother called it. But he hadn't tracked down two international gangs accidentally, had he? True, he'd come across them accidentally, but it had taken a lot of hard work and considerable courage to go after the criminals and get them put away.

As for university, it wasn't unreliability or idleness that had made him leave. The loss of his best friend to a drug overdose had changed his outlook on life. Bowing to paternal pressure, Nathan had been unable to cope and turned to drugs. His death had had two major effects on Quentin – he'd left university shortly after and he hated drugs with a vengeance.

Now, his father appeared to be making an effort to keep his thoughts and opinions to himself, and Quentin vowed not to rise to any bait that was thrown at him. He could be here for a while, so it was up to him to make at least as much effort as his father. Dad, he corrected himself. It was hard to say after twenty-five years.

* * *

'Penny for your thoughts,' Wanda said when she found him gazing into space the next morning.

'They're not worth a penny,' he answered, shaking himself.

'You're thinking about the robberies, aren't you?'

Quentin hadn't been, but now he did. His parents, like other people in the neighbourhood, had increased the security of their home by fitting front and rear sensor lamps, bolts on the doors and additional locks on the windows.

'Don't want hooligans breaking in here,' his father said when he pointed out the extra measures later that day.

'I shouldn't think it was hooligans,' Quentin said, forgetting his vow not to contradict him. 'Hooligans would trash places, probably pinch anything they can get their hands on. You said only good stuff was stolen – jewellery, paintings sometimes, even some porcelain figures, Mum said. Not the kind of stuff kids or hooligans would know what to do with. This is a select area, where most people can afford nice things. These burglars, they–' He stopped at the impatient click of his father's tongue.

'Yes, yes, I realize that,' Herbert blustered. 'Any burglar's a hooligan to me. I'd like to get my hands on the blighters, I can tell you. Give them a good hiding.'

Quentin flinched, remembering the times he'd received a good hiding, though he had to admit he'd often deserved it.

'Let's try not to think about the break-ins,' Rosemary said. 'Everyone's been told to let the police know of anything further, and lots of people have had alarms fitted, so there's not much more we can do. Quentin and Wanda have come all this way to see us, so we should be entertaining them, not talking about our problems.'

The quavering of her voice and the nervous turn of her head undermined her brave words. Quentin put his arm round her shoulders.

'You don't need to entertain us, Mum. We're having a great time just being here in the sun. Howard wants me to go running with him next weekend, and I can always go for a run in the park, keep in practice.'

'Yes,' Wanda agreed, 'and tomorrow we're going into town to see Shelagh's salon, then do some sight-seeing. We can do a bit each day. We've got plenty of time.'

'I could do with going into town,' Rosemary said. 'I'll drive you down–'

'No you won't, Rosemary,' Quentin's father interrupted. 'You don't want to be driving in that traffic, and there's not enough parking space near the salon. They can get the bus, and you'll be going into town on Friday when you have your hair done. They don't want us tagging along with them all the time.'

Rosemary looked disappointed but said nothing. Guessing she didn't want to go against her husband in front of him and Wanda, Quentin bit back a sharp retort.

'The bus stops at the end of the road,' Herbert carried on. 'It goes right into the centre, but *I'll* take you down if you'd rather, my dear.'

For a moment Quentin saw himself waiting at the bus stop while Wanda whizzed by in his father's Audi, giving him a regal wave as she passed.

'That's sweet of you, Mr Cadbury,' Wanda replied, 'but we'll be quite all right on the bus, won't we, Quentin?'

'Of course. We often use the bus or underground in London. It's less hassle than driving.'

'Quite so. There you are, Rosemary, all settled.'

Putting on her sweetest smile Wanda said, 'That'll be fine, Mr Cadbury, but I'd like Rosemary to come with us some days. I need some new clothes. I'm sure she could show me the best places to shop, and she's got such good taste.'

Quentin gazed at Wanda, admiration swamping him. In a few sentences Wanda had put his father gently in his place and made his mother smile, a small triumphant smile.

'Thank you, Wanda. I'd love to come shopping with you.'

'Yes, well, I know you women like shopping. Rosemary goes with Shelagh sometimes, don't you, Rosemary?' Herbert said this as if he was trying to prove that his wife was allowed a life outside the house. He cleared his throat, coughed, then turned to Wanda again. 'Call me Herbert, my dear. No need to stand on ceremony.'

'Herbert,' said Wanda softly. 'What a good old English name. Strong.'

Turning away, Quentin hid the roll of his eyes. He knew Wanda disliked the name Herbert as much as he did.

The phone rang and Rosemary went to answer it. She came back into the lounge holding the portable handset and looking solemn.

'It's Ed Grayson. He's been burgled.'

Herbert looked startled. 'Edward? I thought he was in Brisbane.'

'He was, he's just got back and–' Rosemary hesitated before carrying on '–they've taken Joan's jewellery and… his army medals.'

Quentin saw his father's pale blue eyes bulge with anger.

'That's despicable!' he roared. 'Stealing a man's medals that he's risked life and limb for, and a dead woman's jewellery – it's– it's– despicable!'

'Has he called the police?' Quentin asked, wondering what difference it made if the owner was dead.

'Yes. They told him they'd be there as soon as they could. I said you'd call him back.' She passed the handset to her husband, but he waved it away.

'I'll go over there,' he said. 'Got to support a fellow officer.'

'Ed was a colonel in the army,' Rosemary explained when her husband had left the room. 'He and Joan came over here ten years ago, but Joan died last year. He invited your father to join the ex-servicemen's club not long after we came.'

Quentin whirled round and walked into the hallway, where his father was putting on his jacket. He couldn't remember ever seeing him go out without a shirt, tie and jacket in England, but it seemed the Australian summers had forced him to forego the tie and settle for open-necked shirts.

'I'll drive you, Fath– Dad. You said you'd sorted the insurance.'

Looking surprised, his father said, 'No need, my boy, it's not too far.'

'I'll come with you, then.'

'What for? You don't even know Edward.'

Wanda's low, sultry voice reached them from the doorway. 'I think what Quentin means, Herbert, is that he might spot something, some clue that might help to identify who these burglars are. He is a detective after all. I'll stay here with Rosemary.'

Quentin saw his father look from him to Wanda and back again. 'Well, I suppose it wouldn't hurt,' he said. 'If you're coming, my boy, you might as well drive.' He picked up the keys from the hallstand and passed them to Quentin.

'Right, let's go,' said Quentin.

They had agreed on a complete break. No agency, no case to work on, no danger. But how could he let the opportunity pass?

Chapter Four

The ten-minute drive took them through pleasant suburban streets lined with modern detached houses and bungalows, most sporting open-plan front gardens. Jacaranda trees, heavy with vibrant pink and orange blossom, filled the roads with colour.

Colonel Edward Grayson, OBE, was formerly a member of the Queen's Fusiliers, Quentin learned on the way, and had been mentioned in dispatches several times. A capital fellow and an efficient army officer who'd befriended an ex-serviceman and made him feel at home.

Quentin was relieved to find that Grayson was indeed a capital fellow. He was white-haired, slim, quietly spoken, and, apart from mentioning the loss of his medals, made no reference to his former rank or service. Despite his distress at the robbery there was an air of authority about him that made Quentin believe that men would respect and follow him. His manner was as far removed from his father's as anyone's could be.

'Edward,' Herbert boomed as soon as he was inside the house. 'Damned awful business. So sorry, old chap.'

Grayson nodded and looked at Quentin enquiringly.

'My boy, Quentin, over from the old country,' Herbert informed him.

Quentin extended his hand. 'Nice to meet you, Colonel Grayson.'

'Ed will do,' Grayson replied, shaking his hand. 'I'm not in the army now.'

Quentin saw the disapproval on his father's face, and wondered whether he should use "Mr" instead of "colonel" or "Ed". It seemed wrong to call someone nearly forty years his senior, whom he'd just met, by his Christian name. He'd only been calling his father "Dad" for a few days.

'The police are on their way,' Ed Grayson was saying. 'Not that I hold out much hope of them catching anyone. These people are damned clever.'

'Yes, well, that's why Quentin's here—' Herbert coughed, as if embarrassed to go on.

'I'm a private detective, Mr, er, Ed. I wondered if you'd like me to have a look round, see if I can spot anything to give us a clue.'

'A private detective? Now I think about it, I'm sure you've mentioned that, Herbert. In the papers, wasn't it, a big case in London? Your boy helped catch the ringleaders.'

Quentin raised his eyebrows. He couldn't recall his father saying anything positive about him to anyone before.

'Yes, yes,' his father blustered. 'They couldn't have done it without him. Helped the Met, you know, got a contact in Scotland Yard.'

Looking suitably impressed, Grayson said, 'Well, you're more than welcome to look around and ask any questions you like, except shouldn't we wait until the police have been?'

'Don't worry, Mr Gray– I mean Ed, I won't touch anything. I'll just look, at least until the police have finished.'

Grayson nodded. 'Feel free. Anything to catch these bastards. It's not what the things they've taken are worth. It's sentimental value. My wife's jewellery – I was going to pass that on to my granddaughter.'

'Must be worth a bit,' Herbert said. 'And your medals. Can't replace them.'

A pained look crossed Grayson's face. 'No. Still, at the end of the day they're only lumps of metal.'

Quentin looked at his father, expecting him to object to military medals being described as lumps of metal.

'Fetch a good price in the right market. Worth a lot to a collector. These people must know that,' his father said.

'Can you show me where the stolen items were kept?' Quentin asked. 'Were they in a safe?'

'No. We've never had a safe. Never felt the need.'

'No alarm?'

'No. We had one in England, when I was away on duty, for my wife's sake, but we never bothered here. There's a security lamp at the front, but these houses are well spaced out. A neighbour isn't likely to spot one going on in the middle of the night. And it's not as if the jewellery was worth millions, though it was insured for quite a few thousand. It was in a box in a drawer in Joan's dressing table. Stupid. I should have given it to my granddaughter after Joan died, but I didn't have the heart to part with it. This way. Mind the suitcase.'

Quentin stepped round the suitcase, apparently left in the hall when Grayson had first come in. His father moved forward as if to follow them, but Quentin stopped him.

'Better not, Fath– Dad. We don't want to contaminate the scene too much.'

'Pah!' said his father.

'He might be right, Herbert,' Grayson added. 'As far as I can make out, they didn't go in the kitchen. D'you mind waiting in there? I could do with some tea, and there's a bottle of whisky in the cupboard.'

Quentin followed Grayson into a medium-sized room. Obviously once a bedroom, there was a white dressing table against one wall, a stool and a low chair covered in grey velour. White fitted wardrobes lined the opposite wall, their doors open and their contents spilling out. A drawer in the dressing table had been pulled out and lay askew on the floor. The jewellery box sat open on the dressing table, empty apart from one earring and a keyring showing that the owner had given ten pints of blood.

'We couldn't find the other earring,' Grayson explained. 'I suppose one's no good to anyone, that's why they left it.'

'What about the medals?' Quentin asked.

'They were in my bedroom. I– I moved the bed in there when Joan died. Couldn't face seeing her things every time I woke up.'

Going into the next room, Grayson indicated an open drawer. 'They've taken the box as well. Probably get more for them if they sell them as a set.'

'Maybe,' Quentin agreed. 'It makes them easier to trace like that, so that's a bonus. The police can put a description out to anyone dealing in that sort of thing. That's what they'd do in England anyway.'

Careful not to touch anything, Quentin walked about the house. He looked at the windows, their panes, handles and sills, but there was nothing to see. The sliding patio doors at the back of the house looked shut but Quentin could see a narrow gap where they met. 'They got in through here,' he said. 'I—'

He stopped as the room was striped with intermittent flashes of blue and red, and he heard his father's voice calling, 'The police are here.'

'Right,' said Quentin. 'Better let them in, let them do their job. I'll have a proper look later, when they've gone, or I can come back tomorrow if you'd rather.'

'Whatever suits you,' Grayson said, and went to open the door.

* * *

While the police were making a note of all the relevant details, the senior constable eyed Quentin and his father enquiringly.

'My friend, Herbert Cadbury, and his son, Quentin,' Grayson explained. 'Quentin's a private detective.'

Quentin groaned inwardly, wishing he'd told Grayson not to mention his occupation. The senior constable raised his eyebrows and gave Quentin a sceptical look.

'A private dick, eh? I hope nothing's been touched.'

'No, Constable, everything's exactly how it was. I haven't touched a thing.'

'So we won't find your prints all over the place, then?'

'Possibly in the hall, but nowhere else.'

'That's right,' Grayson said. 'He was the one who insisted on nothing being touched.'

Apparently satisfied but still looking sceptical, the senior constable nodded. An hour and a half later, when all the usual procedures had been carried out, the senior constable said, 'That's all we can do at the moment, Mr Grayson—'

'It's Colonel Grayson, you know,' Herbert interrupted. 'Colonel.'

Grayson shot him a withering look. 'Herbert, I keep telling you, we're not in the army now. Carry on, Constable.'

'It's Senior Constable, actually,' the police officer said with a deliberate look at Quentin's father.

'Mr Grayson,' he continued, 'as I said, we'll do everything we can to catch these criminals and recover your stolen items. We'll question the neighbours, see if anyone noticed someone hanging around. These burglaries have been going on for six months, and this is the sixth break-in to an empty property, so they must have known the house was empty somehow. If anything else has been taken, something you haven't missed yet, or if you think of anything you haven't told us, let us know. You too, Mr Cadbury,' he added, directing his gaze towards Quentin.

'Don't worry, Senior Constable– sorry, I didn't catch your name?'

'Peterson.'

'Well, Senior Constable Peterson, I'm always happy to help the police.'

With a dismissive nod, Senior Constable Peterson repeated his reassurance to Grayson and advised him to ring his insurance company, which Grayson did as soon as the police had left.

'They're not sending anyone round,' he said when he'd ended the call. 'They've had several claims for similar thefts. I might not get the full value because I didn't have an alarm. The thing is I've been away three months. There was one break-in before I went, but if I'd known about all the others, I'd have had one installed.'

'Suppose I should,' Herbert said. 'I'll get on to them first thing tomorrow.'

'Good idea,' Quentin agreed, though he thought it unlikely the burglars would continue to target the area for much longer. With the amount of robberies that had already taken place, people would be on their guard and increase their security even more.

The doorbell rang. It was a neighbour who'd seen the police car and come to enquire if Grayson was all right. While they were talking, Quentin resumed his examination of the scene. He went round the house again but, apart from the bedrooms, nothing seemed to be out of place. Drawers and cupboards had been opened, their contents obviously rifled, but there was no damage to the property, nothing ruined like there had been when he'd been burgled. There were no tell-tale signs, no convenient clue for him to find. The sliding doors where entry had been gained led onto a paved patio, and there was a concrete path all the way round to the front of the house. There were no footprints to be found, no scraps of material caught on bushes, nothing to give him a lead. Bugger it, he thought. Looks like they've covered their tracks completely.

'There's not much to go on,' he told Grayson. 'What's bugging me is how did they know the house was empty? Who knew you would be away?'

Grayson spread his hands. 'Lots of people, I suppose. I mean, I was going for three months and I had the mail redirected to my daughter, so the post people would know. I told my immediate neighbours, and your father and Rosemary. No one else that I can think of. Did you find the whisky, Herbert?'

'Here you are, old chap. Already poured.'

While his father and Grayson sipped their whisky, Quentin drank tea and mulled things over. It was baffling. According to the police this was the sixth robbery in six months, all carried out on properties whose owners were away and only jewellery, cash or high-value items taken. That ruled out kids or opportunists.

His detective instinct aroused, Quentin felt frustrated. With no clue to get him started there wasn't much he could do, and anyway, Grayson hadn't asked him to investigate. Should he offer? Better not. He didn't want to appear presumptuous, and he didn't think his mother would appreciate him starting work on a case just a few days after he'd arrived. Oh well, he mused as they drove back to Hibiscus Crescent, he would just have to leave it to the police and get on with his holiday. At least Wanda would be pleased.

Wanda was pleased, and so was Quentin when his mother suggested that she and his father should take the casserole she'd cooked to Grayson's house to share with him.

'I rang and invited him here,' she said, 'but he says he doesn't feel like going out after all the upset. We'll pop over, make sure he eats something. We won't stay too long, and I'll put enough aside for you and Wanda. Help yourselves.'

'That's fine, Mum,' Quentin assured her. 'I'm sure he'll appreciate it. We'll be all right here.'

Later, when they'd gone, Wanda set the food on the table and poured some wine.

'It's a real mystery, then, these robberies. Do you think the thieves knew about the medals and the jewellery? I mean, if nothing else was taken they must have done, mustn't they? How on earth did they know?'

Quentin shrugged. 'Don't know,' he said between mouthfuls. 'They must be getting a tip-off from someone, unless they're just sussing out which houses are empty and taking pot luck.'

'That must be it,' Wanda said. 'They can't be getting tip-offs – who would know when all these different people were going away?'

'Don't know that either.'

Wanda speared a piece of chicken with her fork. 'Hmm. Curiouser and curiouser. Still it's not our problem, is it? I mean, I know you're itching to get your teeth into it, but we can't. We're in another country and the police have it in hand. It's not as if we've been asked to investigate. Lovely casserole, isn't it? Your mum's a good cook.'

'So are you.' Quentin gazed at her, his hunger forgotten. 'And that's not all you're good at.'

'Really? What else am I good at?'

Laying down his fork, Quentin reached across and took her free hand. 'You know damned well.'

Taking a slow, deliberate mouthful of food, Wanda looked at him from under her lashes.

She swallowed. 'In your parents' house? What if they come back early?'

'They won't be back yet. I don't care anyway.'

Wanda dabbed at her mouth with a napkin. 'I don't know.'

'I do.' Quentin pushed his plate away, stood up, walked round to her side of the table and held out his hand.

His pulse quickened when she smiled and said, 'Oh well, I suppose we are consenting adults.'

She rose to face him and he kissed her, tasting the sweetness of her lips and drinking in her heady perfume. Then he took her hand and led her upstairs.

Chapter Five

The following day Quentin and Wanda went into Sydney by bus, taking in as much of their surroundings as they could. As they drew nearer the city, the modern houses gave way to smaller, less spaced-out ones, reminding Quentin of the streets in Oxford where he'd grown up.

Shelagh's salon was situated in a row of shops north of the centre, with a florist's on one side and a Turkish barber's on the other. Above the glass front a bold sign spelled out "Shelagh's Chic Salon". The decor inside was all in pink and cream, and Quentin could see that Wanda liked the place immediately.

'It's so tasteful,' she said, looking appreciatively at the two glass chandeliers hanging from the ceiling. 'And there's a beauty room. I could do with a facial.'

Immediately Quentin imagined rows of women caked in mud, with slices of cucumber on their eyes. No such image greeted him when Shelagh showed them into the small treatment room, however.

'There's no one else booked in until after lunch,' she told them, 'but we're busy on the hairdressing side all day.'

The salon buzzed with activity. Shelagh led them into a staff room and made them coffee.

'Mum's coming in for a colour on Friday,' she said. 'I must say you did a good job of talking her into having it highlighted in London, Wanda. I'd been trying to persuade her to have it done for ages.' She stopped as a plump girl of about nineteen with short red hair came into the room.

'Can I take my break now, Shelagh?' Her accent was pure Australian and she spoke rather breathlessly, as though the effort of shampooing and blow-drying hair had worn her out. 'My next lady's not due for twenty minutes.'

'Yes, Linda, but don't be late back.'

'I won't. Thank you.' With only a nod at Quentin and Wanda, the girl left.

'Linda's only been here six months,' Shelagh explained. 'She's a bit flighty but she's a good hairdresser and the clients seem to like her. I've also got Suzy, she's coming on well. Then there's Dina, she's been here since we opened.'

'You've got a lovely place, Shelagh.'

'Thanks. It's a bit small now we've taken some of the space for the beauty room, but it's big enough for me to cope with at the moment.'

'Well, we'd better go and let you get on,' Wanda said.

On the way back through the salon Shelagh stopped briefly at a workstation to introduce them to Dina, the senior stylist, then again at the reception desk, where a dark-haired girl with huge brown eyes and bright lipstick was putting down the telephone.

'This is Suzy,' Shelagh said. 'Suzy, this is my brother Quentin, and this is Wanda.'

Wanda smiled. 'Hello, Suzy.'

Suzy smiled back, then switched her gaze to Quentin. Her eyes grew even bigger and she gave a small intake of breath when he said, 'Hi there, Suzy.'

For a moment she seemed to freeze. Then she said, 'Oh, em, hi. Shelagh's told us a lot about you.'

'Don't believe a word she says,' Quentin joked. 'I'm nowhere near as bad as she makes out.'

Suzy didn't seem to know how to answer that. She blushed, then said, 'Em, nice to meet you. And you,' she added, as if realizing that Wanda was still there.

The door opened and a woman came in. 'Here's my next lady,' Shelagh said. 'Bye then, you two. See you later.'

'Well,' Wanda said when they were outside, 'you made an impression there.'

'What do you mean?'

'You know very well – with Suzy. She couldn't take her eyes off you.'

Quentin smirked. 'I can't help women falling for my charms. After all, I'm young, fit, good looking–'

'All right, Romeo, that's enough. Colin called me this morning, by the way.'

Quentin clicked his tongue and beat back a stab of annoyance. Colin, a long-term friend of Wanda's and a serious contender for her affections, sometimes helped them with their detective work. 'On a voluntary basis only,' he'd stipulated when he'd agreed to help them. 'I don't want any money. The excitement and satisfaction are enough.'

Quentin was sure the excitement and satisfaction came from working with Wanda. Colin, he decided, would use any excuse to be near her, a fact that still caused Quentin to feel jealous, even after more than two years and Wanda's repeated assurances that Colin was, and would remain, only a friend.

'What did he want?'

'Just to see how we were, and let us know that Magpie and Mozart are OK. He's doing us a big favour, you know.'

'Yeah, I know,' Quentin said, somewhat mollified. 'So how are they? Mozart and Magpie I mean.'

'Mozart seems to be all right, but he's keeping Magpie indoors in case he tries to get back to your house. Cats do that sometimes.'

Quentin nodded, picturing the black and white cat he'd adopted not long after his move to Greenwich. Mozart, Wanda's white West Highland terrier, had known Colin for some time and had appeared quite happy to be left with him. He wondered why Wanda had mentioned Colin immediately after the conversation about Suzy. Was it just to make him jealous?

Dismissing the idea, he walked a few feet to the adjacent Turkish barber's and looked through the window. Two men, one young and the other older, were attending to their clients, while three more customers sat waiting.

'They look busy,' Wanda said, coming to join him.

'Yeah,' Quentin said. 'I knew someone who went to a Turkish barber regularly. He said they don't just cut hair – they shave you and do all sorts. I've always wanted to try one but I've never had the nerve.'

Wanda laughed. 'They don't dance round you like whirling dervishes or shave you with swords, you know. Why don't you book an appointment?'

Quentin wrinkled his nose. 'Maybe I will, when I need a haircut. So, what shall we do now? Where do you want to go first?'

'The Opera House,' Wanda said at once, reaffirming her love of opera. 'I'd love to see something. They might even be doing some Mozart. And they don't just do opera. They put on plays, too.'

'OK, we'll start there. Lead on, Macduff.'

* * *

Sydney's famous attractions did not disappoint. The city was buzzing. On the way to the Opera House they passed through streets lined with shops and department stores, their windows already dressed for the Christmas season. It seemed strange seeing festive decorations and tinselled trees sparkling with lights when the temperature was almost thirty-two degrees.

'Lovely shops,' Wanda said, stopping to admire a window display.

'Hmm,' Quentin agreed, hoping she wasn't going to spend the rest of the day shopping. If it got any hotter, though, he might be lured inside by the air conditioning. He was anxious to get nearer the water, where it might be cooler. 'Come on,' he said, guiding her along the busy pavement. 'You'll have plenty of time for shopping with Mum or Shelagh.'

When they'd visited the Opera House and taken a leaflet detailing forthcoming events, they wandered down to the harbour, where people queued for ferries to north Sydney and various destinations. They could see the bridge, an imposing sight in itself, but were surprised at the number of people actually walking across it. It was like watching ants on a garden path.

'We should go across there one day,' Quentin said. 'Think of the view.'

He checked his watch. Five o'clock. After a short discussion they decided to stay in the city, so Quentin rang his mother and said they would eat out, to which she promptly replied that she would keep the lasagne she'd made for the next day.

They walked to the waterfront, found a bar where they freshened up, claimed a table under an awning and ordered two beers. Wanda didn't normally drink beer, but Quentin guessed she'd want something long and cold today. He was right. She downed half her drink in one go.

The waterfront teemed with people, customers from bars and restaurants spilling out onto the pavements.

Cooking smells of all kinds filled the air, and the place hummed with activity. Backpackers and tourists in shorts and skimpy tops mingled with the general population; people from all over the world were enjoying the atmosphere or seeking respite from the heat in the cool of the bars or the shade of an awning.

Two hours later, when the heat of the day had ebbed, Quentin felt more comfortable than he had since they'd arrived. A breeze cooled his bare arms, and he marvelled that he was able to be outside in just shorts and a T-shirt in November.

'Well, it's early summer here,' Wanda remarked when he mentioned it. 'It'll probably be boiling by Christmas.'

Christmas. Would they stay that long? But it was only seven weeks away. His mother would love him to stay, he knew, and he didn't relish the thought of returning to England while the threat against him remained. He clung to the hope that the perpetrator would somehow miraculously be caught while he was away. Unlikely, he mused. He'd evaded capture for years.

It was probably just as unlikely that running away would solve anything. If someone really wanted to find him, they would track him down sooner or later.

'But no one knows where we are,' Wanda reminded him when he voiced his thoughts. 'I haven't told any of my family. We haven't even told Colin. The only contact we left was our mobile numbers. So we flew to Sydney. All that means is we're in Australia somewhere. And Australia's a big place.'

That thought comforted Quentin, and he drew on his natural optimism and told himself that things would be all right in the end. When the end would be, he had no idea.

He glanced across the water as daylight began to fade and stars began to twinkle, giving the ambience of the place a different feel. Yes, he thought, sitting back and sipping his drink. Lovely. And we're here, so we might as well stop worrying and make the most of it.

Chapter Six

On Saturday afternoon, Shelagh joined them at the botanical gardens looking distracted. Little Michael ran up to Wanda as soon as he saw her and she scooped him up and kissed him.

'Michael!' she said. 'What a nice surprise. I thought you were staying with Daddy today.'

'Howard was invited to a cricket match, so he dropped Michael off at the salon,' Shelagh explained.

Wanda walked on along the path, still carrying Michael.

'I hope he's not late back,' Shelagh said to Quentin. 'We're going out tonight.'

'Are you? Somewhere nice?'

'To a friend of Howard's. He's got a promotion so he's celebrating.'

A glimmer of an idea formed in Quentin's head. 'What about Michael? We could stay with him if you like.'

'It's all right, we'll take him with us. We're staying overnight. But we'll be back early tomorrow morning. We thought we'd take you over to Manly for the day. It's nice there and you and Howard can have a run.'

Quentin's vision of a whole night with Wanda faded as quickly as it had appeared.

'Have you had a good morning?' Shelagh was saying. 'You must have seen a fair bit of Sydney by now.'

'Yes, we have. Mum and Dad came out with us yesterday, and Dad insisted on taking us to the Anzac Bridge. It was interesting, though.'

As they drew level with Wanda and Michael, Quentin said, 'Anything wrong, Shelagh? You look worried.'

Shelagh pulled a face. 'Linda might be leaving. Apparently her boyfriend's going to Melbourne.'

'Really? Do you know why? Is he going to work there?'

Shelagh shrugged. 'I don't know. He works next door in the Turkish barber's. It's his father's business. He opened it just after I opened mine. If Linda leaves, it's bad timing for me, what with the baby due in January. December is always busy at the salon with the Christmas rush. It'll be difficult trying to get a replacement hairdresser.'

Setting Michael down Wanda turned to Shelagh. 'Has she actually given notice?'

'Not yet. It's not definite.'

'Well, if she goes while we're still here I'll come in and help out. I'm not a hairdresser, but I don't mind answering the phone or making appointments.'

Shelagh looked at her gratefully. 'Thank you, Wanda. I'll bear that in mind. Another thing – one of my customers came back off holiday last week and guess what?'

A premonition planted itself in Quentin's brain. 'What?'

'She's been burgled.'

'Another burglary!' Wanda said. 'I wonder if it's connected to the ones where you live, Shelagh. Does the customer live near the salon?'

'She lives out at Canterbury-Bankstown. I used to do her hair when I worked in a salon there, and when I got my own place she followed me. Several of my clients come from out of town. We've built quite a good reputation, especially since we opened the beauty side.'

'When was this – the burglary, I mean?'

Shelagh shrugged. 'She doesn't know. She was away for two weeks, so it could have been anytime when the house was empty.'

'What was taken, did she say?' Quentin asked, his curiosity aroused.

Shelagh thought for a moment. 'A set of cameos, a brooch, a ring and earrings, quite old she said, and some other jewellery, worth quite a bit from what I can gather.'

Quentin blew out a long breath. The same burglar. It had to be.

'And a sheepskin jacket and a brand-new laptop,' Shelagh went on. 'Still in the box apparently.'

Quentin's assumption disintegrated. Not the same burglar, then? Or burglars, if there was more than one.

'Oh,' he said, feeling a vague sense of disappointment. 'It's not the same as the others. They only had small, valuable items taken.'

'A brand-new laptop's worth a lot,' Wanda pointed out. 'Still, who would want a sheepskin jacket in this climate?'

'You'd be surprised,' Shelagh said. 'It gets chilly in the evenings in the winter. Michael, come back here.'

She lumbered after her son, who had run round a clump of shrubbery. When she returned with him wriggling in her arms, they continued their stroll through the gardens.

'It's usually busier here on a Saturday,' Shelagh told them. 'Come on. I'll show you the biggest spider you've ever seen. And you see that tree up ahead? The one with the big, dangling, brown leaves? Well, they're not leaves, they're bats. They eat the leaves and when they're gone, they fly off at night in search of more food.'

'I bet that's quite a sight,' Wanda said. 'Don't you, Quentin?'

'Hmm? Oh yes, I expect it is.'

A sheepskin coat and a computer. It didn't fit the pattern. Stop it, Quentin told himself. Concentrate on… what was it? Oh yeah. Bats.

* * *

It was about six o'clock that evening, back at his parents' house, when they were surprised by an unannounced visit from Edward Grayson.

'I hoped you'd be in,' he said, eyeing the food on the table. 'Sorry, I didn't mean to interrupt your meal. I should have rung.'

'It's all right, Ed,' Rosemary assured him. 'Have you eaten?' When Grayson shook his head she carried on, 'Join us. I'll get another plate. And before you say anything, it's no trouble. I bet you haven't been eating properly since you came back from your daughter's.'

'Not really,' came the answer. 'Thank you, Rosemary.'

'No need to thank us, old chap,' Herbert put in. 'Fellow officer's welcome anytime.'

Quentin almost squirmed at his father's words. What the hell did it matter if Grayson was a fellow officer? Surely the fact that he was a friend was enough for him to be welcome?

Grayson appeared impervious to his father's military reference. 'To tell you the truth, this break-in business has knocked the wind out of my sails,' he said, taking a seat at the table. 'I keep thinking about Joan, how upset she'd be at losing that necklace. She said she wanted Sarah to have it the minute she was born.'

'Sarah?' Wanda queried.

'My granddaughter. I know it's stupid, but it makes me mad to think that someone else will be wearing what should have been hers.'

'I can understand that,' Wanda said.

'I was wondering,' Grayson said turning to Quentin, 'whether you could do something. I haven't heard any more from the police. Anything you can do would be a help. I'll pay you, of course.'

A thrill ran through Quentin. A challenge always exited him. 'I'd be pleased to help, and I wouldn't dream of taking money from a friend of my family's.'

This earned him a look of approval from his father. 'Quite so,' he barked.

'Thank you,' Grayson said. 'I would appreciate it.'

'The trouble is,' Quentin continued, 'the only clue we have is the fact that only empty properties are targeted.'

'It's not just people who are away on holiday,' Rosemary said. 'The people in the next road to Shelagh were only away for a long weekend.'

'That's the connection, though,' Wanda said. 'Empty properties.'

'And the items that are stolen,' Quentin added. 'There's a pattern. So that's where we have to start. Find out how they know when the house owners will be away, and the rest will follow.' Maybe, he thought, hoping he hadn't sounded too blasé. 'Have you got a photograph of the necklace or the medals, Ed?'

Grayson nodded. 'Yes, we went to a big do just before I left the army. Joan wore the necklace and it was the last time I wore my medals. I gave a copy to the police. I can do one for you, drop it round tomorrow.'

'Yes please, that would be useful. Thanks.'

The conversation lulled as they ate. Glancing round the table, Quentin saw the glimmer of hope in Grayson's eyes, the pride on his mother's face, the doubt on his father's and the *so you've done it again* on Wanda's. He didn't have to worry about Wanda, though. Now the investigation was official, he knew she would do whatever it took to stop these thefts. He caught her eye and she sent him a resigned smile.

Dear Wanda. She was a brick, shoring up his wall of confidence and, despite their constant banter, making him feel good about himself.

It struck Quentin that all the best treatment he'd had in his twenty-five years of life had come from women. His mother when he was growing up, the girlfriends who thought the sun shone out of his eyes (well, every part of his anatomy) and now Wanda. He was grateful for their belief in him. All he had to do now was avoid letting them down.

* * *

After dinner that evening, Quentin and Wanda went for a stroll along the roads in the area. Quentin thought how aptly the road where his parents lived was named –

Hibiscus Crescent. The scent of hibiscus hung in the air and a light wind rustled the leaves on the jacaranda trees.

'It's so peaceful compared to the city,' Wanda said. 'It's a shame the peace had to be disturbed by these burglaries. Poor Ed Grayson. He's quite upset about it all.'

'Strange really, when you think of what he must have seen in the army,' Quentin mused aloud. 'I mean, he didn't get an OBE and mentioned in dispatches for sitting behind a desk. He's seen action, according to my father.'

Wanda nodded. 'Yes. It's different when it's personal, though. And he's older now, and on his own. I wonder why he doesn't move up to Brisbane to be near his daughter.'

'Perhaps he will now. And I've been thinking.'

'Sounds ominous.'

'Not really. It's just– well, we know that somehow the burglars know when people are away, but there is something else we can start with.'

'I think I know what you're going to say.'

Raising his eyebrows, Quentin looked at her. 'Reading my mind now?'

'No, why should I? I'm perfectly capable of working it out for myself.'

'Come on, then, clever clogs. What was I going to say?'

'That we should check any places where the stolen goods might be passed on to, especially things like miniature paintings and those medals. We should be trying to find dealers who would buy that sort of thing.'

'Yes, we should. It'll be quite a search. I bet there's loads of places willing to take what they can get without asking where it came from, and even if they ask they can be told a pack of lies.'

'There's the internet,' Wanda said. 'I expect the police have someone on that. Lovely job, sitting in front of a computer trawling through all the relevant sites.'

'They won't risk selling anything online,' Quentin decided. 'Not if they've got any sense, and judging from the way these burglaries have been carried out they're not silly. You have to put a description and a photo of the goods online. No, they won't do that.'

'You're probably right. That still leaves a lot of time on the internet to find various shops or markets that might take the stuff, or leafing through the telephone book. They might not even dispose of the goods in Sydney. They might take them somewhere else. And don't look at me like that. You're the one who took the case on.'

Quentin groaned. 'I know. I must want my head seen to. We've got to try, though. We've cracked more difficult cases than this.'

Wanda reached for his hand and squeezed it. 'We'll be all right. Anyway, we're out all day tomorrow. We don't want to cancel our arrangements with Shelagh and Howard. We'll start properly on Monday.'

'Good idea,' Quentin agreed. 'I've been looking forward to having a run with Howard all week.'

They had reached a small area of parkland on the edge of the estate.

'You can always have a run here,' Wanda said as they perched on a bench. Quentin slipped his arm round her shoulders.

'I'll wait for you if you want to do a few circuits now,' Wanda offered.

'Actually,' Quentin said softly, 'I can think of better things to do on a lovely evening like this.'

'Oh, can you, now? And what would that be?'

Not bothering to answer, Quentin cupped her face in his hands and kissed her. When he released her she drew back and whispered, 'I'll tell your parents if you don't behave.'

'You can't blackmail me like that. I thought you liked me being naughty.'

'Hmm. Well, perhaps I'll let you off just this once.'

Snaking her arms around his neck she kissed him, a long lingering kiss. Quentin felt the beginnings of a tingle. His hand went to her breast and she pushed him away.

'Not here,' she whispered. 'We'll have to wait.'

Bugger it, he thought. Looks like another cold-shower night.

* * *

They got back just after seven to find Rosemary on the phone.

'Oh, hold on dear, they're back. Just a moment.'

'It's Shelagh,' she said, looking at Quentin. 'They've changed their minds about taking Michael with them. They want to know if you and Wanda will go over and stay the night with him, if you can get there by eight-thirty. I'm sure Herbert will run you over there.'

'We'd love to, wouldn't we, Quentin?' Wanda said at once.

'Yes, of course. Tell her we'll get there as soon as we can. We're going out with them tomorrow anyway, so we'll go straight from theirs.'

Ignoring a look from his father that he couldn't interpret, Quentin collected some overnight things with a smile on his face. A whole evening alone with Wanda. Not a cold-shower night after all.

Chapter Seven

'You're not annoyed, are you, because your dad pays attention to me?' Wanda asked when they were curled up on Shelagh's sofa later that evening.

Quentin laughed. He was used to Wanda being fancied by men of all ages, but the only one he had concerns about was Colin. It hadn't surprised him that his father had taken to Wanda the first time he'd met her. She had charmed him, and for all his hard exterior, his father's old-school upbringing had taught him to show respect to women. Past experience had made Quentin believe that his father genuinely loved his wife. He was bossy, laid down the law on many occasions, but he'd always looked after her, and, as far as Quentin knew, had never had an affair.

'Of course not,' he said. 'He can't help it if you've bewitched him. You bewitch everyone else – why should he be any different? I can't make up my mind whether he can't understand what you see in me or whether he's envious of me – you know, being young, handsome and having you.'

Wanda landed a playful punch on his shoulder. 'You forgot modest. Does he know now, then? Has he said anything?'

'Not in so many words, but from the way he looks at me I think he must do.'

'Oh well, he had to know sooner or later. It was nice of Shelagh to suggest us coming over here tonight. I'm sure she only asked us so we could be on our own for a bit.'

Quentin grinned. 'Yes. I offered this afternoon but she said no.'

'Well, I expect she wanted to check with Howard first. I'm quite looking forward to going out with them tomorrow, and to the shops with your mum later in the week. At least we'll see the real Sydney, not just the tourist attractions.'

'Talking of attractions,' Quentin said, nuzzling her neck, 'I always find them better if I have an early night.'

A noise from behind made him turn. Michael stood there, all tousled hair and sleep.

'Where's Mummy?' he asked, looking confused.

Wanda sprung up and went to him. 'She won't be long, Michael. Did you forget that we were here? Come on, let's get you back to bed.'

'Want a drink,' Michael said, not moving.

'All right, we'll get some milk.'

Quentin watched as she led him into the kitchen. Sweet kid, he thought, gazing after his nephew. Yeah. Sweet kid. Bad timing.

* * *

After a delightful time with Wanda when Michael had gone back to sleep, Quentin slept deeply. He didn't know what woke him. A noise?

Careful not to wake Wanda, he slipped out of bed and, in just his boxer shorts, padded out of the room. It was the guest bedroom at the back of the house, two doors along from Michael's. He paused outside Michael's door but heard nothing from inside. Another sound came, from downstairs he thought. There was a low-powered plug-in light close to the landing floor, allowing him to descend the stairs without putting on the main light. The stairs were situated in the corner of the open-plan lounge, and at the bottom he turned to where he thought the sound had come from – towards the patio doors.

He felt for the light switch on the wall and flicked it on. There was another noise, a crash like something breaking, right outside the doors now, and he moved forward, pulled the blind across and looked out. He thought he saw something move, but the light from the room reflected in the glass and he couldn't be sure. He fiddled with the lock, slid the door open and stepped out onto the patio, slipping on a piece of broken flowerpot. Cursing, he righted himself. At that moment came the sound of a car engine being started. Running back through the house Quentin reached the front window and peered out. All he saw was the beam from a car's headlamps as it drove away.

'What's going on?' Wanda's voice was thick from sleep as she came downstairs.

'I'm not sure,' Quentin said slowly, 'but I think I've just stopped someone breaking in.'

'What?' Wanda's voice lost its sleepiness. 'Someone tried to break in?'

When Quentin told her what had happened, she gasped.

'There was a car?' she said. 'At this time of night?'

'What is the time?' Quentin asked.

'Don't know. Hold on.' Wanda went to the kitchen and returned a moment later. 'Two-thirty.'

Quentin strode to the doors and out onto the patio. In the light from the lounge, he saw the broken flowerpot, obviously knocked over as whoever was trying to break in fled when the light went on. He went back inside and found a torch, then looked across the patio and went round the side of the house to the front. There was nothing to see. He gave it up and went indoors.

'We should call the police,' Wanda said. 'And Shelagh and Howard.'

Shaking his head Quentin said, 'Can't see the point. Whoever it was has gone, they didn't get in and nothing's been taken.'

'But we should call Shelagh and Howard. It's their house.'

'We'll call them first thing in the morning, and we'll go to the police station and make a report. They won't do anything tonight unless it's an emergency.'

'What did you do to your hand?' Wanda asked, catching hold of his wrist and looking at his palm from where blood was oozing.

Quentin gave a rueful grin. 'I slipped and scraped in on the wall when I tried to stop myself falling. Bloody flowerpot. That's what you get for rushing outside at half past two in the morning.'

Wanda washed and dressed his grazed skin. 'Thanks, he said. 'I'll have a proper look round outside in the daylight. Let's get some sleep.'

Sleep, he thought as they crept into Michael's room to find him lying crossways on the cover, a soft teddy bear in the crook of one arm. Dreamland.

Wondering what would have happened if the burglar had broken in, Quentin followed Wanda back to the bedroom.

* * *

After relating the night's events to Shelagh and Howard the next morning and spending an hour making a report at the police station, they decided to go over to Manly as planned.

'I need to do something to take my mind off it,' Shelagh said on the ferry. 'I'll be paranoid now. I'll be glad when the burglar alarm's fitted. That's if it will do any good. My client had an alarm and the burglar managed to drill a hole in it and fill it up with foam so it couldn't go off.'

'We'll make sure it's placed up high,' Howard assured her. 'They could hardly risk climbing a ladder in the dark. They're not likely to come back, anyway. They'll try somewhere else. And it can't be the same people that did all the others. Just kids, probably.'

'Why can't it be the same people?'

'Because,' Quentin told her, 'all the other houses were empty. Yours wasn't.'

'That's right,' Wanda said, trying to lift Shelagh's spirits. 'Everyone else was away on holiday, or away for some reason, for at least a few days.'

'Anyway, we've reported it, so that's all we can do at the moment,' Howard said as they approached Manly Wharf. 'We should get going on that run, Quentin, before it gets too hot.'

'It's too hot already,' Quentin said, though he was looking forward to the run.

Shelagh had thrown a picnic together and Michael had brought his bucket and spade and a blow-up beach ball.

Leaving the girls and Michael at Manly Cove, Quentin and Howard jogged along the Corso together.

'Nice place,' Quentin said between breaths, noticing the cafés, pubs and shops as they passed them.

'Popular, especially on a Sunday,' replied Howard, not breaking his stride.

'Looks like you and Shelagh have made a good life for yourselves.'

'Yeah, Shelagh's a great girl.' Howard spoke in the distinct Australian drawl. 'I wish she wouldn't work so much, though.'

'She'll have some time off, though, when the baby comes?'

'Oh yeah, but she'll go back as soon as she can. I've told her, we can afford to get a manager for the salon but she won't have it.'

'She always was strong-willed,' Quentin said.

Howard grunted and Quentin glanced sideways at him. He got the impression Shelagh's decision to stay at work was a bone of contention between them.

'She's upset about last night, of course,' Quentin said. 'But don't worry too much. I gave the would-be burglar a fright when I switched the light on. I don't suppose they'll chance their arm again.'

'I hope you're right. I told Shelagh it was probably kids, but I don't think it was really. I know the house wasn't empty, but it should have been. If we hadn't asked you and Wanda to stay, there wouldn't have been anyone there.'

Quentin had thought of that himself. 'Did anyone know you were going out and taking Michael with you? Anyone who thought you had something worth stealing?'

'Well, there isn't much, except my grandmother's pearls. Only the people at the party knew we were going. It wasn't a party really – just a few friends. I've known them for years. Your mum and dad and you and Wanda, that's all who knew we'd be out.'

'What about Shelagh? Would she have told anybody?'

'Shouldn't think so. We only got invited yesterday morning.'

They reached a tree-lined promenade where people were walking, running, cycling, even roller-skating.

'Come on,' Quentin urged. 'Let's get some real running done before I'm too tired.' Breaking into a sprint he called, 'Race you to the end.'

Fit though he was, Quentin was no match for Howard. Used to the heat, Howard passed him with a laugh and a wave. At the end of the promenade he stood, hand on hips, waiting for Quentin.

'What kept you?' he jibed when Quentin caught him up.

'Bloody hell!' Quentin panted. 'You're like a bat out of hell.'

They ran back towards the cove where they'd left Wanda, Shelagh and Michael, stopping at one of the outdoor showers to refresh themselves and cool down.

Bliss, thought Quentin as the cold water splashed over him.

'Hello,' said a voice behind them. 'I thought it was you. Quentin, isn't it?'

Stepping out from the spray of water Quentin whirled round. A girl in white knee-length shorts and a green top stood there, her hair pulled back into a ponytail. He recognized her from Shelagh's salon, remembering the dark hair and large eyes, although the bright lipstick wasn't in evidence today.

'Hello,' he said, struggling to recall her name.

'You're Shelagh's brother,' she said, fixing her doe-eyed gaze on him. 'We met at the salon.'

'Yes, I remember.'

Howard came to his rescue. 'Hello, Suzy,' he said, coming out of the shower on the other side of Quentin.

'Oh hello, Mr Prince.'

'I'm just going up to the toilets, Quentin,' Howard said.

'OK, Howard. I'll wait here for you. I haven't a clue where we left the others.'

Quentin turned to Suzy. 'On your own?'

Suzy nodded. 'My sister couldn't make it, but I thought I'd come anyway. I like it here. I used to come here with– I used to come here a lot.'

She looked suddenly forlorn, and Quentin felt sorry for her.

'Why don't you join us?' he offered.

'That's nice of you, but I'll have to be getting back soon. I'm going out tonight.'

'Oh? Somewhere nice?'

'To the cinema with my parents. We're going to see that new Tom Cruise film.'

'Well, enjoy it,' Quentin said, and watched as she walked away.

When Howard returned, Quentin followed him over the sand to the spot where Shelagh was lounging in a deck chair and Wanda was on a blanket watching Michael make sandcastles.

'Did you have a good run?' Shelagh asked. Before either Quentin or Howard could answer she splayed her hands over her belly. 'This little devil's playing football again.'

Wanda leaned over and placed her hand near Shelagh's.

'I can feel it. It's wonderful. One of life's miracles.' For a few seconds her expression was so wistful that Quentin wondered whether she regretted not having children of her own. The moment passed, and Wanda straightened up.

'I'm glad it's not me, though,' she said. 'I'm not one for changing nappies and night feeds.'

'I don't mind that,' Shelagh said. 'I'm just afraid Linda might leave before Christmas. I don't want to turn people away.'

'No worries, love,' Howard assured her. 'We'll sort something out.'

'Like I said before, I'll come in and do reception work,' Wanda said. 'I don't even mind coming in if she doesn't leave, just over Christmas, to help you out.'

'Thanks, Wanda. That would be a help.'

'We bumped into Suzy, or rather Suzy bumped into Quentin.' Howard grinned as he said this. 'I reckon you're in there, mate, the way she was looking at you. Not that you'd be interested,' he added hastily, 'with a beautiful lady like this in your life.'

Wanda said nothing. Instead she grabbed Michael's bucket and led him down to the water's edge, where she knelt and scooped up some wet sand. The tide was ebbing, and she sat with Michael digging a moat around mounds of upturned sand.

Quentin's emotions were mixed. Only a few days ago she'd told him for the umpteenth time that he should be meeting people nearer his own age. We're free agents, she'd said when they'd first met. Yet when someone nearer his own age showed an interest she didn't seem to like it. Perhaps she didn't like it right under her nose. Who knew, with Wanda? He doubted he would ever know everything about her, or even how she really felt about him.

Does it matter? He asked himself. No. Yes. He wanted to know, but he didn't need to know. As long as she stayed with him, that was all he cared about.

Chapter Eight

The following morning Quentin lay in bed, the current spate of burglaries uppermost in his mind. He'd promised Edward Grayson that he'd do what he could to put a stop to them and bring the perpetrators to justice, and despite his fondness for a challenge he was apprehensive about it.

Firstly, he had very little to go on, and secondly, he was going to have to conduct this case under the noses of his family. What if he failed? Would they still rate him as a detective? Or would the recent rise in his father's opinion of him come crashing down? Since the attempted break-in at his sister's house it felt more important than ever to crack the case. If only he had a proper starting point. Oh well, he thought, I won't solve anything lying here.

He was about to fling back his covers when there was a peremptory tap on the door before it opened and his mother appeared.

'Oh, you're awake, dear. I've brought you some tea.' Setting the tea on the cabinet she perched on the side of the bed. 'I'm glad you're taking these robberies on. I think Ed Grayson feels better now he knows someone is doing something to get to the bottom of it, someone apart from the police, I mean. And poor Shelagh was nearly burgled.'

Quentin rubbed his eyes. 'Well, I'll do my best, Mum, but I can't promise anything. These people seem to have everything sewn up.'

'If anyone can do it, you can, Quentin. I've got confidence in you.'

'Thanks, Mum.

'And–' Rosemary hesitated, her eyes searching her son's face. 'And thanks for making an effort with your father. I know how difficult he can be at times, and I know, well, I know sometimes you keep your temper for my sake...'

Laying a hand on her arm Quentin said, 'It's all right, Mum. Don't worry, I won't... upset the applecart.'

A look of understanding passed between them, and Quentin saw the relief on her face.

'I know you won't. I'm glad Wanda came with you. She's such a nice person, and she's obviously good for you, Quentin. I hope it works out for you both.'

Quentin felt a flush rise in his cheeks. He shared a close bond with his mother but the conversation was making him slightly uncomfortable.

'Thanks for the tea,' he said, reaching for the cup.

Rosemary stood up. 'It's so wonderful to have you here. My lovely boy.' She turned and left the room.

Quentin stared after her, a warm glow enveloping him. Dear Mum. She believed in him. So did Wanda. Feeling more like his optimistic self, he sprang out of bed.

The first thing he did after breakfast was to hire a car. Relying on relatives or public transport was fine for sightseeing, but he knew they would need their own car if they had to do a lot of mileage or wanted to get somewhere in a hurry.

It was mid-morning before he drove a blue Nissan Micra onto his parents' driveway. Wanda greeted him with, 'That'll do. I'll make you a coffee, then we'd better get started.'

'You could have started without me.'

'I was talking to your mum. I thought I should offer to cook tonight, as we could be out chasing criminals for the foreseeable future.'

'We've got to find the criminals before we can chase them,' Quentin grunted. He followed her into the kitchen and sat thinking while she made coffee.

'Right,' Wanda said when they'd finished their drinks. 'You check the internet and I'll go through the local business directory.'

Quentin pulled a face. 'Is it worth going through the directory? Surely all businesses have a website these days?'

'Probably, but you never know. There may be some smaller shops that haven't. It's worth a try, anyway.'

'OK. Here we go, then.'

Quentin walked into the L-shaped lounge. Like the rest of the house it was open and airy, and some of the furniture, shipped over from his parents' elegant 1930s house in England, looked incongruous against a background of plain ivory walls and wide modern windows. The computer, a recent acquisition after pressure from Shelagh, sat on a small desk in the corner with a dressing-table stool in front of it.

They'll have to get a proper chair for this, he thought after half an hour. My back's aching already.

He made a list of all the dealers in the area that might trade in the kind of items that had been stolen. After comparing notes, he found six names on Wanda's list that didn't appear on his.

'Not a complete waste of time, then,' he said. 'So, next step. What do you think, phone or visit them all?'

'Phoning's quicker,' Wanda answered, 'but I think we're more likely to get a response face-to-face. We should ring first, to check the owner or the buyer is there. We'll have to split up. We'll be at it for days otherwise.'

'It'll probably take days anyway. Still, we've got to start somewhere. OK, let's sort them into areas, and decide where to go first.'

By the time they'd had lunch, discussed which shops they were going to visit and downloaded maps showing the routes to various places, it was nearly three o'clock. Then Wanda remembered she was supposed to cook dinner that evening so they decided that Quentin would make a start on his own.

Taking a list, a map and the photo of the necklace and medals Grayson had left for him, Quentin drove the Micra into the city. Within half an hour he'd found one of the shops on the list, parked and made his way to it. It was in one of the older parts of the town, with residential streets branching off the main road. I should have phoned like Wanda suggested, he thought as he walked. Let's hope the person I need to speak to is here.

The shop looked small. He hovered outside for a moment, wondering what he should say. What could he say? Have you bought any stolen items lately? Has some dodgy bloke been here selling you second-hand goods? The bell clanged as he pushed the door open. It smelt of old furniture and dust, and Quentin could see that although it was narrow it went a long way back. A glass counter showing antique-looking jewellery and a variety of watches stood just inside. A middle-aged man was stooped over something on the counter but looked up as Quentin approached.

'Can I help you?' he asked.

'Em, I hope so. Are you the owner?'

'Yes, why?'

Quentin took out Grayson's photo and passed it over the counter. 'Have you seen this necklace or these medals?'

'Who are you?' said the man sharply.

'My name's Quentin Cadbury. I'm a private detective.'

'Got any ID?'

Quentin fished for his wallet and took out his driving licence. 'Sorry, I haven't got my business cards with me.'

'It doesn't say you're a private detective on this. You're a pomme, aren't you?'

'I'm British, if that's what you mean,' Quentin said, feeling a prick of irritation. 'Look, I'm making enquiries on behalf of a client. These items were stolen last week and I'm just trying to find out anything I can about who might've taken them.'

The man, still stooped even when not bent over the counter, looked at him suspiciously. 'I've already told the police I haven't seen them,' he said.

'OK, but if anyone tries to sell them to you could you let me know? My client would be very grateful. These things had great sentimental value for him. I'll give you my number.'

He felt in his pocket for the wodge of paper and the pen he'd brought, making a mental note to buy a proper notebook and have some cards printed. After writing down his name and mobile number he passed it to the shopkeeper and left.

'That went well,' he muttered as he walked away. 'Let's hope not everyone's as helpful as that.'

After two more visits he decided to call it a day. The last two shopkeepers were polite but couldn't tell him anything, except that they, too, had been questioned by the police. That reassured him a little – at least it proved the police were doing something.

'It could be a long haul,' he told the family over dinner.

'Never mind, dear, as long as you're trying,' his mother said. 'You won't put yourself in danger, though, will you?'

'Don't worry, Mum, I'll be sensible. If I need help or find out anything important, I'll call the police. This is delicious, Wanda.'

'Yes, very nice, my dear,' agreed his father, brandishing his fork in Wanda's direction.

Rosemary raised her eyebrows. 'Praise indeed, coming from you, Herbert.'

Herbert looked flustered. 'Well, your cooking's always good, Rosemary. No need to keep telling you. Stands to reason.'

Quentin wondered what reason stood to justify taking someone for granted, but supposed it was common enough. He'd probably done the same when he'd lived with them.

'I'm going in to have my hair done again on Friday, Wanda,' Rosemary said. 'Do you want me to ring Shelagh and see if she can book you in as well? Or will you be too busy?'

Wanda looked at Quentin. 'We can probably take a few hours off on Friday. You could come, Quentin, and go to that Turkish barber.'

Turkish barbers were the last thing on Quentin's mind.

'You go,' he said. 'I might come into town with you, if things go well for the rest of the week.'

He didn't really want to think about the rest of the week. Trudging round asking questions wasn't the most exciting part of detective work. Like every other job he'd worked at, detection was mainly routine, which was why he jumped at any chance to take on something that promised at least some kind of action. But, as he knew well enough, action alone didn't always reap results.

* * *

51

Edward Grayson rang Herbert the next morning to say he'd rung the police to see if they'd made any progress, but had been told they were doing all they could.

'Great comfort that is,' Quentin commented. 'The thing is, only valuable things have been taken; things that would fetch a good price and give whoever stole them a good return for their time and trouble. You don't get people paying the price they want at your local market or car boot sale, so where do the police start looking? The stuff could be sent anywhere.'

Later, when they were alone, Wanda said, 'I've thought of something else.'

'Have you? Go on.'

'One of the houses that was targeted was in this road, you know, the house where the police were the day we arrived. Your parents know them, don't they?'

'And your point is?'

'Well, we know that somehow the burglars are finding out when people's houses will be empty. I thought if we talked to those who have had items stolen, they could tell us who might have known they would be away and if anyone knew they had something worth stealing. It might give us something to follow up.'

'Good thinking,' Quentin said, annoyed that he'd forgotten about the break-in so close to his parents. 'When did you have this bright idea?'

'Earlier, when we were all talking.'

'Why didn't you say something, then?'

Wanda looked at him from beneath her lashes. 'You're a detective. Work it out.'

'You didn't want my parents to know? You think we should get their permission to question their neighbours? You–' He broke off. Wanda's expression told him it was neither of these suggestions. Light dawned, and he swallowed hard before carrying on.

'You're trying to make it look as though I'm the brightest star in the sky, trying to make me look good in front of my parents.'

Well of course she was. She took every opportunity to boost his confidence when his father was present.

'Thanks,' he murmured, feeling the colour rise in his cheeks. 'But we are partners, you know. You're entitled to contribute as much as me. Anyway, it doesn't matter what they think, well, what *he* thinks.'

Gazing at her, Quentin was tempted to expand this point, to explain more about his family than he'd revealed since meeting her, but she had already moved away from the subject.

'So, what do you think?' she was saying. 'Shall we go and see them, the people along the road?'

'OK. Though I asked Ed Grayson who knew he was going away but it didn't give us anything. Still, no stone unturned and all that. We'll ask Mum to introduce us.'

'When?'

'No time like the present.'

'Right, then. Let's go.'

* * *

'Hello, Janet,' Rosemary said when her neighbour opened her front door. 'This is my son, Quentin, and his partner, Wanda.'

'Hello,' Janet answered. 'Nice to meet you. Rosemary said you were coming to stay. Come in.'

When they were settled in the kitchen-diner, they were introduced to Bill, Janet's husband.

'I was wondering if we could ask you some questions about the robbery,' Quentin said. 'I know you've told the police, but–'

'Quentin and Wanda are private investigators,' Rosemary interrupted, a note of pride in her voice. 'Ed Grayson, Colonel Grayson, a friend of Herbert's from the ex-servicemen's club, he was burgled too. He's asked Quentin to investigate the case for him.'

'That's right,' Wanda said. 'The thing is, there's a common theme with these burglaries, and we thought you might be able to tell us something to help us work out what the connection is.'

Janet looked at her husband, who pulled a face. 'I don't know what we can tell you that we haven't already told the police,' he said. 'Still, I don't mind answering questions if you think you can do anything to catch these people.'

'Thank you,' Quentin said, pleased to be doing something proactive. After half an hour of questions and answers, though, he'd learned nothing new or helpful.

'Right, OK,' he said standing up. 'If you think of anything else, can you let me know?'

'Of course.' Bill shook Quentin's hand and nodded to Wanda.

Janet followed them to the front door. 'Goodbye,' she said. 'I hope you find something useful soon.'

'That wasn't much help, was it?' Wanda said as they walked back along the road.

'Never mind, dear,' Rosemary said. 'I'm sure something will come up soon. We'll go and have a nice cup of tea.'

Tea, Quentin thought. I need a bit more than tea to get my head round this case. Oh well, it looks like we're back to footslogging for the rest of the day.

Chapter Nine

Footslogging over the next few days got them nowhere. Most of the people they approached had already been questioned by the police and had nothing further to add to their original statements. Wanda seemed to get a better response than Quentin, a factor that he put down to her feminine wiles, especially when the dealers they spoke to were male.

'We're going round in circles,' he complained when they met up in a car park at the end of a long day. 'There's got to be something else we can do.'

'Yes,' Wanda agreed. 'Either no one we've spoken to knows anything or they're very good at covering things up. Of course, not all the receivers are fences. People could buy things not knowing they're stolen. Not here, necessarily. Some may be passed on further afield to spread it out a bit, lessen the chances of them being traced. No wonder the police haven't got anywhere.'

'Hmm. Well, we've covered practically every shop and dealer in Sydney. Unless something comes up to give us a lead, we'll have to try somewhere else.'

Wanda sighed. 'Where do you suggest we start? In case it's escaped your notice, Australia's rather big. They might even be sending stuff abroad.'

Abroad. Something clicked in Quentin's head. 'That's quite a possibility,' he said slowly. 'Yep, quite a possibility. All the items taken are small, jewellery, medals, miniature paintings.'

'Except for that one Shelagh told us about. They took a laptop.'

Quentin spread his hands. 'And a sheepskin coat. Forget that one. I don't think it's connected to the ones we're investigating. As I was saying, small items can be easily concealed in luggage. If the carrier was challenged, they'd only have to say they bought them and were taking them home, or that they were a collector, as long as they didn't take too much at once—'

'Or,' Wanda interrupted, 'they could be taken to other towns in Oz, by train or coach, or even—'

'Or even what?' Quentin asked, though he guessed she'd had the same idea as him.

'Well, they could even be sent by post. I read somewhere that diamonds are sent by post because it's the safest way. Perhaps there's a way we can find out if anyone is sending packets on a regular basis.'

'I've thought of that, but you have to fill in a customs form to send things abroad. Still, they don't have to say what's really inside. They could make something up. It would be all right as long as it wasn't opened en route or lost in the post.'

So many possibilities, Quentin thought. The burglar could be a one-man band or a member of an international organisation. He groaned inwardly. Somehow, they had to get a lead, something more than speculation.

'Anyway,' Wanda was saying, 'I think we can give ourselves a break tomorrow. I'm going to have my hair done. You could come – Shelagh could give you a quick trim if she's got time, or Suzy will. I'm sure *she'll* make time for you.'

Quentin gave a half-laugh.

'Come on,' he said, pulling out his mobile phone. 'Let's go and have a drink somewhere. I'll call Mum and say we'll eat out.'

* * *

'I think I'll try that Turkish barber,' Quentin said when he drove his mother and Wanda to Shelagh's salon the next morning. 'I'll see you two later.'

While he waited for them to get out he caught sight of Suzy through the window. She looked up from the reception desk, smiled at him and waved. She had a nice smile, he decided. He waved back, and wondered if she really did have a soft spot for him.

When he'd parked the car, he walked to the barber's. He was greeted at the doorway by a short, beaming middle-aged man, his belly pushing against the buttons on a black waistcoat.

'Good morning, good morning, come in,' he said effusively. 'You wish haircut, shave?'

'Just a haircut please, if you can fit me in.'

'Good, good,' the man said, shuffling Quentin towards several leather-covered chairs. 'You sit here. I get coffee.' He headed to an opening at the back of the room, the kitchen Quentin assumed, though his view was obscured by a black beaded curtain which chinked as the greeter passed through it.

Quentin hoped that the offer of coffee didn't mean he was in for a long wait. He looked around, taking in his surroundings. There were four workstations, though only two were in use. Each chair was positioned in front of a huge, black-framed mirror, contrasting starkly against the white walls, and the floor was checked in black and white tiles. The back wall was almost completely covered by an oversized black and white photograph of the Blue Mosque with the Bosphorus in the background, and traditional Turkish music played softly. The two barbers that Quentin had seen through the window, the young, slim man and the older, more rotund man, were dressed the same as the man who had greeted him – in black trousers and waistcoat and a white shirt. The black and white theme made the place look clean and light and gave an illusion of space.

The volume of the exotic music increased at the same time as the beaded curtain rattled and Quentin half expected to see a belly dancer come through it. Instead, the man who had ushered him in came back with the tiniest cup and saucer Quentin had ever seen. It looked ridiculous in his big hands.

'Er, thank you,' Quentin said as he took the coffee. He stared into the cup, not knowing what to make of its contents. Oh well, he thought, in for a penny in for a pound, and took a sip. The thick, syrupy liquid was strong, and he screwed up his face.

'Turkish coffee very good, yes?' the greeter beamed.

'Er, yes, thank you,' Quentin spluttered.

When the man moved away and picked up a broom, Quentin glanced around for a place to put the cup out of sight. Seeing nowhere, he planted it firmly back onto the saucer and nursed it, hoping he could get away without drinking any more. He turned his attention to the seat in front of him, where a man was lathered up for a wet shave. The younger of the two barbers stood behind him, a shaving brush in one hand. Next to him the older barber, olive-skinned and balding, was holding a mirror behind another client, reflecting the back of his head. When the client nodded his satisfaction, the barber looked over at Quentin and smiled.

'Good morning, sir, I shall be one minute only.' His accent was thick but his words were clear. Turning back to his client he went on, 'Thank you, Mr Giles. You come again next month?'

'Yes, Ahmed, book me in for four weeks today.'

The barber called Ahmed went to the reception desk and wrote in the appointment book. When the customer had paid and left he turned to Quentin.

'You wish a haircut, yes?'

'Yes please.'

The barber put on an exaggerated sorrowful expression and waved his hands. 'Alas, I must go out, but, my son, Halim there, will finish soon.'

Halim looked over and nodded.

'You have been to us before?' Ahmed continued.

'Er, no.'

'You handsome gentleman,' Ahmed gushed. 'You have full works. You will enjoy. You have time, yes?'

'Yes,' Quentin answered, mildly amused by the older man's enthusiasm. He had no idea what the full works entailed, but he guessed it would be more expensive than the simple haircut he'd come in for. Still, he reasoned, I've got to wait for Mum and Wanda so I might as well be in here.

Ahmed spoke to his son. 'I get my keys, Halim, then I go. This gentleman needs full works.'

Halim nodded, but Quentin couldn't help noticing the look of resentment that crossed his face. He detected a definite undercurrent of tension between them. His father gone, Halim finished with his customer and sombrely gestured Quentin towards the empty chair. Gratefully abandoning his coffee cup in the waiting area, Quentin plonked himself down in the still-warm black chair at the workstation. He glanced in the mirror at Halim who, Quentin guessed, wasn't particularly happy in his work. He seemed efficient, had sulky, dark, good looks and was polite, but he lacked his father's effusive personality and ability to put his client at ease. He spoke little as he placed a black cape around Quentin's shoulders.

Before they'd even discussed what type of haircut he wanted, Quentin felt the buzz of an electric razor on the back of his neck. He'd been having a grade four all round, short on top with a side parting, since he was ten years old.

As if noticing his look of alarm, Halim said, 'Don't worry, mate. I know what will look good on you. You're having the full works so sit back and enjoy.'

His use of the Australian's favoured address of "mate" highlighted the difference between him and his father. His English was perfect, with no trace of a Turkish accent.

A few moments later Halim relinquished the clippers for a cut-throat razor.

'I don't need a shave,' Quentin said, eyeing the razor warily. 'I had one this morning.'

'I can see that,' Halim said, 'but we use an open razor for other things.'

Quentin's eyes widened and he held his breath as Halim wielded the blade to cut away the stray hair around his sideburns. Then, before he knew what was happening, the cut-throat was just millimetres away from his left eye as the barber cut around his eyebrow. Quentin had never had his eyebrows shaped and didn't think they needed doing, but with the blade uncomfortably close, now didn't seem the time to mention it.

'You still want a parting?' Halim asked as he finished off the right eyebrow.

'Ah-ha,' Quentin murmured, and before he'd taken another breath Halim was back with the razor. He stared in horror at his reflection as Halim began to cut a parting into his hair. 'I usually just comb the parting in,' he said as he watched a thick white line being carved into his head.

'It's better this way,' Halim told him. 'No need for a comb after this haircut.'

After replacing the razor Halim picked up what looked like a foot-long earbud and dipped it into a small jar of something blue. Then he produced a lighter, flicked it on and held the flame to the end of the earbud. It ignited immediately and before Quentin could say anything the burning stick was thrust into his ear. A singeing smell reached Quentin's nostrils. Bloody hell, he thought in disbelief, I'm on fire! Seconds later the offending stick was pulled from his ear and the procedure was repeated on the other side.

'Perfect,' Halim announced, apparently pleased with his efforts.

Relief swept through Quentin. His ordeal was over, and he had to admit his hair looked good. Having made it clear he didn't want a shave, he was about to get up when the meet-and-greet man emerged from the beaded curtain carrying a tray with something white and steamy on it. Halim flicked a lever on the chair and Quentin was jolted backwards, his head rebounding against the backrest. Now lying almost flat, he gazed up at a grinning Halim as he took the corners of what Quentin could see was a steaming hot towel. In a quick twizzling motion Halim slapped it over Quentin's face.

Quentin's surprised gasp was muffled by the towel, which covered the whole of his face. Bloody hell, they're suffocating me, he thought in panic. At that moment a hole big enough for his nose to poke through was made between the folds of the towel.

'This is good for the complexion,' Halim assured him. 'We'll just leave it on for a minute or two.'

Shifting uncomfortably in his seat, Quentin felt like an Egyptian mummy. He was just wondering if Halim did embalming in his spare time when he heard the shop door open and someone come in. Unable to see, Quentin assumed it was another customer, though the effusive welcome by the greeter was absent. He was surprised to hear a woman's voice. It sounded familiar but he couldn't place it.

'I haven't got long,' the voice said breathily.

'I'll just be a moment, mate,' Halim said. The swish of movement and a rattling sound told Quentin they had gone through the beaded curtain. He lay in his towel mask trying to match the voice to anyone he'd met recently. That breathy voice – yes, the plump, red-haired girl from Shelagh's salon. Linda. He recalled Shelagh saying that Linda's boyfriend worked at the barber's.

Hushed voices filtered through the curtain, and from their tone Quentin could tell they weren't exactly whispering sweet nothings. He only got snatches, but he heard Linda's breathy voice.

'I haven't forgiven you for that. I told you to stay away from hers, and you did it anyway.'

'OK, OK, I'm sorry,' Halim said. 'Look, we'll be in Melbourne soon. We can start again.'

'I don't know if I'm going yet.'

Halim's reply was lost as their voices grew fainter, as though they'd moved further away. Unable to hear, Quentin tried to find the lever to enable him to sit upright. Reaching out blindly he knocked over Halim's work trolley, sending it clattering to the floor.

The noise caused Halim and Linda to come into the room.

'Sorry,' Quentin said, feeling their presence beside him, 'I just need to sit up, my back's killing me.'

He must have sounded stupid, but Halim pushed the lever on the chair and Quentin was catapulted upright. What the hell's going on, he thought with an inward groan.

I'll really have a bad back now. Miraculously his face towel was still in place.

'I've got to go, Halim,' he heard Linda say. 'We'll talk later.' He heard the door open and close before Halim turned his attention back to him and began to unwrap the cooling towel from his face.

'Bad back, eh, mate?'

'Yeah, long plane journey.' A half-truth anyway.

'I can help with that. It's not usually included, but as you didn't have a shave…'

Quentin felt a hand push against his shoulder and another grab his wrist. Then, with a quick, hard tug, Halim practically yanked Quentin's arm out of its socket.

'Ouch!' yelled Quentin, screwing up his face and staring at Halim incredulously. This was no ordinary barber. He must have been trained in torture. Quentin was tempted to sit on his hands in case Halim offered to give him a manicure.

'There,' Halim said when he'd repeated his action on the opposite shoulder. 'That'll help you realign.'

It was the weirdest haircut Quentin had ever had in his life. Who would pay to go through this on a regular basis?

'Just a little product to smooth your skin and you're good to go.'

Halim squirted a sweet-smelling oil onto his hands, slapped his palms against Quentin's cheeks and massaged it in.

'All done,' he said, wiping his hands on a towel. 'Happy with it?'

The man who'd greeted him earlier called from the reception desk. 'Is very good.'

Quentin gazed at his reflection. With the treatment he'd had, his face glowing and his parting resembling a chalk track in an earthen field, he wouldn't describe his feelings as happy.

'Well, it's a different look for me, but yeah, I like it,' he lied. 'I couldn't just use your loo before I go, could I?'

He wanted time to get used to his new look before inflicting it on Wanda and Shelagh. God, what would his parents say?

'Through there,' Halim told him, gesturing to the opening.

Quentin walked to the opening, parted the beaded curtain and entered a short corridor. There were three doors – one on either side of the corridor and one at the end, which stood open and showed the kitchen area. Neither of the other doors was marked as a toilet. He pushed open the right-hand door and took a step in. It was small, lit by a window set high up in the wall at the end. There were boxes on the floor and shelves with similar hairdressing products and oils to those Quentin had seen outside. A stockroom he realized. He was about to go out but stopped. Something had caught his eye. A box. A box half-hidden behind another but with a picture showing on the part that was visible. He stepped closer, tilting his newly cropped head to read the label. Toshiba. A brand-new laptop, still in its box.

Quentin's heart hammered against his ribs. Don't be stupid, he told himself. Why shouldn't they have a new computer? Perhaps they were intending to do the business accounts on it. He turned to leave, and his heart hammered even more. There was something else, something hanging on the back of the door.

A sheepskin coat.

Chapter Ten

'Let me get this straight,' Wanda said that afternoon when she sat with Quentin in the café of a department store. 'You're saying there was a laptop and a sheepskin coat in the barber's stockroom? And you think they could be the things stolen from one of Shelagh's clients?'

'Yes.' Quentin looked round to make sure his mother wasn't coming back from her browse round the cookware department. 'It's not just that, it's what Linda said to Halim.'

'Linda? You think she's in on it?'

'She must be. She said she told him to "stay away from hers", but he did it anyway.'

'*Hers*? You mean the person the things were stolen from?'

Leaning forward, Quentin placed his elbows on the table. 'Possibly. But think about it. We may just have found the connection between the robberies.' Seeing Wanda's blank look, he continued, 'Who else was burgled, or would have been burgled? Someone Linda knows?'

Wanda gave a sharp intake of breath. 'Oh my word, Shelagh!' She paused, chewing at her bottom lip as she let this sink in. Then she said slowly, 'I see what you're saying, but it doesn't follow. All the other robberies have taken place at empty properties, and only jewellery and small items were taken. Maybe Halim did commit one of the burglaries, but he can't be behind the others. Why would he break the pattern and steal a computer and a coat if he was? And Shelagh wasn't away from home as such. She only stayed out overnight, and they only arranged it that day.'

'Exactly. So who would know, on that very day, that the house would be empty that night? Shelagh was at work in the morning – she had a call to say they'd been invited out. She probably mentioned it, said they would be taking Michael with them. In the afternoon she was with us at the botanical gardens, then she went home. She couldn't have told anyone else.'

Shaking her head, Wanda said, 'I can't believe Linda would stand by and let the person she works for get robbed. That's awful.'

'I don't think she did. I think that's what she meant when she said she told him to stay away from "hers" – she must have mentioned it to Halim for some reason, but forbade him to do anything. He went against her wishes.'

'Wow!' Wanda said. 'Shelagh's going to be really upset.'

'Don't tell her,' Quentin warned. 'Or Mum or my father. Not yet. I think we should be sure of our facts first. We'll think it through. Perhaps we can come up with something to prove our theory. Oh, here's Mum. Don't say anything.'

They spent another hour in the shop. While Rosemary and Wanda tried on clothes Quentin meandered around the music department, looking at the CDs but not really seeing them. His mind was still on what he'd seen and heard in the barber's.

What had he seen? A computer and the sheepskin coat. What had he heard? Very little. He could have misconstrued the whole thing. Was he on the wrong track? Gut feeling told him otherwise. Linda. Linda was the link. If she had told Halim about Shelagh being out, she could also have told him about the client who had the computer and coat stolen. What had Shelagh said? A client had returned from holiday and found she had been burgled. What better place to learn when people are going on holiday? Regular customers, people who had their hair done weekly or fortnightly, would cancel their bookings because they would be away. Could Halim have committed all the robberies? Was his father involved, too? Quentin's head ached with trying to piece things together. He wished he could go for a good long run to clear his mind.

Before dinner that evening, he decided to do just that. He changed into a vest top, shorts and running shoes and sprinted to the park area at the end of the road. He made several circuits of the place, then ran around the adjacent streets until he re-entered the road where his parents lived from the other end. When he came round the corner and reached Janet and Bill's house, he slowed down. He thought back to the day he'd asked them about the break-in. Nothing they'd told him had helped. There was nothing to connect that burglary to either the near break-in at Shelagh's or the one at her client's whose computer had been taken. Or was there?

Unable to dislodge the possibility that had planted itself in his mind, he brought the subject up over dinner that evening.

'Mum, does Janet go to Shelagh's salon?'

'Yes, dear, she's been going there for a while now. I recommended it.'

Wanda jerked her head up, picking up on the implication immediately. 'Janet goes to Shelagh to have her hair done?'

Rosemary glanced from her son to Wanda. 'Why?' she asked. 'Is that important?'

Quentin cut into a potato. 'I'm not sure yet. It's just a thought.' He felt his father's intense gaze and waited for the question he knew was inevitable. His father may be belligerent and bigoted but he wasn't stupid.

'You think the burglaries are connected to Shelagh's salon?' Herbert asked sharply.

Rosemary looked worried. 'How can they be?'

'It just seems odd, that's all,' Wanda said. 'Two of Shelagh's client's being burgled, and Shelagh herself nearly being broken into.'

'That's just coincidence, surely?' said Rosemary. 'I hope so, anyway. Shelagh's got enough to cope with, with the salon and the baby coming–'

'Shush, Rosemary.' Turning to Quentin, Herbert said, 'That can't be right. I don't know what you're basing your theory on. There's been more than two robberies, and all the victims don't go to the salon. What about Edward Grayson? You're barking up the wrong tree there.'

'I don't suppose–' Wanda broke off, as if uncertain whether to continue. 'I mean, do you know where Ed goes to have his hair cut?'

'Same place as me, British chap here in Roseville, ex-forces. What's that got to do with anything?'

Wanda looked at Quentin questioningly and he shook his head almost imperceptibly.

'We have to look at every possibility,' Quentin said, guessing that Wanda had been trying to ascertain whether Grayson had ever used the Turkish barber's.

Herbert harrumphed and carried on eating; Rosemary said no more but still looked worried.

So another of the victims used the salon, Quentin thought. Linda could have overheard Janet saying she would be away and then told Halim. But Ed Grayson? No connection there.

Herbert waved his fork at Quentin. 'Don't go worrying your sister with this,' he growled. 'Don't want her upset.'

Quentin tried to remember when his father had ever been considerate enough not to upset *him*, but couldn't.

'I wasn't going to. We'll get some concrete evidence, if there is any. Otherwise, we'll try something else.'

'Don't worry, Mr Cad– Herbert, we wouldn't dream of saying anything to Shelagh until we're sure of our facts,' Wanda said, flashing him a smile.

She was rewarded with a nod. 'All right, m'dear, if you say so.'

For the umpteenth time Quentin sent silent thanks to Wanda for her innate ability to smooth the waters between him and his father. Without her conciliatory approach he probably would have lost his temper by now. Oh well, he thought as he finished his meal, when we've solved this case, we'll move on and have a look round other places until we can go back to England. When it's safe to go back, that is.

Does it matter if we don't go back? he thought as he lay in bed that night. We can operate the business from here just as well. But in his heart, he knew he would go back. Despite it being so far away from his family, he loved London; the hurly-burly of it, the red buses, myriad theatres, the Houses of Parliament, the river, the rain, everything. He thought of his Greenwich home and Magpie, and wondered how his cat was coping in a strange house with a dog. On the spur of the moment he switched the bedside lamp on and looked at the clock. It would be morning now back home. After a moment's hesitation he did something he'd never done in the two years he'd known Wanda – he rang the long-standing rival for her affections simply because he wanted to talk to him.

'Colin? Sorry, I hope I didn't wake you.'

'Quentin? Anything wrong?' Colin's surprise was evident.

'No, just wondered how Magpie was, that's all.'

'I told Wanda the other day, he's OK. He's here now, on the settee next to me.'

Quentin felt suddenly envious. Colin was sitting at home with *his* cat by his side. He beat back his jealousy and comforted himself with the thought that always made him feel superior to Colin. Colin may have a nice house in Wanstead, a loving daughter, a good career behind him with a decent pension to look forward to, the remains of a redundancy pay-out and at the moment, Quentin's cat; but he didn't have Wanda.

'He's still finding his feet, but I think Mozart being here helps. They scrap occasionally, but at least being together they have a common link. Is that the only reason you phoned?'

'Yes, except have you been to Greenwich and picked up my post?'

'I went a few days ago. There was nothing that looked important, only adverts and a notice from the Inland Revenue.'

'Nothing at Wanda's either?'

'No. What were you expecting? A cheque?'

Quentin sighed. 'No such luck, unless my one and only premium bond has come up. I just wondered, you know, the reason you took Magpie and Mozart to your house instead of staying at mine or Wanda's–'

'Oh, the man who threatened you? A poison pen letter or something? No, and I wouldn't think he'd be nosing round Greenwich looking for you. He'll be lying low for a while. He wouldn't dare risk surfacing again so soon.'

No, but he could send someone else to do his dirty work, Quentin realized, thinking of the man who had escaped justice several times and who blamed him for breaking up the criminal rings he'd masterminded.

'So how are things where you are?' Colin was saying. 'Wanda said something about some burglaries. Not getting involved with that are you?'

'Sort of,' Quentin admitted.

'So you are, then. I don't suppose you've rung for my advice. You've never taken it before.'

Quentin imagined Colin's grey eyes behind his dark-rimmed glasses, his high forehead creased into a frown. 'You've been helpful in the past,' he said, hoping he didn't sound too patronising.

'Well, what an admission. Why don't you tell me what's going on, then – a fresh pair of ears and all that?'

Ridiculous, Quentin thought. How could anyone help from ten thousand miles away? Nevertheless, he gave Colin a brief outline of the case.

'Tricky,' Colin said when he'd finished. 'Well, if you think there's a common thread stick with it. Just because you can't find it doesn't mean there isn't one. This barber – did he have anything else apart from the computer? Any of the missing jewellery?'

'Not that I saw. Jewellery can be easily hidden. I only spotted the computer because it was just inside the door of the room I went into by mistake.'

There was a pause, as though Colin was trying to think of something to say. Then, 'Well, if you've been in there once you can go again.'

'Brilliant idea,' Quentin quipped. 'What do you suggest, I break in during the night, or just saunter in and say, "Hey old man, mind if I look in your stockroom?"'

'Use you head, Quentin. Create a diversion, and while it's going on nip in and have a thorough search.'

Quentin sat bolt upright in bed. 'You know, Colin, that *is* a brilliant idea. I might just try that.'

A snigger sounded in his ear. 'I'm full of good ideas, me. It's a pity you don't take more notice of them. Don't you go putting Wanda in any danger, mind, or you'll have me to reckon with.'

'I won't, but you know Wanda. She won't be left out of anything. I'd better go, Colin. It's midnight here. Bye for now.'

When he'd ended the call Quentin lay down and tried to sleep. Colin's words went round and round in his head. Because we can't find a common link doesn't mean there isn't one. If he found jewellery at the barber's, he would have proof of the link. Colin was right. He needed to search that stockroom thoroughly, and he needed a diversion. So how could he create one?

Chapter Eleven

'Of course,' Wanda said the next day when Quentin mentioned his conversation with Colin, 'there is another way anyone can find out when houses are empty. Choose a nice area, one where people have a bit of money and likely to have nice things, and hang around for a bit. They'd soon see which houses have activity and which don't.'

Quentin shook his head. 'Be a bit conspicuous, wouldn't they?'

'Not necessarily. They could walk by a few times, or drive round, cycle or run. After all, you run round the roads.'

They were strolling through the park area at the bottom of the crescent. As they came to the entrance gate, Quentin looked along the road they'd just walked along. It was more like an avenue, with trees punctuating the pavements on both sides.

'Hmm,' he said. 'I'd have to run at quite a slow pace to notice every house, and I'd have to do it over a longish period to ensure the occupants were away. They could be away for weeks or just a few days. How would I know when it was safe to break in?'

Wanda nodded. 'I suppose you're right. So you think you should have another look in the barber's stockroom? How are you going to do that? Break in?'

'Not if I can help it. I thought we'd create a diversion, something long enough for me to slip in unnoticed and make a search. Perhaps I could be in the shop already, or something could happen to make me go in.'

There was a lull while Wanda mulled this over. 'Yes, that might work. Good idea, Quentin.'

Quentin grinned. 'I'm full of good ideas, me,' he said, quoting Colin. Ignoring an irritating prick of conscience, he went on, 'So all we have to do is think of something.'

Wanda pushed a hank of fair hair behind her ear. 'I'm sure I could create a diversion.'

Quentin eyed her appreciatively. 'Well, all men find you diverting, so I shouldn't think Halim or his father will be any different. But you can't just go in and start flirting with them.'

Putting on a pained look Wanda said, 'Me, flirt? I never flirt. I charm.'

Quentin pursed his lips. 'I think you'll find some men will take it as flirting.'

'They can take it any way they like. Anyway, I was thinking of something more diverting than that.'

'Don't tell me you're going to shout fire or something.'

'No, I was thinking I might faint, you know, overcome by the heat, need a rest and a drink of water.'

'Yes,' agreed Quentin, warming to the idea, 'and I could get the water then slip back to the stockroom, or…'

'Or what?'

'I can't remember seeing a back door.'

Wanda frowned in concentration. 'I should think there is. There's got to be a second exit, surely? I'm sure I saw one at Shelagh's, and all those buildings are more or less laid out the same. Why?'

'Well, if there is I could leave that way. No, that won't do, not if I'm in having a shave or a haircut. I couldn't just leave. I wouldn't exactly be inconspicuous with shaving cream all over my face or wrapped up in towel either. If I come in just as you faint, though, perhaps with some other people, they may not remember I was there.'

'Other people? You mean customers?'

'We could choose a time when several customers are in the shop, and we could add to the confusion, say, if we can get someone else to come in with us. The more the merrier.'

'Who are you thinking of, Shelagh? We'd have to tell her why.'

'No, not Shelagh,' Quentin replied after a moment's thought. 'We'll play it by ear.'

'How long do you think you'll need in the stockroom?'

Dredging his memory, Quentin tried to recall the layout of the room. 'At least ten minutes, fifteen if possible.'

Wanda nodded. 'OK. I'll faint, but I'll come round straight away – I don't want them calling an ambulance. I can keep them fussing over me long enough for you to do your bit. What about if I faint outside the shop, you know, in the doorway? They'd have to come out to help me and no one would see you go to the stockroom.'

'I don't think that's a good idea. Passers-by would see you and they might stop to help.'

'That's what we want, isn't it? The more the merrier, you said.'

'Yes, but if passers-by are helping you, then Halim and anyone else in the barber's might not bother. They'd see you were OK and carry on working.'

'Not if I've already been inside.'

Quentin raised a quizzical eyebrow. 'That'll be a first. A woman having the full treatment in a Turkish barber's. I can just see you lathered up for a nice close shave.'

'Very funny. Not a treatment, not for me, but I could be there making an appointment for somebody else. You, for instance.'

Quentin's amusement faded as her words sank in.

'Do you know, that might just work. You go in, make an appointment, throw a bit of your charm about, then collapse just as you're going out. A few people might stop and gather round, including me. When you come round, they are bound to let you sit inside until you are well enough to go. That'll keep Halim and his father occupied.'

They reached a bench and sat down. Bees buzzed round the surrounding bushes and a variety of colourful birds hopped around the paths, pecking at the ground for any morsels of food dropped by picnickers. Quentin raised his face to the sun, letting its rays suffuse him while he thought things through. Their plan could work, but something wasn't right about it.

'I've got it,' he said, straightening up. 'Don't make the appointment for me. Use a fictitious name, say it's for your brother or someone. Halim doesn't know who you are, but if he knows I know you, then he'd expect me to stay with you when you faint.'

'Of course he would,' Wanda agreed. 'But you're forgetting about Linda. She knows we're a couple and she's Halim's girlfriend.'

'True, but we'll make sure she's not there at the time. She's got no idea I know anything anyway. She didn't recognize me that day she came in to talk to Halim – I was covered up. And, if I find anything incriminating in the stockroom, we might be able to put Halim behind bars before either of them realizes our connection.'

The conversation lulled. Quentin could almost hear the cogs going round in Wanda's head.

'Well? Come on, Wanda, what do you think?'

'I think,' she said slowly, 'that it's risky, but… unless we can come up with anything better, we should go for it.'

A grin spread over Quentin's face. Alleluia! Some action at last.

* * *

The next day Shelagh, Howard and Michael came over for tea. It was a British tradition Rosemary liked to keep up, especially when she had guests – Sunday roast at lunchtime and tea in the late afternoon. China crockery, delicately cut sandwiches and home-made cake. Unless, as often happened, they were invited to a barbecue. Quentin guessed her fondness for barbecues didn't match her fondness for sitting at a table eating "properly", as she called it.

Today's cake – lemon – was delicious, and when they had finished eating Shelagh began clearing the table. Quentin picked up a pile of plates and followed her through to the kitchen.

'How's Linda?' he asked. 'Has she given her notice in yet?'

Shelagh shook her head. 'No. She seemed a bit happier yesterday. Her boyfriend didn't go away this weekend.'

'Does he go away a lot, then?'

'He had a spate of going every few weeks, but he hasn't been so much lately. I don't know where he goes. Linda says he's been looking for somewhere to live.'

Or somewhere where he can pass on stolen goods, Quentin thought, wondering how many questions he could ask without Shelagh querying his sudden interest in Linda's boyfriend.

'And no other juicy titbits from clients?'

Shelagh put the tray she was carrying on the draining board. 'Juicy titbits? I'm a hairdresser, not the editor of *Heat* magazine.'

'I bet you hear all kinds of things. You said one of your customers had been burgled.'

'Yes. No more of those, thank goodness. That's not juicy, it's horrible. Not as horrible as someone breaking in when you're there, though. The thought that someone might have got into our house while you were asleep, with Michael there…' She shuddered before she went on. 'We've ordered a burglar alarm, by the way. I know it's like bolting the stable door, but still… The police say there's probably no connection with these other robberies. They think it could just be kids. Well, you know, teenagers.'

That was still a possibility, Quentin realized, but whoever it was had a car. Also, in his experience, kids or teenagers didn't often break into houses alone. Of course, there might have been someone in the car waiting to drive the culprit away, but gut feeling told Quentin teenagers weren't involved. He was convinced his theory about Linda telling Halim that Shelagh would be out that night was right.

Before he could say anything else his mother joined them, bearing leftover sandwiches and cake. 'I'll wrap these up for you, Shelagh. You can take them for your lunch tomorrow.'

'Thanks, Mum. Oh, Suzy asked after you, by the way, Quentin.' Shelagh's anxiety about the attempted robbery seemed to slip a little, and her voice took on a teasing tone. 'She definitely likes you.'

'Maybe,' Quentin answered, 'but she shouldn't get her hopes up. I'm not interested.'

Shelagh grimaced. 'I remember when you were delighted to have girls falling over you.'

'That was before he met Wanda,' Rosemary interrupted. She looked from Quentin to Shelagh. 'I know she's older than Quentin, but I think they're ideally suited, and anyway he should follow his heart, not what convention dictates.'

Sharing a look of understanding with her, Quentin blessed his mother silently. He could always count on her to support him.

'For heaven's sake, it was only a joke,' Shelagh answered. 'Of course I think you and Wanda are fine together. You should know that by now, Quentin.'

A squeal from the lounge reached them, followed by laughter, causing them to go to see what was going on. Michael lay on the floor while Wanda knelt beside him, making faces and pretending to be a monster. Then she tickled him until he squealed again.

'They get on so well, those two,' Shelagh said softly and Quentin guessed at her thoughts.

Wanda should have children, but she was coming up to forty. Lots of women have babies at forty, Quentin knew, but what were the chances of he and Wanda having children? That's what Shelagh had been hinting at, he was sure. He shook himself. He liked children, but he'd never envisaged having any. And Wanda... Wanda had never even hinted that she wanted children. All she'd told him was that her husband had died and it had been a childless marriage. He'd assumed she didn't relish the thought of nappies and night feeds – just as she'd said on the beach at Manly.

His thoughts were interrupted as the phone rang. It stopped, and his father's voice boomed, 'Edward? Good to hear from you. Going to the meeting next week? What? That's preposterous, absolutely preposterous! What happened?'

Wanda stopped tickling Michael and Howard scooped him onto his lap and made a shushing motion with his fingers. Shelagh, Wanda and Quentin fell silent, trying to gain the gist of the conversation. Another burglary, Quentin predicted, but he wasn't prepared for what his father said when he came into room, still clutching the telephone.

'Someone's broken into the ex-servicemen's club,' he choked, his face beetroot. 'They've taken all the medals.'

Chapter Twelve

'Medals?' Quentin said, thinking his father looked as though he might have a heart attack.

'All the service medals that people have donated or left in their wills. It's despicable, absolutely despicable.'

'Oh, Herbert,' Rosemary said. 'That's awful. Is Ed still on the phone?'

Herbert nodded and thrust the handset at Quentin. 'He wants to speak to you.'

Taking the handset Quentin said, 'Ed? I'm sorry to hear about this. How do you know about it?'

Ed Grayson's voice sounded agitated when he spoke.

'I'm a designated key holder for the building. My name's on the list of people to be notified in the event of a fire or – or a break-in. The thing is, the police seem to think it could be connected to these other robberies.'

'Really? Did they say why?'

'Only because the club's been closed for refurbishment. All events and meetings have been suspended until next week. The work is finished now, so the cleaner's been in to get the place up to scratch ready for the next meeting. That's who found the medal case open – it's one of those free-standing glass display cases. The glass was broken.'

'No alarm?'

A snort sounded in Quentin's ear. 'Yes, but only on the doors, not on the case. The alarm at the back was immobilized. The workmen have been going in and out every day for a month. Lots of things were removed before the work started, for safe keeping, but the medals, well, the case was locked and covered up so they were left there.'

'I see. So the place was empty every night? No one hanging around after the workmen left? No caretaker?'

'We don't have a caretaker as such. We take it in turns to lock up after meetings.'

'Could it have been one of the workmen, do you think?'

'The police have taken fingerprints, so if they match any of the workmen's they'll soon find out.'

'Right. Did the police give any indication that they suspected anybody?'

'Unfortunately not. I did ask, and all they said was they'd increase surveillance, send out an extra car to drive round the affected areas. The club's not in the same area as the other burglaries. It's in the middle of town. There is a CCTV camera covering the car park at the rear, but it was sprayed with black paint so no footage.'

Quentin thought for a moment. 'Could I go down and have a look?'

There was a pause, as though Grayson was deciding what to say. 'I could take you along, but I don't think it will do any good. The police have been over it.'

'I'd like to see it, though, get the layout of the place. It might help.'

'All right, I'll take you tomorrow. How are your investigations going? Any progress?'

Quentin hesitated, wondering how much to reveal. 'We think we're onto something but we need more proof. It's a slow process I know—'

'Well, I hope you can do something soon. This is getting out of hand.'

Yes, Quentin thought. If the burglar's got any sense they'll stop now, before they get caught. They're getting overconfident, and if they're overconfident they'll start making mistakes.

'OK, Ed. I'll see you tomorrow.'

* * *

The ex-servicemen's club was in a road just east of Kings Cross in the centre of Sydney. It was accessed via three steps up to the front door and was bound on either side by other properties, one a solicitor's office, the other a real estate agent. Access could also be gained via a driveway further along, leading to a small car park. From there were paths up to the rear of each property.

Ed Grayson was proved right about Quentin's examination of the crime scene. It yielded nothing except how and where entry had been gained – by forcing the lock on the back door. The medal case stood against a wall, empty except for shards of glass that had fallen inside. Quentin's father, who had insisted on going with them, looked at it in dismay that gave way to anger; his mouth twitched, his eyes bulged and his fingers curled into balls.

'I'd like to get my hands on whoever did this,' he muttered. 'I'd teach them a thing or two. Some of those medals were awarded posthumously. People died.'

Quentin stared at him, remembering the callous way he had dismissed the death of his friend as an unfortunate statistic. Perhaps if Nathan had been in the army instead of at university, his father would have been more sympathetic.

'Had the cleaners done anything before they discovered the robbery?' Quentin asked.

Grayson shook his head. 'No, that's why there were so many fingerprints.'

'OK,' Quentin said. He went outside again and looked at the properties either side. The two men followed him.

'So they got in through the back entrance when all the businesses in this row had closed,' Quentin said. 'There are no flats or apartments above these, so no danger of anyone hearing or seeing anything, and if the club was closed it would make things easier. Assuming the thief or thieves aren't among the workmen–'

'Why assume that?' Herbert interrupted. 'Easiest thing in the world – take the medals, hide them in a tool bag, take them away.'

'Yes, but unless they were all in on it whoever it was would have had to be on their own. I'm guessing they tried to force the lock on the case but the glass shattered. Their workmates would have heard it if they'd been there and they'd have to explain the broken case, unless they hid all the glass and covered the case up. Was the case uncovered when the cleaners found it?'

Grayson nodded. 'That's what she said. It was the first thing she noticed.'

'She? Are there any male cleaners?'

'No, there's only Mrs Barker.'

'Only one? Could she have taken the medals?'

Grayson looked indignant. 'Certainly not. I've known her nearly ten years. She couldn't be part of a gang, and what use would she have for medals?'

What indeed? Quentin thought. 'Right. So how many workmen were there, and did any of them have a key? That doesn't make sense, though. If they had a key, they wouldn't need to break in.'

'I'll check with Peter Harrison,' Grayson said. 'He oversaw things while I was away – they might have collected the keys from him each day. If they didn't have a key, it still could have been one of them – they could have come back later and broken in.'

'Of course they could,' Quentin agreed. 'Can you let me have all their names?'

'I'll ask Peter, but the police are already running checks on them.'

Quentin felt he was swimming out of his depth. He couldn't see how this robbery was connected to the others – it was in a business area, not a residential one, and the workmen had to be considered as suspects.

Now he thought about it, it was quite likely to be one of the workmen. How else would anyone know there was anything worth stealing in a property undergoing refurbishment? The windows were blanked out. The interior couldn't be seen from the outside. And there was no connection whatsoever between the ex-servicemen's club and Shelagh's salon. The only similarity with the other robberies was what had been stolen – medals. He supposed that's why the police thought there was a link – Ed Grayson had lost medals.

Bloody hell, he thought, it's getting more confusing than ever. 'Ed,' he said at last. 'Is there anyone you could have told about the medals being left here while the work was going on?'

Grayson looked blank, then said, 'I told you, I was away when the work started.'

'What about since you've been back?'

'No, no one.'

'Nobody would have known except the committee members and key holders,' Herbert put in. 'That's why it has to be one of the workmen, or just a chancer. Stands to reason.'

'OK,' Quentin said. 'I'll just have another look round, make sure I haven't missed anything.'

Going back inside he toured the building again. It smelled of new wood and paint and every room except the kitchen was tidy. Cups and plates had been left on the draining board, and a canister of sugar with its lid askew crawled with the biggest ants Quentin had ever seen. The workmen had swept the floor and removed all their tools. He could see nothing to give any clues about the break-in. There weren't even any bags of rubbish. Quentin guessed they had either been disposed of or taken for examination by the police.

'There's nothing else I can do here,' he admitted when he rejoined the others. 'Thanks for bringing me, Ed.'

'Fat lot of good it did,' his father barked irritably, and for once Quentin agreed with him.

* * *

'So you don't think there's a connection, then?' Wanda asked later when Quentin described his visit to the club. They sat in the garden back at Hibiscus Crescent, drinking coffee and eating slices of cheese and onion quiche.

Quentin swallowed before answering, 'If there is one, I can't see it.'

'No, nor can I. Perhaps we're too hung up on our theory about Shelagh's salon. The burglaries could be committed by totally different people, the ones who are taking small, valuable items, and the ones who take whatever they can, like the computer and the coat.'

'Or,' Quentin said slowly, 'it's the same person who got greedy, saw the computer and coat and decided to break their rule and take something extra, something they wanted to keep for themselves instead of passing it on.'

Wanda chewed at her lip. 'Maybe. Not the club, though. That doesn't fit at all. The fact that medals were stolen could just be coincidence.'

Coincidence. That didn't ring true to Quentin, but as there didn't seem to be any other connection except the medals, he decided to accept it, for now at least.

'There's something else,' he said. 'We're only talking about the break-ins we know about. There's the client Shelagh mentioned, Janet and Bill, and Shelagh's near break-in, but the other robberies can't have come through the salon. Still, I suppose some clients might not mention they've been burgled. I'd like to know exactly how many have been reported to the police.'

'Well, short of asking them, I don't see how we can find out. All we can do is work with what we've got.'

'I could ask them. If I offer to help, share any information I get with them, perhaps they'll share some things with me. The copper who came to Ed Grayson's knew I was a private investigator. I'm sure he would have made a note of it. Come to think of it, I think he said Ed's was the sixth burglary in six months.'

Wanda considered this. 'Hmm. I don't see how you can go cap in hand and expect them to tell you anything. When we've got something concrete to tell them, then they might.'

'OK,' Quentin said, deciding she was right. 'Let's go back to our plan for checking Halim's storeroom. When are we going to try it?'

'Well, Shelagh said Thursdays, Fridays and Saturday mornings are the busiest in the salon, so it's probably the same in the barber's. Shall we make it Thursday?'

Taking the last piece of quiche, Quentin said, 'I don't know if we should wait that long. He might have got rid of the stuff by then.'

'He might have got rid of it already for all we know,' Wanda countered.

A definite possibility, Quentin thought. Then he remembered what Shelagh had said the day before. Linda was happier because Halim hadn't gone away that weekend – the weekend just gone. Presumably Halim was working on weekdays, so he probably hadn't had time to get rid of the goods. In which case they would still be in the stockroom and it would be fine to wait until Thursday. Or perhaps it wouldn't. Anything could happen before then, and he wasn't prepared to sit around doing nothing.

'I can't see the point of waiting,' he said. 'Let's just go for it. It's quite busy there, plenty of people milling about. We'll go down tomorrow, get the lie of the land and if we don't think the time or circumstances are right, we'll leave it.'

'All right. We'll see who's in the barber's and in the street. It may take a couple of days before we decide to go ahead. We might have to change the plan – like you said, we'll play it by ear.'

'Play what by ear?' Rosemary approached them with a plate of biscuits.

'Oh, just what to do tomorrow,' Quentin said, helping himself to a chocolate cookie. 'We're probably going into town.'

How it happened Quentin wasn't sure, but five minutes later he'd agreed to take his father on a cooling trip to the coast while his mother took Wanda to her flower arranging club.

Bloody hell, Quentin thought. A whole afternoon alone with my father!

'Great,' he said after his mother had gone indoors. 'What on earth are we going to talk about for four hours?'

Wanda raised an immaculate eyebrow. Despite the heat she looked cool in pale blue shorts, open-toed sandals and a sleeveless white cotton top.

'I'm sure you'll think of something. It won't hurt you to make an effort.'

'Make an effort? I have been making an effort.'

'I know, but really, he's been very good since we've been here. I mean, we've said things he hasn't agreed with, but he's held his tongue.'

Quentin sighed. 'All right, you've made your point. I'll do my duty like a good little boy.'

'Well done,' Wanda said standing up. 'You can go for a run while you're there. After all, what else have you got to do this afternoon?'

He caught his breath as she stood before him, slim and sensual, and he felt the beginnings of a tingle. 'I could think of at least one thing I'd rather do.'

Wanda laughed. 'It's far too hot for that. I'm going to have a quick shower, then it'll be time for me to go.'

'OK.' Quentin watched her leave, beating back his desire and wondering what his father would make of him offering to take him out for the afternoon. Wiping his forehead, he groaned. There was only one way to find out.

* * *

During his run along the path from Balmoral Beach to Chowder Bay Quentin tried to keep his mind off the burglaries and what he and Wanda were going to attempt tomorrow. After a surprised reaction to his offer, his father had agreed to accompany him. Quentin had brought a fold-up chair and carried it to a convenient spot, where his father had settled himself in the shade of a eucalyptus tree. He seemed quite happy to read his military magazine while Quentin went off on his run.

A few other people had the same idea as himself and were jogging against the breeze, which was brisk and cooling. Most people were strolling, singly or in couples, some in family groups. Quentin cursed silently as he broke his stride to avoid a dog before noticing how much it looked like Mozart, Wanda's West Highland terrier. His thoughts turned to Magpie and home, and he wondered how cold it would be there now, with winter setting in and the days growing shorter.

When he'd taken a glug from his water bottle he turned and ran back to where he'd left his father. Collapsing onto the grass, he sat panting until he got his breath back.

'Told you it was too hot for running,' Herbert said. 'Should have waited till tonight. Nice here, though. Good spot to watch the world go by.'

Quentin nodded. He was unused to seeing his father watching the world go by. In England, when he wasn't working or away with the army, he'd been active, or at least he'd looked active. As far as Quentin could remember a lot of his activity seemed to involve walking about in military fashion, laying down the law and making sure his opinion was heard. And felt.

'What are you doing about this robbery business?' his father said now. 'Can't see what good you've done so far. What about this theory of yours – about Shelagh's salon? Can't be right – facts don't fit. Hope you haven't said anything.'

'We haven't, and we won't until it's absolutely necessary.'

Herbert snorted. '*If* it's necessary, you mean. So what are you doing? Got any plans?'

'Possibly,' Quentin said cautiously. He didn't want to reveal his plan for tomorrow.

'Possibly? What does that mean? Either you have or you haven't.'

'It's just an idea at the moment.'

'An idea? Does Wanda know about it?'

'We've discussed it, yes.'

'Huh. Can't see why you can't tell me. Handled all sorts of situations in the army.'

Quentin closed his eyes and counted to ten. For Christ's sake, he wanted to shout, you're not in the bloody army now.

'I appreciate that, and if I thought you could help, I'd tell you. But the army was your business and detecting's mine. Just because things are taking a while to work out doesn't mean we won't work it out. After all, the police have every resource at their disposal and they haven't managed to catch anyone, have they?'

His father grunted. 'That's true, my boy. Comes to something when you're frightened to leave your house in case it's burgled. Glad that alarm's coming soon.'

'Yes. Well, you're not planning on going away for a while, are you, so you should be all right. Still, an alarm's a good idea. It'll give Mum some peace of mind.'

Quentin thought of the alarms that had been made inoperative, one at the ex-servicemen's club and one at Shelagh's customer's house. But they were on single-storeyed buildings. An alarm high on a double-storeyed house should be fine.

A silence fell between them, and Quentin wondered how soon he could suggest going home. He took another swig of water, then offered the bottle to his father.

'Could do with a cold beer,' was the response.

'There's a bar not too far away,' Quentin told him, remembering the one he'd seen on his run. 'Why don't we go and get a beer?'

This earned him an appreciative look. 'Now that is a good idea. Fold this thing up, will you?'

Yes sir, no sir, three bags full sir, Quentin mumbled as he folded up his father's chair. He started to walk, then stopped when his father called to him. Turning back to face him, Quentin saw he looked slightly uncomfortable, as though he was embarrassed about something.

'Been meaning to say, glad you decided to come out to see us. Means a lot to your mother.'

Temporarily stunned, Quentin fought for words. 'Well,' he said after what seemed like an age, 'I'd have come sooner, but you know how things are.'

'Yes, yes, building up the business and all that. I know.'

No, you don't, Quentin thought. You haven't got a clue. Nevertheless, he grinned and fell into step with this awkward, blinkered man, and decided that spending the afternoon with him wasn't as bad as he'd thought it would be. As least he was getting a beer out of it.

Chapter Thirteen

The diversion proved easier than they'd hoped. At ten o'clock the next morning the city was already bustling, and after parking their hired car Quentin and Wanda walked to the parade of shops where the salon and the barber's were situated. The pavements were full of people going about their daily life, and Quentin was glad to see that the barber's shop door was open, presumably to let some air inside. Not all the smaller shops had air conditioning, he'd noticed.

Ambling nonchalantly by, he glanced through the window. Halim's father, Ahmed, was there, in an animated conversation with a man Quentin took to be a customer, possibly trying to persuade him to have "the full works". Halim stood with his back to the window putting the finishing touches to a haircut. Quentin wondered if the customer was booked in for a shave as well, and would end up swaddled like he had been. Two other men sat waiting on seats at the front.

Carrying on along the road, Quentin passed Shelagh's salon, walking quickly so as not to be spotted by her or any of the staff. When he got past it, he turned and waved to Wanda, who stood on the opposite side of the street. She waved back, signalling that she would take her turn at going past the barber's. A swathe of people rounded a far corner and began to walk towards him. Now might be a good time. He hesitated – should there be more people inside the shop to cause more confusion? But then, given the size of the shop and with only two people and the greeter working, it was probably as busy as it could be.

Stepping into the road he saw Wanda look through the barber's window, then turn towards him, nod and begin walking to the door.

She's going in, he thought, panic setting in. What if this doesn't work and we make fools of ourselves? We should have planned it more carefully. Oh well, too late now.

Passing the barber's window again, he saw Wanda at the reception desk talking to Ahmed, who finished writing something in the appointment book then looked up and beamed at her. She smiled and started backing away. When she got to the door she turned, caught Quentin's eye, and when he nodded she duly feigned a collapse, groaning loudly and banging her handbag against the wall. She lay on the pavement, slumped across the shop doorway and blocking the entrance. Several passers-by stopped and gathered round her. Quentin stepped over her and called into the shop.

'We need some help here!'

He bent down, making a show of feeling for Wanda's pulse. The older barber appeared, followed by Halim, then the big-bellied greeter and the customers.

'She's fainted,' Quentin said, not looking up. 'Probably the heat. Get her inside and I'll fetch some water.'

'We'll call an ambulance,' Ahmed said, at which Wanda stirred and her eyes fluttered open. 'Hot,' she murmured. 'So hot.'

'Bring her in,' said one of the men who'd been waiting to be attended to. 'I'm a doctor.'

Quentin saw a flicker of panic cross Wanda's face. Bloody hell, he thought. A doctor – that's all we need.

'I'll get the water,' he muttered, pushing past them and heading to the back of the shop. He was glad Halim or his father didn't seem to recognize him from his previous visit, although today they hadn't really been looking at him. Going through the beaded curtain to the kitchen, he grabbed a mug and filled it with water, trusting that no one was paying enough attention to query how he knew where to go. Then he went back and handed the mug to the customer who'd been having his hair cut.

'Give her this,' he muttered.

By now, there were about ten people in the shop and Wanda was being sat in a chair. With everyone focused on her, Quentin slipped back through the curtain and made for the stockroom.

Let's hope we're not wasting our time, he thought as he pushed the door open. Closing it quietly, he felt the sheepskin coat swinging from the hook on the back before he saw it. At least that was still here. So was the computer, still in its box. He cast his gaze around, wondering where to start.

As before, the shelves were mainly filled with hairdressing and shaving products, as well as a neat stack of towels and various razors, scissors and leather strops. He moved along until he spotted a heap of capes on a shelf in the corner, like the one he had worn when he'd had his hair cut, not neatly stack like the towels, but spread out more. Placing his hand on them Quentin felt something underneath. He pushed the capes aside to reveal a blue linen bag, about twelve inches square, with an outline of several mountains and the words "The Blue Mountains" printed in black across the middle. Its surface was made uneven and lumpy by whatever it contained. After picking it up and resting the base on the shelf, he drew open the drawstring and peered inside. His breath caught in his throat as he recognized what he was looking at. Not jewellery, not bracelets or miniature paintings. Medals.

His mind whirling. He drew one out and stared at it, wondering if it was one of Ed Grayson's or one from the clubhouse. No time to think about it now. He had to get out before–

He jumped as he heard voices coming closer. Hastily he dropped the medal back in the bag, pushed the bag back into place and covered it with the capes. Then he darted to the door and flattened himself against the wall so he would be behind the door if it opened. It opened a fraction, but whoever was pushing it stopped in response to a voice from further away, as though it was calling from the other side of the beaded curtain.

Quentin recognized Halim's voice as he answered. 'The facial oil? All right, I'll be two minutes.'

Quentin held his breath, expecting Halim to enter the room and planning how he could make a dash through the door without being seen. Instead of coming in, though, Halim changed direction. Quentin heard the door immediately opposite, which he remembered was the toilet, open and shut. Halim was obviously taking a comfort break before carrying on his work. Did that mean Wanda had gone, or had the two barbers decided to leave her with the doctor and get back to their clients?

There was no way of knowing, but Quentin knew two things for certain. He'd have to leave the medals – the police would need to find them here as evidence – and he mustn't be caught in the storeroom.

Seizing his chance, he slipped silently out of the room, remembering to leave it slightly ajar as Halim had. He heard the flush of the toilet and froze. He couldn't risk coming face-to-face with Halim in the narrow passage, and now he was doubtful about going back through the shop – if people had left and it was less crowded, he wouldn't be able to sneak back unobserved. Making a snap decision he hurried the few paces to the kitchen area, keeping away from the opening through which part of it could be seen. He heard Halim go from the toilet to the storeroom, praying that he would go straight back into the shop.

Looking round for somewhere to hide if Halim came into the kitchen, he noticed a back door. Moving to it, he tried the handle. Locked. He couldn't believe his luck when, just above the worktop on his left-hand side, he saw a row of hooks, two of them sporting sets of keys. One held just two keys, so Quentin tried these first. Alleluia! he thought as the first key turned in the mortise lock. The second key turned easily too, and the door swung open.

A minute later Quentin was running along the communal alleyway, past the waste bins and piles of discarded boxes, until he came to the passage that led to the front of the parade of shops. Slowing to a walking pace, he ran his hand through his hair and smiled a triumphant smile. That was close, he said to himself.

Sauntering along the pavement, he glanced in at the barber's as he passed, wondering if Wanda was still there or had made a miraculous recovery and left. Hoping that neither Halim nor his father noticed him, he spotted Wanda sitting to one side, the mug of water still in her hand. He willed her to look his way, but she was gazing towards the back of the shop as though she expected him to come through the beaded curtain. He carried on, crossing the road to avoid Shelagh's salon. Then he doubled back and strolled past the barber's again. This time Wanda spotted him, her face lighting up in surprise. He walked on and waited across the road until he saw her emerge, then waved and called to her. When she joined him, he guided her swiftly along the pavement until they came to a small café on the corner of the parade. They sat at a table around the far side, so they couldn't be seen from the barber's or the salon, and ordered coffee.

'That was neat,' Wanda said when the waitress had taken their order. 'How did you manage it? Don't tell me – the back door just happened to be open.'

'Nearly right.' Quentin grinned.

'Well, did you find anything?'

'You could say that.'

'Don't be so infuriating. What did you find?'

'Well, the coat and computer are still there.'

Wanda picked up a packet of sugar and threw it at him.

'Come on, then,' she demanded. 'Was it jewellery?'

Deciding she had waited long enough, he said, 'No, not jewellery. Only medals.'

'Medals!' Excitement rose in Wanda's voice. 'You found medals! So we've got proof of that at least.'

Quentin's earlier flippancy receded. 'It's proof enough for us. Not for the police, though. They'll only have our word for it.'

'True, but I'm sure they'll investigate if you tell them what you saw. After all, they know medals have been stolen. I don't suppose you thought to take a photo, did you?'

'Didn't get time. I'd just found them when I heard Halim coming. I don't know how long I was in there.'

Wanda rolled her eyes. 'It seemed ages to me. It wasn't easy, I can tell you, pretending to be ill to a doctor–'

'Oh, I don't know,' Quentin interrupted. 'I daresay thousands of people try it on to get out of work.'

'Maybe, but I'm not one of them. Anyway, the doctor was really nice. He took my pulse and said it was racing, but that otherwise I seemed all right. I think he bought the heat explanation. He told me to make sure I kept hydrated and to wear a hat. So, what are we going to do now? Go to the police?'

Quentin shook his head. 'I still think we need more proof, something we can show them.'

There was a lull as the waitress brought their coffee. After she'd gone Wanda asked, 'How can we do that?'

Quentin grinned again. 'Easy. We go back in and either take one of the medals or take a photo.'

Wanda leaned back in her seat and eyed him coolly. 'Do we? And how do you expect to do that, get me to have another fainting fit, or perhaps you'd prefer to break in during the dead of night like the burglars.'

'Break in? As if I'd do such a thing.'

'As if,' Wanda mocked, sending him a look that said she knew he already had something in mind. 'All right, spill. How are you going to do it?'

'Simple,' he told her, reaching into the pocket of his shorts. 'With these.'

Chapter Fourteen

Wanda gasped. 'You took the keys?'

'Let's just say I borrowed them. The door was locked, so if I'd opened it and left the keys there, they would have known something was wrong. I locked it from the outside, so now they'll just think they've mislaid the keys. It's easily done. When we go back, after we've taken a medal or a photo, we'll lock the door again from the outside. They'll never know we've been there.'

Looking doubtful, Wanda said, 'I suppose you could always go in for a shave or something later on and leave the keys in the shop somewhere for them to find.'

'Yeah,' Quentin agreed, though he didn't relish the idea of Halim putting an open razor anywhere near him.

The story of Sweeney Todd came to him fleetingly before a couple with a dog and two children rounded the corner and sat at the next table. Leaning closer to Wanda he said, 'I suppose we could always get a duplicate set of the keys cut.'

'Good idea.' Wanda's voice was low. 'Then, when you go back to the stockroom, you could leave the original set for them to find and still lock the door from the outside.'

After draining his cup, Quentin called for the bill. 'Time to go.'

Wanda stood up. 'Go where? Shelagh's?'

'Not yet. We don't want to burden her until we have to, and we don't want to give Linda or Halim cause to think we suspect them. Let's just walk, go somewhere where we can think things through.'

They meandered through the streets, eventually finding themselves in Kings Cross.

'There's enough here to take our mind off things,' Quentin said when he realized where they were. 'This is the red-light district.'

'Really?' Wanda cast her gaze alternately to either side of the road. 'It doesn't look seedy enough to be a red-light district.'

'Well, it is. Shelagh told me about it.'

The main road through Kings Cross looked like any other city street, at least now in the daytime, with nothing obvious betraying its night-time activities. It was wide and pleasant and lined with shops and clubs, with a large, round, steel sculpture resembling a dandelion clock half-way down on one side. The pavements were as full of people as any other part of town, some staring curiously in shop windows, others just walking by as though ignorant of what the shops sold or afraid to be seen looking.

'Ooh la la!' Wanda laughed when they passed a window displaying skimpy underwear. 'Perhaps I should walk on and leave you to browse, Quentin.'

'What for? That sort of thing only interests me if you're wearing it.'

'Right answer. When we've got this case under our belts, I'll see what I can do.'

'Really? I'll hold you to that.'

'Fine. Remind me not to bring your mum here when she offers to take me shopping.'

They looked at each other and laughed. 'Come on,' Wanda urged. 'Let's go down to the front and go for a long walk, blow the cobwebs away.'

'I quite like my cobwebs the way they are,' Quentin told her. Nevertheless, he matched her quickening pace, thinking again how lucky he was to have this wonderful woman by his side.

* * *

The wind picked up as they walked along, ruffling their hair and cooling their glowing faces.

After getting a duplicate of the barber's keys cut, Wanda wanted to go to the Opera House to see if there was any change in the programme. On the way, Wanda's mobile rang, and she stopped to answer it. 'My mother,' she mouthed, and leaned against a convenient railing.

Quentin stood a few feet away, imagining Wanda's mother on the other end of the line and realizing he'd only met her once. The meeting hadn't gone well. It was clear that Wanda's mother didn't approve of her daughter's relationship with a younger man. Quentin didn't really care, though he'd been upset that his charm and charisma hadn't won her over.

'All right?' he asked when the call ended.

Nodding, Wanda said, 'Ah-ha. My brother's got a promotion – again. I think she just rang to sing his praises.'

'Bully for him,' Quentin quipped. 'Let's hope he makes enough money to keep her in her old age.'

Wanda shrugged. 'She can't help it. He's done well for himself. It's only natural that she's proud of him. Come on, we'll walk a bit further then turn back.'

They carried on in silence. Suddenly Wanda said, 'If we're going to do it, I think we should do it tonight.'

Quentin understood exactly what she meant. The case hadn't been mentioned for two hours, but he knew it wasn't far from either of their thoughts.

'Before he can get rid of the medals, you mean? I was thinking the same myself, although if my theory about why he often goes away is right, I don't think he'll pass them on till the weekend. Still, the sooner the better, I suppose. What time does the shop shut, do you think?'

'I don't know. Probably about half five, the same as Shelagh's. Why? We can't go that early. Not everyone leaves their business as soon as it closes.'

'I was thinking about eight.'

Wanda looked baffled. 'Eight? But it'll still be light.'

'All the better. No risk of any security lights coming on.'

'But more risk of someone seeing us.'

'Not us, Wanda, me. One person isn't as visible as two. Anyway, I'll need you on the outside.'

'But you said "us", and you know I won't be left out.'

'You won't be left out. You'll be somewhere nearby with your phone and the car in case I need to get away in a hurry.'

Wanda gave a wry smile. 'So I'm your getaway driver now, am I? We sound like two burglars planning an escape.'

'I suppose we are, technically. I mean, we're going into someone else's property without their knowledge or permission, to take something that isn't ours, but for the right reasons. After all, the police raid or break into places if they think they'll find evidence of criminal activities, so why shouldn't we?'

'Because we're not the police, that's why. You should have joined the police force, Quentin. It would have been a good career for you.'

Detecting a note of sarcasm in her voice, Quentin stared at her. Was she mocking him?

'Don't look so peeved, Quentin. You told me Steve Philmore said you wouldn't make a bad copper.'

Quentin thought of Detective Chief Inspector Philmore, whom he had assisted on previous cases in London. 'Not being a bad copper doesn't make you a good one. You know as well as I do that I couldn't stand their rules and paperwork.'

Wanda laughed. 'You mean your methods are too haphazard? But if you'd joined you would have learned to cope with all that.'

Would I? Quentin thought. I don't think so. There's thinking outside the box and there's ignoring it altogether.

'Still,' Wanda went on, 'if you had, I wouldn't have met you, and anyway I like you the way you are.'

Was that true? Quentin wondered. They were two of kind, he realized that, but if he were in a secure job with a regular income and a pension to look forward to, would she agree to his suggestion that they move in together, maybe even marry, become a couple in the proper sense? Bugger it, he thought, annoyed that he'd allowed himself to be distracted from the case.

'OK,' he said. 'Let's go home, have dinner, charge our phones and come back about eight. I can't wait to have an uninterrupted look in that stockroom.'

* * *

Wanda was just complimenting Rosemary on the chicken and herb bake she'd served for dinner when Shelagh arrived with Michael.

'Can I leave Michael with you?' she blurted, looking flustered. 'Howard's brother's had an accident and he's in hospital. Howard's gone over there. His mother's in a state and I feel I should be there for her.'

Jumping to her feet, Rosemary put her arms around her daughter. 'Oh, Shelagh, how awful. What happened?'

'We're not sure yet, but it sounds like he went off the road and hit something. A tree or a lamp post, I suppose. It was just Stephen. There wasn't another car involved, apparently.' Shelagh dumped a bag on the floor. 'I brought Michael some things.'

'How far is the hospital?' Quentin asked. He thought his sister looked pale. Her ankles were slightly swollen, and she rubbed her lower back, clearly in discomfort. She must have been on her feet all day, he realized.

'Quite a way. I hate driving there – it's a pain.'

'We'll drive you, won't we, Quentin?' Wanda said.

Quentin caught her eye and understood the coded message. We don't have to go to the barber's tonight. Tomorrow will do.

'There's no need–' Shelagh began.

'Yes there is,' Herbert barked. 'You look all in. I'll come with you.'

'Thanks, Dad, but really, there's no need for us all to go. On second thoughts, though, Quentin, I would be grateful for a lift. I don't really feel like driving all that way. You don't have to stay – I can come back with Howard.'

'Of course,' Quentin said. 'No problem, sis. I'll get my keys.'

'Have you eaten?' Rosemary asked Shelagh, all concern. When Shelagh shook her head, she went on, 'There's some chicken left. It's no good you rushing off on an empty stomach. You need your energy. Sit down and I'll get you something.'

Shelagh did as she was told. She looked drawn, and Quentin wondered whether Howard was right – perhaps she was overtaxing herself, running the house and the business with Michael to look after as well.

While Shelagh swallowed a few mouthfuls of chicken, Michael grinned happily through half-chewed cake, smudges of chocolate on his chin and pyjama top.

'Anyway,' Shelagh said when she'd finished eating, 'it's just– since Howard's dad died Irene's on her own. We see quite a bit of her but Stephen lives nearer and he pops in every day to make sure she's all right.'

'Don't worry, Shelagh,' Wanda said. 'Quentin will take you. Leave Michael here.'

'I'll go with you, Shelagh,' Rosemary suggested. 'I know Irene, and a bit of feminine comfort might help her.'

'That's a nice idea, Mum,' Shelagh said. 'You could go in for a bit, then come back with Quentin, if Wanda doesn't mind playing mum for a night.'

'Of course I don't mind.' Wanda held her hand out to Michael. 'We'll have a fine old time, won't we, Michael?'

Accepting her hand, Michael nodded solemnly. 'And Granddad,' he said, pulling his hand away and climbing onto his grandfather's lap.

Amazement swamped Quentin. It was the first time he'd noticed any affection from Michael towards his grandfather.

'Hey ho, my lad,' Herbert said gruffly, looking surprised. 'Show you my coins if you're a good boy.'

Quentin vaguely recalled his father's coin collection, gathered from the various places he'd visited whilst in the army, some of which were, as his father never tired of telling him, quite valuable. As a child he'd been banned from touching them after he'd removed one and tried to clean it with furniture polish.

'Right,' Quentin said, all hopes fading of going back to the barber's shop after he'd dropped Shelagh off. 'I'm ready when you are.'

* * *

As they entered the hospital, Quentin was struck by the tasteful décor and the efficiency of the staff in the main reception area. The place seemed bright and clean, but in Quentin's eye's nothing could disguise the fact that hospitals only existed because people got sick. As far as he was concerned, the less time he spent in them the better.

They found Howard in the corridor, nursing a polystyrene cup of cold coffee and looking distraught. He seemed relieved when he saw them.

'Thanks for coming,' he said. 'Mum could do with some support. She's at her wits end with worry.'

'How is he?' Shelagh asked, looping her arm through her husband's.

'Pretty bad. They've taken X-rays and say he's got multiple fractures of his leg and a damaged pelvis. The air bag saved him from chest and abdomen injuries, but they think he was thrown sideways and hit his head. They don't know what on – could have been the metal seat belt bracket, or maybe something came through the window. He's got a nasty gash on his head.'

'Poor Stephen,' Rosemary said, her voice laden with sympathy. 'Do you know what happened?'

'Not really. He hasn't said much. I think he's in shock. He keeps losing consciousness. I'll take Shelagh in to see him, Rosemary, and my mum can come out and talk to you.'

Quentin watched them disappear behind a set of swing doors. Shortly afterwards a big-boned woman with red-rimmed eyes came from the ward towards them. Quentin heard his mother's soft voice as she embraced her, then led her to a seat further along the corridor. He hovered on the periphery, not wanting to interrupt them.

As they drove home later that night Rosemary was quiet.

'Cheer up, Mum,' he said, trying to lift her spirits. 'They'll sort him out in no time. They can put anything back together these days.'

She nodded and pursed her lips, and later he caught her looking at him. He knew, beyond a shadow of a doubt, that she was imagining how she would feel if it was him lying in a hospital bed with multiple injuries. A mother's love, he mused. Is there anything else like it in the world?

Chapter Fifteen

He was awoken the next morning by a shake from Wanda. 'Shelagh phoned,' she said, perching on the edge of the bed.

Yawning, Quentin sat up and rubbed at his eyes.

'They didn't get back from the hospital until late and she's shattered,' Wanda continued. 'She's asked if I can go into the salon today, to man reception. Your dad's offered to take me, and I said he could. It'll make him feel useful. You can pick me up when I've finished if you like, or I can get the bus.'

'I'll pick you up. Ring me when you're ready.'

'All right.' Wanda planted a kiss on his cheek then turned to go. Quentin called her back.

'Perhaps we'll eat out tonight,' he said, struggling to get his thoughts together. 'I'll pick you up, we'll get some food and then we'll do what we were supposed to do last night.'

'Yes, good idea. I must go now or I'll be late.'

As she walked from the room Quentin gazed after her. A whole day at home with his parents. What was he going to do all day?

A sudden shrill whoop answered his question. Michael. Michael was still here, awake and playing by the sound of it. Loud repetitive thumps drifted up to him, as though a ball was being bounced under his window. He lay down and pulled the pillow over his head, but the thumping persisted. Oh well, he thought, it's time to get up anyway.

By the time his father returned from taking Wanda to the salon Quentin had showered, shaved and eaten breakfast. He spent the morning playing with Michael, surprised at how well the boy threw and caught the tennis-sized ball.

'I see a future cricketer before me,' he said. 'England had better watch out for The Ashes in a few years' time.'

Quentin didn't follow cricket or any ball games. He'd never really been a team player. He enjoyed running much more.

'Granddad, you play,' Michael called, throwing the ball as his grandfather came into the garden.

It went flying past Herbert, who retrieved it and sent it back to him. Quentin watched them, a twinge of something he didn't understand stabbing at him. He couldn't remember his father ever playing with him like this.

He pulled himself up sharply. It doesn't matter, he reminded himself. It doesn't matter now.

* * *

Before it was time to meet Wanda, he rang her to arrange a pick-up place.

'I'll meet you at the end of the road, by the café where we were yesterday,' he said. 'I don't want to come to the salon in case Halim sees me. I don't want him to connect me with you, in case he puts two and two together.'

'All right.' Wanda spoke in hushed tones, as though she was trying not to be overheard. 'I've been on the lookout for him, too. I thought he might go past or come in to see Linda and recognize me – not that it would matter. There's no reason why I shouldn't be here. I didn't have to tell him I knew the owner of the salon when I was in there.'

'No,' Quentin agreed, 'but everyone in the salon would think it was strange if they found out you'd fainted in his shop and not told them, or at least told Shelagh. Stay away from the window if you can. I'll see you at closing time.'

With nothing else to do, Quentin left Hibiscus Crescent at three-thirty. At four-fifteen he parked the car as near to the salon as possible and walked in the opposite direction, to where the shops ended and a church was set back from the road. Finding a bench in the grounds behind the building, he sat and waited, his mind on what they had planned that night.

It was almost five-fifteen when he rose to walk to the café where he'd arranged to meet Wanda. He ambled towards the church, reaching the nearside corner just as two people emerged from the other side of the building: a young woman, tugging on the arm of a dark, slim man. Before they had a chance to notice him, Quentin hastened to the corner then stopped, dropping to his knees and peering between the wall's edge and a tall gravestone. He strained to hear what they were saying, but couldn't make it out. What he saw, though, threw him into confusion.

The man was trying to shake free of the woman's grip, but she clung on and whirled round in front of him. She spoke for a while, her face upturned to his. Whatever she said, it seemed to change the man's attitude. Instead of trying to get away, he pulled her to him and kissed her.

Bloody hell, Quentin thought, that's a turn-up for the book. The man was Halim, but the woman wasn't Linda. It was Suzy.

* * *

Quentin arrived at the café to find it had closed at five. He stood outside and waited, impatience setting in when Wanda wasn't there fifteen minutes later. He was about to ring her when she appeared, her blonde hair held behind her ears with diamanté clips and her usually perfect complexion slightly reddened.

'Sorry I'm late,' she said. 'I had to cash up and tidy up as well. Suzy rushed off as soon as she finished her last customer.'

'Yes, I know.'

'Do you? How?'

Quentin explained what he'd seen in the churchyard.

Wanda raised her eyebrows in surprise. 'So Halim's a two-timer now?' she asked.

'Not sure really. To me it looked as if Suzy was doing all the running. Maybe she was trying to get Halim to hook up with her instead of Linda.'

Quentin paused, thinking of Suzy's doe eyes lingering on him, and the ego boost he'd felt at the suggestion that she was sweet on him. How wrong could anyone be?

'She obviously persuaded him, at least for now, judging by that kiss,' he concluded.

Wanda sighed. 'Are you thinking what I'm thinking?'

'Yes. It could be Suzy who's giving Halim information. Perhaps I misheard what Linda said to Halim in the barber's. Maybe she said, "I told you to stay away from her", not "I told you to stay away from hers". Maybe she meant stay away from Suzy.'

'Suzy doesn't strike me as the type to have an affair with a colleague's boyfriend,' Wanda commented. 'Still, people surprise you, don't they?'

Quentin nodded. 'This throws a spanner in the works, just as we thought we were getting somewhere.' He gestured towards the café door. 'We'll have to go somewhere else to eat. They're closed.'

'So I see. We'll go down to the waterfront if you like. Halim's father is still there.' Wanda jerked her head in the direction of the barber's shop. 'I had a quick look as I left. The florist on the other side is all shut up, but not everyone goes home on the dot of closing time. We'll go back about eight like you said.'

As they made their way through the city Wanda asked, 'How's Howard's brother, have you heard?'

'He's a bit better today,' Quentin said, remembering a phone call from Howard's mother. 'They've operated on him, he's conscious and he's had something to eat, so that's a good sign.'

They reached the waterfront and chose a bar that offered a decent menu. Resisting the temptation to gain some Dutch courage from a glass of whisky, Quentin settled for coffee and a bottle of water. He didn't know why he was nervous – he'd broken into a property before. But then it had been on the spur of the moment, an action born of necessity. Having time to think about it was different, like waiting for a tooth extraction or the build-up to a difficult exam.

When they'd finished their meal, he sat tapping his fingers on the table, stopping only to lift his hand and check his watch.

Wanda, refreshed and looking more like her serene self, gazed at him thoughtfully. 'We don't have to do this, you know, if you're worried about it.'

'We do, and I'm not worried.'

'You look it.'

'It's the waiting around. I just want to get on with it.'

'Yes, well, I've got something for you.'

'Really? What?'

Reaching into her bag Wanda took out something black and hairy. Quentin stared at it. For a fleeting moment he thought she was handing him some sort of animal. Then he gave a half laugh.

'A wig! You took a wig from Shelagh's salon?'

'Borrowed,' Wanda corrected, her face deadpan. 'If you can borrow someone's keys then I can borrow a wig. Shelagh won't mind and I can return it tomorrow.'

'OK, enough of the games. What's it for?'

'You, of course. I've got these too.' Wanda dived into her bag again and pulled out a spectacle case, from which she extracted a pair of dark-rimmed glasses. She leaned forward and lowered her voice. 'As you said it'll still be light. If anyone sees you, at least they won't recognize you.'

'A disguise? What's wrong with a trench coat and a newspaper?'

Wanda gave an exasperated *tsk* and put the glasses back in the case.

'There's gratitude for you. Look, I know the shops in that parade will all be closed and there shouldn't be anyone around, but you never know. Someone might be staying late or stocktaking or something. They'll only see you from a distance, at least I hope they will. If you look different there's no chance of them connecting you to Shelagh or– or anyone.'

'Point taken,' Quentin said, mildly amused. 'All right, I suppose it is a sensible precaution. And the wig's black. From the back I could be Halim. Right. By the time we get back it should be safe enough to carry on. What?'

Wanda was frowning, and chewing at her bottom lip as she did when she was thinking things over.

'How will we know there's definitely nobody there?' she said at last.

'Well, it's a small shop. I'll check the front for activity, then do the same at the back.'

'OK. Unless they're in the loo or the stockroom, you'll see them.'

'Right,' said Quentin, standing up. 'Let's do this.'

Chapter Sixteen

Quentin was surprised what a difference a wig and a pair of spectacles could make. When they had gone back to where he'd parked the car Wanda arranged the wig on his head, making sure there were no tell-tale strands of his own hair showing. He donned the light jacket he'd brought with him, placed the glasses – plain glass – on his face, looked in the vanity mirror and grimaced.

'I feel like I'm going to a fancy dress party.'

'Stop complaining. It's no worse than wearing a hat and it won't be for long. Let's get going before the light fades enough for the security lights to come on.'

'I didn't see a security light when I went out the back door,' Quentin said as Wanda started the engine. 'There might be an alarm, though.'

Wanda shook her head. 'Shouldn't think so. They're all small businesses along there, not that much worth stealing, not like a supermarket or bank. There's not even a jeweller's. Shelagh hasn't got an alarm in the salon.'

'No,' agreed Quentin. 'Oh well, I'll just have to risk it. At least there's room to park at this time of night. Pity these shops haven't got their own parking. Here we are. Drive past slowly, so I can look inside, then stop by the alley.'

He gazed through the barber's front window as they drove by.

'Can't see anyone. No lights on. No sign of an alarm either.'

They pulled up at the entrance to the alley. There was no one in the immediate vicinity, just some boys at the far end walking away from them.

'Keep hold of your phone and be ready to drive off as soon as I come back,' he said, opening the passenger door.

It took him exactly two minutes to walk up the alley and along the backs of the single-storeyed shops. It was quiet, with no signs of activity except for a cat that crossed his path and scrambled over the fence into a garden. Quentin cursed under his breath. Although it was unlikely he would be seen by anyone from the shops, he'd forgotten that the alley backed onto the gardens of a row of houses. If someone was looking through an upstairs window, he might be seen. Better to be as swift as possible.

Approaching the back of the barber's cautiously, he sneaked a look through the kitchen window for any sign of movement. Nothing. Outside the back door he paused, listening. Still nothing. Glad that they'd had duplicate keys cut, he took them from his pocket and opened the door, grateful that it swung open effortlessly. He slipped in and closed it behind him. He stood just inside for a moment, listening again for any sounds. Then he went through the short hallway and into the stockroom. The small window gave some light, but it was starting to fade and the room was dim. Not too dim to see immediately that the sheepskin coat no longer hung on the door and the box containing the computer wasn't there. He looked around in case it had been moved further along, but found nothing. He hurried over to where he had seen the linen bag.

'Bugger it!' he muttered. The capes which had concealed the bag now hung from a hook on the wall, and the space on the counter where the bag had been was empty. The medals had gone.

* * *

'Now what do we do?' Wanda asked when they were driving back to Hibiscus Crescent. 'Are you sure there was nothing else there?'

'Not that I could see. I had a pretty thorough search.'

'Right. So, what do we do now?'

Quentin shrugged. 'Don't know what we can do without any proof. If only we'd gone in last night.'

'It's no good worrying about that now. Stephen's accident couldn't be helped. We'll just have to work round it.'

Casting her a withering look Quentin said, 'Work round it? How are we supposed to do that?'

'I don't know. Something will come up. You're a detective. Think of something.'

'You're a detective, too. Why can't you think of something?'

'All right, keep your hair on!' Wanda glanced askew at him and laughed. 'On second thoughts take it off. You'll give your mum a fit.'

Snatching the wig from his head, Quentin scowled. What a waste of time. Ed Grayson was going to think he was sitting around twiddling his thumbs instead of making investigations into the robberies, and his father was likely to say as much.

'Did you leave the keys there? The original set?' Wanda was saying.

'Yeah. I dropped them into a gap between the kitchen units. They'll find them soon enough.'

'Right. Let's hope they haven't checked there already, then. Anyway, as I said, if we don't think of something soon, we'll be charged with perverting the course of justice. We've got information and we haven't told the police.'

'It's not information. It's only our theory.'

'Yes, I suppose,' Wanda agreed. 'I think it might be time to go to the police, though, tell them what we know. Let's sleep on it and decide what to do tomorrow.'

Tomorrow, Quentin thought. Always tomorrow. It's been over a week since Ed Grayson asked me to take the case on, and still nothing concrete to go on.

They arrived back at Hibiscus Crescent to find the house empty. There was a note on the table to say that his parents had taken Michael home and were staying at Shelagh's until she and Howard returned from the hospital.

'Good.' Quentin grinned, his depression about their lack of progress disappearing in a blaze of anticipation. 'We've got at least an hour.'

'Don't even think about it,' was the answer. 'I've been at work all day, and anyway your parents could be back at any time. Visiting finishes at eight.'

Quentin groaned. He knew it was useless to try to persuade her when she had that look on her face. Just as well, he thought as he heard a key in the door.

His parents came in, Rosemary looking more cheerful than she had yesterday.

'Stephen's a lot better,' she said when she saw them. 'It'll be a long haul, but they think he'll be all right.'

'That's a relief,' Wanda said. 'Does Shelagh want me at the salon tomorrow?'

'No. She says she'll be going in.'

'Howard doesn't want her to,' Herbert growled. 'Think he's right. She should be at home.'

Whether his father meant Shelagh should be at home because she was pregnant, or because he thought every woman's place was in the home, Quentin didn't know, and right now he didn't care. At least Howard's brother seemed to be better; the only positive thing that could be salvaged from this otherwise negative day.

Chapter Seventeen

'We need to do some brainstorming,' Wanda said the following morning. She looked as cool and collected as ever, in the same shorts as yesterday but the top changed for a V-neck, apple-green T-shirt.

Tearing his gaze from her, Quentin said, 'My brain's done so much storming it's a wonder I haven't been struck by lightning. All I get is thunder in my head. I can't think straight.'

'Exactly. That's why we're going out for the day, or for the morning, anyway.'

'Really? Where are we going?'

'On a boat trip.'

'I thought you didn't like boats.'

Wanda pulled a face. 'I wasn't planning a world cruise. Just a tour round the harbour, give us something else to think about. There's one at ten-thirty, so we'll take that one, then we'll have a brainstorming session.'

What they should be doing, Quentin realized, was giving Ed Grayson a run-down on everything they'd learned so far, but he had no concrete proof. All he had was his own account of what he'd seen, and if he admitted that, Grayson would insist he took the information to the police. Which he should do. Which he would. But not yet.

He was procrastinating, but he couldn't help it. He wanted to provide evidence, evidence that the police couldn't ignore.

So, a boat trip? What the hell, he thought, sighing. A boat trip sounds good.

* * *

The breeze on the boat was bracing. Quentin tasted the salty sea spray as he stood by the rail, feeling small and insignificant against the blue of the sea and sky, the soaring white shells of the opera house, the green of the parks. He could see why his family loved it here.

'Fabulous, isn't it?' Wanda said, coming up beside him. 'Beats winter in London anytime.'

'Do you think so?'

'Not really. It beats winter, that's for sure, but I love London. I wouldn't want to live anywhere else, not permanently.'

Quentin nodded, knowing she was thinking of the reason they had come here in such a hurry.

'It'll work out,' he said, though he had no idea how, or even if it would.

Another passenger came to stand next to them. 'Come on,' Quentin said, taking Wanda by the elbow and leading her further along the deck. He didn't want anyone listening to their conversation. They found a spot with fewer people, though they had to talk over the noise of the engine.

'So is your brain working or is it as blank as mine?' he asked.

'I can't really think of anything else we can do except go to the police,' Wanda said. She moved closer. 'Look, I know it's annoying not to have any evidence, but we shouldn't keep things to ourselves any longer.'

'I know, but–'

'But nothing. If we go to them, tell them what you saw, they'll have to do something. They can't ignore it. And all the time we're dallying, someone else could get burgled.'

A light went on in Quentin's head. 'Wanda, you're a genius!'

'Am I? Why does that make me think you've got an idea that will delay us going to the police?'

'Because,' Quentin said triumphantly, 'if someone else gets burgled they'll stash the stuff in the stockroom. Then we can go in again. I've got the duplicate keys. This time I'll be sure to get something concrete.'

Wanda's mouth tightened. 'No, Quentin. You can't risk it again, and it could be weeks before there's another robbery. Even if there is we might not hear about it. No. Enough's enough.'

Not for me it's not, Quentin thought, but he said, 'You're right. OK. We'll go and tell them what I saw, but we won't say I took the keys and went back to have a look. We'll say I went in again during working hours – that I was in there having a shave or something.'

'Yes, good idea.' Wanda flicked her hair back from her face. It was immediately blown back again. 'It's too windy here. We're nearly back anyway. Let's get nearer the gangway.'

They had docked and were slowly shuffling their way down the gangplank when Quentin spotted someone on the quay. A man, olive-skinned with short dark hair. He was facing slightly away from them, but Quentin clearly saw him putting a bulky cloth bag into a rucksack. A blue bag, and although Quentin couldn't read the wording he could see there was black motif printed on it. His pulse quickened. Halim. Halim was here with the medals.

Halim was fastening the rucksack now. Bloody hell, Quentin thought in panic, if he passes them on, we'll never be able to prove it was him who took them. Halim looped the rucksack straps over his arm and started to walk away, and without waiting to think about it Quentin pushed his way down the gangplank, through the throng on the quayside and began to run after him.

'Hey,' he shouted. 'Hey, stop.'

Mistake. He knew it as soon as he'd said it. Halim didn't even turn to see who was calling. He simply broke into a run, weaving in and out of the crowds until he was away from the dockside. Quentin followed. Not much point stopping now, although he knew he should have followed at a discreet distance instead of calling out. He'd spooked him, made him make a run for it. Well, that's no problem for me, Quentin thought as he dodged between pedestrians. I'm not a runner for nothing.

It wasn't the running that proved difficult, it was the obstacles he had to contend with. People with pushchairs, someone in a wheelchair, a dog's lead he became entangled with and a swathe of people who emerged from a side road in front of him. There was a long line of them carrying banners – a demonstration, Quentin assumed. He pushed his way through, thought he'd lost his man, then saw him turning into a road leading into town. He kept after him, surprised that Halim could run so well. He had a lot of stamina for a barber. Gaining on him, he decided to try to fool him into thinking he had lost his pursuer. If Halim slowed to a walking pace Quentin would be able to approach him without causing a fuss in the street.

They were now well away from the quay, and when Halim looked as though he was twisting round to look behind him, Quentin ducked into a hotel doorway. He waited for a few seconds, then peeked out. It seemed to have worked. Halim was just approaching a small patch of shrubbery and had slowed down. Good, thought Quentin, pleased with his tactic. I'll catch him now.

Putting on a spurt, he went on after him. He had nearly caught up when he tripped over a metal waste bin that had become detached from the wall. It toppled sideways with a resounding crash, and when Quentin had regained his balance and looked up Halim was running again, straight ahead towards the shops.

'Bugger it!' Quentin cursed.

He sprinted on, threading his way through the people until he was nearly on the man he was chasing. Suddenly Halim darted sideways. He'd gone into a shop, Quentin realized, but which one? He slowed his pace and stopped as he came up to the spot where Halim had disappeared. Breathing hard, he stood on the pavement looking into the shop window directly in front of him, then into the windows of the shops either side. A movement made him focus on the one to his left. Posters shielded the interior, but through a gap Quentin saw a pair of dark eyes staring into his. It was less than a second before they moved away, but it was long enough. Turning, Quentin took three paces left, leapt up the two steps to the doorway and went in, expecting to see Halim. He came to a halt just inside the door. Halim wasn't there.

A girl with huge, hooped earrings was looking at him curiously from behind a counter. 'Can I help you?' she asked.

'Er, just browsing,' Quentin said, glancing at his surroundings. The walls seemed to be lined with DVDs and magazines. The girl smiled knowingly. About half a dozen customers were in the shop, all men except for one embarrassed-looking woman of about forty.

'I'll wait outside,' Quentin heard her say. She avoided his eyes as she went past him. Realizing the reason for her embarrassment, Quentin hid a smile. The man she'd spoken to was staring at a female-shaped polystyrene mannequin, dressed in a black leather basque, with a leather collar round its neck and a whip in one hand.

A sex shop, Quentin realized. He was in Kings Cross again, the red-light district. Under normal circumstances he would have at least had a look round to satisfy his curiosity, but his current circumstances weren't normal. He looked about him. It was Halim he'd seen looking at him through the window, he was certain. He must be here somewhere. His gaze fell on an archway in the corner. He flushed when the assistant caught his eye and said, 'Is there anything I can show you?'

'No, but thank you.'

With a shake of the gold earrings and a definite wink, she said, 'We have a bigger selection at the back.' She inclined her head towards the archway.

'Right. Thanks.' Taking a deep breath, Quentin walked towards the archway, his heart beating erratically. He had no idea how he would tackle Halim when he found him. All he knew was he had to get those medals. On the other side of the arch was a largish room with a central display cabinet. A middle-aged man stood nearby, with a strange-looking rubber object in his hand, looking at the display cabinet with a surprised expression. He looked up, raised his eyebrows at Quentin and shrugged in a questioning motion.

For a moment Quentin was paralysed. Halim was hiding, crouching behind the cabinet. That's what the customer was looking at. Quentin put his finger to his lips in a shushing gesture. Then he approached the cabinet stealthily, creeping towards it until he reached one end. Springing round its corner, he flew at the figure crouching there. In the tussle, Quentin managed to wrestle the rucksack away. A cry of pain escaped his adversary as he was pushed over and his head hit the floor. Quentin, about to straddle him and keep him pinned down, dropped the rucksack and gasped as he saw his face. It wasn't Halim.

Chapter Eighteen

The bystander moved away, backing against the wall. Quentin waited, feeling as though time had stood still. The man he had floored sat up, rubbing his head and staring angrily at Quentin. Quentin stared back. He could see why he had mistaken him for Halim – he was about the same height and build, the same olive skin and dark features. And he had that linen bag, the same one Quentin had seen at the barber's. At least, it had looked the same from where Quentin had been standing, in his elevated position on the gangplank.

'Why are you chasing me?' the man asked.

'Why did you run away?' Quentin countered.

The dark forehead creased, and the man moistened his lips. He seemed nervous. It may not be Halim, but Quentin knew he was up to no good.

'I don't like people following me in the street,' the Halim lookalike said.

'I wanted to talk to you. I called out but you didn't stop.'

By now, the sales assistant and a couple of customers from the front room had come to see what the noise was about.

'What's going on?' the sales assistant asked when she saw the two of them sitting on the floor glaring at each other.

'This man attacked me,' Quentin's adversary said, pointing at Quentin. 'That man saw, didn't you?' He nodded to the customer who had witnessed the struggle.

'I did,' said the customer, an amused note in his voice.

Quentin stood up. He eyed the rucksack. 'I think he's got something in that rucksack, something that doesn't belong to him.'

The sales assistant hovered next to them, as if deciding what she should do. Turning to the man on the floor she said, 'Have you got something that doesn't belong to you?'

'No,' came the sullen reply. Getting to his feet, the Halim lookalike said, 'I'm going now.' He picked up the rucksack and started to move away.

'Hold on,' Quentin said, determined to get a look inside the rucksack. 'If you've got nothing to hide, show me what's in there.'

He made to grab the rucksack but missed as the other man jumped backwards, knocking into a free-standing swivel display stand loaded with packets of contraceptives. The stand crashed to the floor, sending the contents in all directions. Reeling from the shock, the man straightened up and whirled round, heading back through the arch. Quentin raced after him, managing to snatch at the rucksack when he reached the other side of the arch. Slipping on some of the contraceptive packets, he grabbed at the nearest thing to stop himself falling – the leather-clad mannequin. The fleeing man tugged at the rucksack and fell backwards when it came away from Quentin's grip. Quentin flung the mannequin at him, his hand yanking away from the polystyrene arm and coming away with the whip.

His opponent once again on the floor, Quentin stood over him with the whip in his hand. Realizing how it must look, he dropped the whip, then grabbed the rucksack, tugged at the zip and tipped it upside down. Out fell a wallet, a mobile phone, a comb, a tube of some sort of sweets, a lighter and a packet of cigarettes. No linen bag.

Quentin stared in disbelief. He had seen this man, who wasn't Halim, put a bulky bag in the rucksack. It was the same man, the same rucksack, he was sure. So what had happened to the bag? I'm going bananas, he thought. He must have got rid of it somewhere along the way. Either that or I'm imagining things.

The sales assistant and the other customers had gathered round them again, the salesgirl blinking at the disarray around her.

'That's enough,' she said. 'Get out, both of you, or I'm calling the police.'

The Halim lookalike scooped up his scattered possessions, pushed them back into the rucksack and stood up. 'I'm going,' he said, backing away.

The customer who'd witnessed the tussle by the display cabinet stepped forward. 'Just a minute,' he said. 'This man grabbed you and tried to take your bag. Don't you want to make a complaint against him?'

With a shake of his head, the man Quentin had spent twenty minutes chasing turned and darted to the front door. He was gone before anyone had time to object.

'Look at the state of this place,' the sales assistant said.

Quentin looked around the shop. 'Sorry. I'll help you clear it up.'

'Don't you touch anything,' the girl snapped, giving him a fiery glare. 'I've a good mind to call the police and report you for criminal damage.'

'I've already called them,' one of the customers told her. 'When I saw them fighting, I thought it might get out of hand.'

'Bloody hell,' Quentin groaned. 'Look, I thought that man had stolen goods in his bag. That's why I was chasing him. If he didn't, why did he run?'

The salesgirl tossed her head, making the gold earrings shake. 'I don't know and I don't care. If my boss comes in and sees this mess, I'll get the sack.'

A uniformed figure appeared in the doorway, followed by another. Oh great, Quentin thought. That's all I need.

Chapter Nineteen

Though he'd never been in a British holding cell, Quentin guessed it was pretty much the same as the one he'd been in for the last two hours. Stark, plain walls, a small, high window with bars and a steel door. His efforts to explain to the uniformed policemen that the fracas in the sex shop had been caused because he suspected a man of being involved with the recent burglaries, and that he'd had no intention of stealing the man's rucksack, fell on deaf ears. He'd been taken to the nearest police station for questioning and was waiting for someone to interview him. He had been allowed to ring Wanda and tell her what had happened, and she'd agreed to come to the station to substantiate his story.

What an idiotic thing to do, he thought as he stared at the blank wall. He must have been mad to chase the guy like that, but he was guilty of something. Quentin could see it in the man's face. Bloody hell, how much longer were the police going to keep him waiting? It was ridiculous keeping him there over nothing. They'd get more trouble with drunks on a Saturday night than his actions that day.

He imagined his parents' reaction if they found out he'd been taken in for questioning. His mother would be upset and his father would be furious. "Damn stupid thing to do", he would say, and for once he'd be right. And Ed Grayson? He'd probably tell him to drop the case and leave it to the police.

His thoughts ended abruptly as a clinking sound came to him. Seconds later the metal door swung open.

'Here you go,' said a cheerful-looking young policeman. 'They're ready for you now.'

About bloody time, Quentin thought, following him through the door. He hoped his earlier request – that someone in charge of the burglary cases be brought in to interview him – had been listened to.

'Thanks,' he said when the officer led him into a small room with a desk sporting a recording machine and three glasses of water. He sat on the chair the officer indicated and waited.

Eventually, two men came in. They wore plain clothes, so Quentin assumed they were detectives.

The older of the two, a man of about fifty with a slight stoop and a receding hairline, spoke to Quentin as he sat down.

'Right, Mr Cadbury, I'm Detective Inspector Jackson and this is Detective Sergeant Wilson. I'm switching on this recording machine. Standard procedure, you understand.'

'Fine,' Quentin said. 'I told the officers when they brought me in. The man in the shop, he–'

'Let's start at the beginning shall we,' the detective sergeant said. 'Your name is Quentin Cadbury, and you are here on holiday from England?'

'Yes.'

'You told the officers at the scene that you're a private detective. Is that right?' DS Wilson's scathing tone made it clear that he didn't think much of private detectives. He had pale, greenish-blue eyes and a thatch of light brown, bristly hair that reminded Quentin of coconut matting.

'That's right, yes. Did Wanda get here? Wanda Merrydrew, my partner?'

'She did.'

'So she can tell you who I am. She's my business partner.'

DI Jackson took up the questioning. 'But she wasn't with you when you were in the shop?'

'No.'

The detective inspector eyed Quentin for a moment, then said, 'All right, Mr Cadbury. Can you tell us why you were fighting with a man in a shop in Kings Cross?'

Sighing, Quentin said, 'Of course I can.'

He related everything connected to the case, leaving out the fact that he had been to the barber's stockroom more than once, kept the keys and made duplicates with the intention of using them to gain unlawful access, and any mention of the salon or Linda and Suzy.

'So,' DI Jackson said when he'd finished, 'you thought this bloke was the one from the barber's, and you think the barber could be responsible for the spate of burglaries we've had recently?'

'Yes.'

'And you base this theory on finding something at his premises by accident?'

'Yes.'

'So, you were nosing around his stockroom when you were supposed to be going to the toilet?' DS Wilson sounded disbelieving.

'Like I said, I went into the stockroom first by mistake. Then I went to the toilet but there was no towel. I remembered seeing some towels in the stockroom, so I went to get one. That's when I found the medals.'

'But you said the medals were under some capes, not under towels,' Wilson persisted.

'Yes, but the towels were next to the capes, and I knocked the pile of towels over and put my hand under the bottom one to pick them up. I could feel something under the capes, so I looked to see what it was. I don't know why. I'm just naturally curious. Call it my detective instinct.'

It sounded implausible, Quentin knew, but he didn't want to mention that it was the computer and the sheepskin coat that had made him search the stockroom. If he did, they'd want to know how he knew those items had been stolen. He wasn't prepared to admit that a client from Shelagh's salon had been the source of this information. They might make the same connection as he had, and he wasn't prepared to involve Shelagh unless he had to, at least not yet. The medals alone should be enough to get them to investigate Halim.

DS Wilson spoke again. 'Why didn't you report this to us?'

Quentin had been expecting that. 'I thought it would carry much more weight if I had proof. Like I said, when I found the medals, I was going to take a photo, but I didn't get a chance. I was going to come to you, but we went on this boat trip and I saw this guy – the one I thought was Halim – with a bag like the one the medals were in. I thought he was on the way to pass them on. If I'd lost him, I'd have had no proof and you might not have believed me.'

The detective sergeant looked at a notebook. 'But it wasn't the bloke from the barber's, this man you chased, and he didn't have the medals in his rucksack. Witnesses said you emptied the rucksack and found nothing unusual.'

Quentin let out a long breath. 'No. He must have dumped the medals somewhere along the way.'

He saw the look that passed between the two men. They think I'm making it up, he thought. Frowning, he went over what he had reasoned out in the holding cell. How could the man have taken the linen bag out of the rucksack and dumped it somewhere? When had he been out of sight long enough to have done it?

'The only thing I can think of is… Well, I lost sight of him a few times, just for a second or two, and– and–' he paused, reliving the route he had taken from the quayside. 'Wait– Yes, there was a patch of shrubbery. He could have chucked it there, or in a bin even.'

Jackson cleared his throat. 'So, if we go to this barber's shop now, you're saying we won't find any medals there?'

'No. I'm sure this guy I thought was Halim had them, like I said.'

'Did you say that?' The detective sergeant referred to his notes again. 'Yes, I think you did.'

Wind the bloody tape back, Quentin thought, frustrated. "Getting nowhere fast" was the phrase that went round in his head.

'Look,' Quentin said, 'if this bloke had nothing to hide why did he run? Why go to the extremes of dashing into a shop and hiding behind a display stand? And why, when he was cornered, didn't he answer any questions? I mean, if he felt intimidated he could have called the police. He was scared, I tell you. He may not have had the medals on him–' Quentin broke off, seeing the items as they fell from the rucksack. What were they? Something jarred in his memory. A phone, a wallet, a lighter, cigarettes…

'That's it!' His exclamation echoed round the room.

Jackson and Wilson exchanged glances again. Quentin leaned forward and put his palms on the desk. 'He had cigarettes. Turkish cigarettes. He was Turkish.'

There was a short silence, as though they were digesting this. Then Wilson said, 'So you think, because he had Turkish cigarettes, there's a connection to this barber?'

Of course I bloody do, Quentin thought, irritated. 'I know it's a long shot from your point of view, but I'm convinced I'm right. I'm sure Halim's the one involved with stealing the medals, but of course there's nothing to prove he's responsible for the other robberies – the ones where jewellery and things were stolen. I didn't find any jewellery. If he had any he'd got rid of it by then.'

Another silence. Quentin heard the tape squeak slightly. Then the inspector spoke. 'OK, Mr Cadbury, we'll investigate your allegations.' He nodded to Wilson, who leaned across and switched off the machine.

Allegations? Is that all they thought they were? Feeling cheated, Quentin looked Detective Inspector Jackson in the eye.

'I *am* a detective, you know. I've worked on some big cases in the UK. If you–' he paused. Should he name-drop? Would it help? 'If you contact Detective Chief Inspector Philmore at Scotland Yard, he'll vouch for me. I've worked with him before.'

Jackson's eyebrows shot up. 'Is that so?'

'Yes. And I was thinking–'

'We don't really need to know your thoughts, Mr Cadbury,' the detective sergeant interrupted. 'Just the facts.'

Quentin decided he didn't like DS Wilson much. Ignoring his comment he blurted, 'If you go in there and spook Halim, you might not find the proof you need. If we leave it a bit longer and he is linked to the other robberies, we might be able to get some proof.'

Wilson opened his mouth but Jackson lifted his hand in a restraining gesture. 'Go on. How do you propose to get this proof?'

Quentin hesitated. The idea had formed during the two hours he'd been waiting to be interviewed.

'Well?'

Quentin straightened up in his chair. 'Em, I thought some sort of trap.'

'A trap?'

Quentin shifted under Wilson's sceptical stare. 'Yeah, a stake-out, or whatever you want to call it. If we pass them some information, they might act on it.'

Jackson ran his fingers round the inside of his collar, then took a sip of water. The overhead fan wasn't doing much to cool the room down.

'Go on.'

'We let them know of a property that's going to be empty,' Quentin said, relieved that Jackson was at least prepared to listen.

'How?' barked Wilson.

Quentin was beginning wonder how DS Wilson could be a detective, the way he needed everything spelt out for him.

'Get someone to go into his shop, have a shave or something and let it out in conversation somehow. Mention a house somewhere in a decent area, you know, a house worth a bit that might have something worth stealing. But the place won't be empty, just look empty. Then if they break in, we'll get them.'

'We?' DI Jackson said drily.

Quentin flushed. He guessed he probably sounded as though he was trying to tell them how to do their job. 'Well, I mean, how you want to arrange it is up to you.'

Jackson gazed at Quentin steadily for a moment.

'That might have been a possibility. But after this unfortunate incident it's hardly likely, is it? Even if you're right about this barber, and the bloke you chased is connected to him, he's bound to tell him what's happened. If they've got any sense they won't risk any more robberies now, not in this town anyway.'

Frowning, Quentin said, 'Yeah, I suppose. The only thing is, the man today doesn't know who I am. He's never seen me before so he won't know what I saw in the stockroom. He won't know I even know Halim.'

'I can't see what difference that makes,' Wilson said. 'It doesn't matter who you are – you chased him and accused him of having stolen goods in his rucksack.'

'I didn't say stolen goods, not to him. I said something that doesn't belong to him. I might have meant anything.'

'But,' Jackson pointed out, 'if he was carrying the medals he would think that's what you meant. He'll tell this Halim and he'll be scared off. And when you say "the barber", is there just one of them?'

Quentin shook his head. 'There's three of them; a greeter – just a general dogsbody really – but it's father and son who are the barbers. The father's called Ahmed, but I don't know if he's involved or not. There's some bad blood between them, I'm sure of that.'

He hesitated, wondering if he should carry on. What the hell, he thought, knowing he was pushing his luck.

'Anyway, surely my suggestion's worth a try? If you rush in and let Halim know he's under suspicion he *will* be scared off, and you'll have no proof. If we can tempt him into another robbery–'

'Give us some credit,' Wilson interrupted. 'Do you think we haven't thought of that? And we can't keep wasting resources sitting in houses in case they turn up. We–'

Jackson shot him a warning look. 'That'll do, Wilson.'

Wilson lowered his head. It was enough to tell Quentin that they'd already tried staking out an empty house and failed.

Quentin looked from Wilson to Jackson. 'You wouldn't need to use your resources, at least not many. I could be there and call you if someone tries to break in.'

Wilson snorted, which earned him another warning look from Jackson.

'OK, Mr Cadbury, we get the picture,' Jackson said curtly. 'I think that's all we need to talk about at the moment.'

'Right,' Quentin said, stiff-lipped. He could see it was useless to press his suggestion further. 'So… am I free to go?'

'Yes.'

Quentin drew a relieved breath. 'What about– about–'

'I don't think the owner of the shop–' began Jackson.

'A sex shop!' Wilson interrupted, a note of accusation in his tone.

Quentin glared at him. 'I just followed that bloke in there. I didn't have a clue what sort of shop it was. Don't suppose he did either.'

Jackson held his hand up again. 'I'll check, but I don't think the owner will want to press charges. It wouldn't be worth their while unless there was some major damage.'

'Will you keep me informed?' Quentin asked. 'Please? I'd like to help. And will you call DCI Philmore?'

Jackson looked at his watch. 'He won't be on duty yet.'

'But you will let me know if I can do anything, or if you get a lead of any sort? I need to tell my client something.'

'Your client?' Jackson sounded bemused.

'Yes, Colonel Grayson. His house was broken into and his wife's jewellery and his army medals were stolen. That's how I knew about the medals. He knew I was a private investigator and asked me if I could do anything.'

Jackson nodded absently. It seemed his mind had suddenly decided to go in a different direction from his body. Quentin knew, though, that because someone didn't appear to be listening it didn't mean they hadn't heard what was going on. Some people could process several things at once. He guessed Jackson was one of these. He hadn't got to be a Detective Inspector by having a single-track mind. Wilson, on the other hand, did not appear to possess such qualities. Quentin thought it unlikely he would make inspector.

'OK,' Jackson said brightly, as if he'd come to a decision. 'That'll be all for now. We've got your contact details. Don't leave the city without letting us know.'

'What about Wanda? Don't you want to talk to her?'

'We have,' Wilson said. 'She's confirmed your name and that you're a private detective. She doesn't seem to know why you ran off after the bloke you chased.'

'No, she wouldn't. I just saw him and took off. Why didn't you say you'd spoken to her?'

Jackson stood up. 'She's given us her number and address. We'll call her in if we need to.'

Quentin stood too, looking uncertainly from Jackson to Wilson, who was fiddling with the recording machine. Why this sudden dismissal? Was it because he'd mentioned

DCI Philmore? A contact in the Metropolitan Police Force carried a lot of weight, especially a Detective Chief Inspector, but somehow Jackson didn't seem the type to be swayed by rank. Perhaps something Quentin had said had given him an idea, a connection to some information he already held. That would be just my luck, he thought, them acting on something they got from me and then taking the credit.

He was escorted from the room to the vestibule, where Wanda sat waiting for him. Thank God, he thought, as she jumped up to greet him. Except now I've got to explain the whole thing again.

Chapter Twenty

'A sex shop?' Wanda queried when Quentin began explaining. They had left the police station and gone to the nearest bar.

'Don't you start,' Quentin said irritably. 'And don't you dare tell my parents. They don't need to know what kind of shop it was. They don't need to know anything about this at all. I need another drink.'

He rose and went to bar. Two whiskies later he had finished his story and felt slightly light-headed.

'We'll get some food,' Wanda said. 'You'll feel better then. I'll ring your mum and say we won't be back yet and to eat without us.'

They ordered lasagne, with salad for Wanda and chips for Quentin. After he'd eaten, Quentin did feel better. They took their coffee to an outside table and sat quietly watching people go by and enjoying the afternoon air.

'So, what now?' Wanda asked eventually.

'Nothing at the moment, thanks very much,' Quentin said. 'I've had enough excitement for one day, being kept over two hours in a police station.'

'Hold on a minute, I'm the one who got abandoned on a gangplank with no idea where you were going or why.'

Giving a rueful grin, Quentin said, 'Sorry, but I didn't have time to explain. I would have lost him. Come to think of it, it might have been better if I had. At least I wouldn't have been hauled off by the police. And now Halim might be spooked. The robberies might stop and we'll never prove he was involved. The police will think I made up that story about seeing the medals.'

Wanda leaned over and squeezed his arm. 'Why would they think that? Don't be so hard on yourself. You only did what you thought was right. The bloke you chased might have nothing to do with the robberies, in which case Halim will carry on.'

What were the chances of that? Quentin wondered. No. There was too much similarity in the circumstances for it to be coincidence. He'd had a bag exactly like the one he'd seen in Halim's stockroom. Where he had managed to dispose of it, Quentin had no idea, but he hadn't imagined it.

'Come on,' he said, getting to his feet.

Wanda scrambled to pick up her handbag. 'Where are we going?'

'Back to that patch of shrubbery. If he threw something in there perhaps it's still there.'

Taking the same route as earlier Quentin stopped at every waste bin and felt inside, hoping to find the cloth bag. When they reached the clump of shrubs, they pulled aside the branches and peered between them. Quentin vaulted the low wall that enclosed the area and searched every inch of ground.

'I've lost my wallet,' he lied when some curious passersby stared at him. 'Nothing,' he groaned when he re-joined Wanda on the pavement. They continued up to the shop where Quentin had been, checking every bin, every nook and cranny where the bag could have been left.

'Either we haven't found it or he picked it up again when he left the shop,' Quentin said.

'That's the most likely,' Wanda replied. 'He'd hardly want anyone else to find it. Once he was away from you, he'd have gone back and collected it.'

'Would he? If I was being chased, I wouldn't risk picking up incriminating evidence again. That's why he ditched it in the first place.'

'Maybe, but no one chased him out of the shop, did they? Once he was sure he wasn't being followed he could have retrieved the goods and disappeared. It's a pity we don't know anything about him, not even his name.'

'Yeah, he was pretty reluctant to say anything. He just wanted to get out of there.'

'Well, he would, wouldn't he?'

They walked back to the patch of shrubbery and sat on the enclosing wall.

'So, what now?' Wanda asked, tipping her face up to the sun.

What now indeed, Quentin thought. I've handed the case to the police on a plate, so where does that leave us? He shrugged, despondency overcoming him.

'Cheer up,' Wanda urged. 'After all, we didn't come here to work. We're supposed to be on holiday.'

'I know but... I suppose I'll have to go back to Ed Grayson and say we can't do any more.'

Wanda sighed. 'We'll tell him we found some vital information which the police are acting on. It's the truth anyway.'

'Is it? They might already suspect Halim for all we know. They don't give much away.'

Quentin frowned, remembering DI Jackson's impassive reaction to his story. His gut instinct was that they hadn't known about Halim. It seemed they'd had no idea how the criminals knew when houses would be empty, or who the criminals were. But now they had a suspect, and they were sure to act on it. Unless… Suppose they didn't act on it, not immediately anyway? It would take time to organise. The shop would be closed in an hour and a half and Halim didn't live on the premises. Of course they could find his home address and arrest him there, or take a search warrant and get him or his father to open the shop so they could search the stockroom.

Another thought occurred to him. Suppose the bloke he'd chased didn't tell Halim about what happened? Suppose he was afraid to admit to being careless enough to be seen, chased and caught by, as he saw it, a member of the public?

'No chance,' Wanda told him when he voiced his thoughts. 'He's bound to tell him. I mean, even if we know nothing about him you've seen him, accused him of having something that didn't belong to him.'

'Yes, but as I told Jackson, I didn't specify what I thought he had, and I didn't say it had been stolen, not to him. It could have been anything. He might think the whole thing was a misunderstanding. Oh all right, I know it's wishful thinking, but even so… OK, so I've seen him. It was a chance sighting and he doesn't know who I am. Sydney's a big city. I could live here another ten years and never see him again.'

'Agreed, but look at it from his point of view. You've had a narrow escape. You were nearly caught with something you didn't want anyone to see. Even if you didn't tell Halim, would you risk taking on another job, carrying another lot of stolen goods to dispose of? I wouldn't.'

Quentin rested his elbows on his knees and cupped his hands around his chin. She was right, yet he couldn't, wouldn't accept that there was nothing else they could do. It was him who'd discovered the computer and sheepskin coat, him who'd risked going into the stockroom to get evidence, him who'd foiled the attempted break-in at

Shelagh's, him who'd spotted a man he was convinced was connected to the case and him who'd spent more than two hours in a police station for his pains. It wasn't right to sit back now and let matters take their course. He straightened up, the idea that was taking shape in his brain refusing to be dislodged.

'I agree with everything you've said, Wanda, but what if my runaway doesn't tell Halim yet? What if Halim still thinks everything is hunky-dory?'

Wanda lowered her head to look at him. 'And your point is?'

'We plant some bait, something Halim won't be able to resist.'

'Bait?'

'Yes, something valuable, in an empty house, a house that will only be empty for tonight, so he'll need to get a move on.'

There was a pause while Wanda digested this. 'And how many houses do you know that will be empty?'

Quentin gave a weak grin. 'None. It won't be empty. But Halim won't know that.'

He felt Wanda stiffen beside him. 'How do I know I'm not going to like this? Whose house did you have in mind?'

Quentin's grin turned to a grimace. 'My parents'. It's all right, I'm sure they'll agree. They can go and stay at Shelagh's, and you can, if you like. Then I'll be there, waiting.'

Wanda sent him the look she reserved for talking to children and animals.

'How can I put this so you'll understand? First off, the likelihood is that the bloke you chased is calling Halim even as we speak and that they've already decided to bring things to a halt, or even worse, Halim might up sticks and disappear. Or the police could be raiding Halim's premises right now. If, by some miracle, none of this happens, and for some reason known only to himself this bloke doesn't tell Halim, how are we going to plant the bait in time for him to make any move before the hypothetical owner returns to the house? And last but definitely not least, how are we going to do this without the say-so of the police?'

Quentin jumped up, her words running off him like flood water down a hillside. He checked his watch: 4.05 p.m. 'Come on,' he said, starting to stride away. 'We've just got time.'

Chapter Twenty-one

'Where are we going?' Wanda asked, hurrying to catch up with him.

'To the salon,' he told her as they broke into jog. 'By the time we've got to the car it'll be just as quick to go on foot. We'll go in, say someone we know is away but will be back tomorrow and make sure Linda and Suzy hear. Whichever one of them is passing on information might tell Halim and he might go for it.'

'Slow down a bit, I can't keep up with you. You can't use your parents' address without their permission, and how do we give out the address anyway? We can't just walk in and casually drop an empty property into the conversation. And what reason can we give for going into the salon?'

'I don't need a reason to go and see my sister, do I? That's your department anyway. Think of something.'

The conversation lulled as they concentrated on getting to the salon as quickly as they could, Quentin wishing he could run ahead. Luckily Wanda was wearing trainers and was able to run reasonably fast, but she was no match for him. He slowed to keep pace with her and they reached the street where the salon was situated at four-thirty. Coming to a halt at the café on the corner, Wanda held her side, panting. Quentin wasn't even breathless, though sweat was streaming down his face, neck and back.

'OK,' he said when Wanda had recovered. 'I'm going to ring Shelagh and tell her we're coming and that I need to speak to her in private. You could make an issue about making an appointment, talk to one of the girls and say... and say...'

'And say what? I thought we agreed not to tell Shelagh about Linda or Suzy.'

'We did, but it's crunch time now. She'll find out soon anyway if the police come after Halim.'

'What if she won't go along with it?'

'She will, of course she will. She might have been burgled herself – she would have been if we hadn't been there. We just need to think of what to say and how to make it convincing.'

Quentin looked at Wanda, who was chewing at her lip thoughtfully. 'I can't believe you made me run all this way and you don't even know what we're going to say,' she said at last.

'We've got to do something and this might be our last chance to get to Halim before the police do,' Quentin reminded her. 'It's a slim chance but it's the only one we've got.'

'I suppose you're right. So... how about we go in with a message for Shelagh, saying that one of her friends who's away wants her to go over to their house for some reason before they come back. We can mention the address. I'll work it in somehow, but Shelagh will have to be prepared or she'll blow the whole thing.'

Quentin pulled out his mobile. 'I'll call her now. I expect her mobile's in the staff room – I've got the salon number here.'

'Wait a moment.' Wanda laid a restricting hand on his arm. 'Chances are one of the girls will pick up. Let me call – I can disguise my voice better than you, then when Shelagh comes to the phone you can talk to her.'

'You can tell her,' Quentin said. 'She'll listen to you. Make sure she doesn't let on it's us who's ringing.'

Wanda's husky, low voice rose several tones as she said in a surprisingly convincing Australian accent, 'Hello? Can I speak to Mrs Prince please? It's about an order she placed for some new dryers.'

Quentin nodded when Wanda turned to him and mouthed 'Linda'.

The Australian accent was dropped, and Wanda spoke again. 'Shelagh, it's Wanda but don't say anything – don't say my name. I'm pretending to be from the company you order the dryers from. Listen, this is important. I'm here with Quentin and we're coming into the salon. Look surprised when you see us. We'll explain why later, but it's connected to the robberies. We think we're onto something. First of all, do any of your staff know your parents' address? Just say yes or no … No? Good, so whatever we say, can you go along with it and not question us about it? It's really important … Great. OK, see you in a few minutes.'

'She's up for it, then?' Quentin had half expected his sister to demand to know the reasoning behind their request. 'OK, have you thought of anything to say, or shall we make it up as we go along?'

'Leave it to me,' Wanda said. 'Just don't contradict me.'

'Right. Let's do it.'

As they walked the few hundred yards to the salon Quentin's chest tightened. What was he doing, dragging Wanda and his sister into a charade for something that, in all probability, would yield no results? But he had to do it. He had to try to get some sort of positive outcome from his own efforts. Damned if he was going to give up now just because the police knew almost as much as he did. They might know a lot more. I don't care, he thought, a new determination settling over him. This is the only thing we can do at the moment, so we're doing it.

It was Wanda who did it, mostly. She rose to the occasion like an actress who'd lost her script and had to improvise.

'Hello, everyone,' she said as they entered the salon and walked past the reception desk towards Shelagh.

Dina smiled and Linda nodded. Suzy, who was scooping colour from a dish on her trolley, turned to greet them, the tinting brush she was holding hitting against her client's head. She lost her grip and it clattered down, splashing blobs of colour on the floor.

Wanda darted forward and bent to retrieve it just as Suzy did the same. Quentin caught a glimpse of a large gold locket as it slipped free of Suzy's tabard and swung from her neck. Blushing as she straightened up, Suzy took the brush from Wanda with one hand and slid the locket back under her tabard with the other.

'Hello,' Shelagh said, coming up to them. 'This is a nice surprise. I'll see to this lady and I'll be with you.'

They waited while Shelagh took money from a customer, then, after an almost imperceptible indication from Quentin, left the reception desk and joined them in the main body of the salon. With the girls having intermittent conversations with their clients and music playing softly in the background, Quentin didn't want to risk them missing anything that was said.

'We were just up the road,' he began loudly. 'So we thought we'd pop in.'

'Yes,' Wanda said. 'We picked up a message on your home answerphone, Shelagh, from your friend, Michelle.'

Shelagh rubbed at her swollen belly, then moved her hand round to the small of her back. 'Michelle?'

'Yes,' Wanda went on. 'She's back from Perth tomorrow and she wants to know if you collected the letters from her post box like she asked. Apparently she's expecting a valuation on some jewellery she just inherited or something?' She paused, looking at Shelagh for confirmation.

Shelagh looked slightly mystified but replied, 'Oh yes, she said something about that.'

There was a lull in the salon's general conversation. Quentin, who was watching both Linda and Suzy as they worked, saw nothing in either of their expressions change as Wanda continued.

'One of the pieces is supposed to be quite unusual – it's got some sort of royal connection apparently. Anyway, she's worried that the letter might have gone to the wrong address. She's at 7 Hibiscus Crescent but sometimes things end up at number 9 by mistake.'

Shelagh's eyes widened, but otherwise she betrayed no sign of recognizing her parents' address. 'Oh, I see,' she said. 'So she's due back tomorrow?'

Wanda nodded. 'Yes. I don't know why she couldn't have waited until then, but maybe she needs to know the value for insurance reasons or something.'

'Yes,' Shelagh agreed, evidently warming to her unexpected role. 'That was it. She took something to be valued but she was waiting for written confirmation. She wants to get it insured as soon as she gets back. Was that all she wanted?'

Quentin sent Wanda a pleading look. *Make that do*, it said. The mythical Michelle was already pushing the bounds of credibility.

'I think so,' Wanda said.

Shelagh raised her voice slightly against the hum of the hairdryer Dina had just switched on. 'OK, I'll pop over on the way home and call her if it's there. Do you want to come through and have a cup of tea? I haven't got anyone else booked in for me today.'

'Yes please,' Quentin said. 'I could do with a cuppa.'

* * *

'All right, what's this all about?' Shelagh demanded as soon as they were in the staffroom with the door shut.

'Sit down, sis, and don't get upset or angry with what we tell you.' Stupid thing to say. Of course she would be upset and angry. 'Well, anyway, don't show it.'

When she'd perched on an old salon chair Shelagh looked from Quentin to Wanda. 'Just tell me. There must be a reason you told that fairy story for everyone to hear.'

As succinctly as possible Quentin relayed what he'd overheard between Linda and Halim, what he'd seen in the barber's stockroom and the churchyard, and the conclusion they'd arrived at. Shelagh's jaw dropped when the full implication of what he was saying hit her.

'You mean either Linda or Suzy have been passing information they've got from here, from my salon, to Halim? And he's the one who has been carrying out all these burglaries? I can't believe it. I mean, I know Suzy was seeing Halim, but that was ages ago—'

'Suzy used to be Halim's girlfriend?' Quentin interrupted.

'Yes, but he's been with Linda nearly six months. If Suzy's been seeing him during that time, I don't know anything about it. I shouldn't think Linda did, either. Come to think of it, I have noticed Suzy giving Linda some funny looks recently, but she's never said anything. Anyway, they wouldn't– I mean, I was nearly burgled – you can't tell me they would risk their own employer getting robbed; either of them.'

'We're only telling you what I saw,' Quentin said.

Shelagh's look of disbelief turned to a look of anger. 'If this is true, I'll– I'll–' She levered herself up from the chair.

'No, Shelagh,' Wanda warned. 'You mustn't do anything now. We don't know which one it is, and accusing them won't do any good.'

'It'll bloody well do *me* good,' Shelagh raged, her face puce. 'Who do you *think* it is?'

Quentin exchanged a look with Wanda.

'We thought Linda initially,' Wanda admitted. 'But after what Quentin saw, and that necklace Suzy was wearing–'

'Necklace?' Shelagh queried. 'I've never noticed a necklace.'

'It's a locket. Perhaps she doesn't wear it often,' Wanda suggested. 'She was pretty quick to hide it. I'm not an expert, but I went to antiques fairs with my late husband and I'm pretty sure it's old. It looks like gold, with diamonds set into it.'

The inference wasn't lost on either Quentin or Shelagh.

'What we should do,' Quentin said, 'is try to photograph it, or at least have a good look at it, so we can give a description to the police to check if one's been stolen. Anyway, whether it's Suzy or Linda, we're hoping they'll pass on what we said in the salon and Halim will go for it tonight at Mum and Dad's. Then we'll catch him red-handed.'

'Do Mum and Dad know about this?'

Quentin gave a rueful grin. 'Not yet.'

'Right. Best of luck with that, then. Still, they want to see an end to these burglaries so I expect they'll agree.' Shelagh sat down again. 'So how are you going to play it? It all seems a bit airy-fairy to me.'

Airy-fairy wasn't how Quentin would have described their plan. A calculated risk, that's how he saw it. And if nothing came of it, they'd lost nothing except a night's sleep.

Wanda interrupted his silent reasoning. 'You need to go back to work, Shelagh, and act normally.'

'Act normally!' Shelagh's expression was thunderous. 'It's all right, I won't give the game away. I wouldn't do anything in front of customers anyway.'

Wanda nodded. 'And is it OK for your mum and dad to sleep at yours tonight?'

'Yes, of course,' Shelagh said. 'I'll go back now. It's nearly time to close anyway.'

Chapter Twenty-two

They made their way back through the salon, Shelagh walking stiffly past Linda and Suzy as the last of the clients left the premises.

'Can I go now, Shelagh?' Linda asked.

'You're supposed to help tidy up before you leave,' Suzy snapped.

'Like you did yesterday?' Linda shot back.

Suzy cast a look at Shelagh, then at Quentin and Wanda, and didn't reply. Instead, she began tidying her workstation, her soft, attractive features set into a hardened expression.

Linda, as if taking Shelagh's lack of response to her request as a refusal, grabbed a broom and started sweeping fallen hair into a dustpan.

Was this exchange just jealousy over Halim? Quentin wondered. Was Suzy still infatuated with Halim, and did Linda know? What if they were wrong about either or both of them? One thing was sure: if anything happened that night, it would prove that one of them told Halim that 7, Hibiscus Crescent would be empty. But which one?

Once outside he and Wanda began walking back to where they'd left the car.

'Suppose whoever it is doesn't tell Halim?' Wanda said. 'Even if they do, he might not go for it.'

'I know, but it's worth a shot. Unless he thinks he's been rumbled there's no reason he wouldn't go for it, especially if he knows tonight's the only chance he's got.'

Wanda made a face that told Quentin she thought the odds were about a thousand to one.

'Well,' she said, 'we've got nothing to lose, except we'll bear the brunt of your dad's temper if he's made to sleep in a different bed for nothing.'

Quentin grinned. 'I'm not worried. I'm sure you can sweet talk him round.'

Wanda shook her head. 'He's not as bad you make out, you know.'

'I don't know any such thing. If he's not, it's only because you're around.'

The wailing of sirens sounded in the middle distance, cutting through the humdrum noise of everyday traffic. Quentin stiffened, half expecting a convoy of police cars to come hurtling up the street and stop outside the barber's shop, ready to burst in and search it. After a few minutes he relaxed. The wailing was still audible but not getting closer. Somewhere in this great metropolis, though, something was going on. A fire? Or maybe an accident.

'That doesn't sound like good news,' he commented. 'Probably much worse than what we're worrying about. Still, I'd be happier if we knew Halim was definitely going to turn up tonight.'

'Let's hope he does, after all this palaver. Quentin. Quentin?' Wanda nudged him as he stared ahead, frowning. 'What's up? Getting cold feet? It was your idea.'

'I know,' Quentin answered, shaking himself. 'It's just... I don't want this case to slip away from me, that's all. I don't want to make a fool of myself either.'

Wanda laughed. 'You've never worried about that before. As I recall you're quite good at making a fool of yourself.'

Quentin searched for a sarcastic reply but found nothing. 'You're right. Perhaps I've been a bit hasty.'

Wanda slipped her arm through his. 'Look, Quentin, it's a long shot but you never know, it might come off. Our long shots have paid dividends before. Oh, I know – it's your parents. You don't want your father to think you're not up to the job.'

Perceptive as usual, Quentin thought.

'Something like that,' he admitted. 'Do you think we should call it off?'

'Certainly not! It's a good idea – a bit rash, but good all the same, and what's the worst that can happen? We stay up all night for nothing – so what?'

Quentin's spirits lifted. Despite pointing out that their ploy had very little chance of success, she was willing to try it and give him the credit.

He looked into her eyes, wishing he could sweep her up and carry her to the nearest bedroom.

'What the hell,' he murmured. 'Let's go for it.'

'That's more like the Quentin I know. Well, come on, then. What are we waiting for?'

Chapter Twenty-three

In his parents' spacious lounge back at Hibiscus Crescent, Quentin stood his ground under his father's incredulous stare. Wanda sat nearby, ready to support him but keeping quiet, while Rosemary was perched on the edge of her chair twisting her wedding ring around her finger.

'You really think one of these women at Shelagh's salon is involved with the burglaries?' Herbert barked.

'Yes. I've told you,' Quentin said. 'It's the only way the bloke in the barber's could know which houses are empty and when.'

'And you're certain this Turkish barber is the burglar? You've got proof?'

'Only what I've seen and heard. We need something tangible, something that will make it impossible for him to deny his involvement. There was nothing on the premises the last time I checked, so if we can catch him in the process of breaking in, then we've got him.'

There was a pause, as though his father was thinking this over. It had occurred to Quentin that Halim may have taken some of the goods home to his private residence, but he dismissed this idea. Gut instinct told him Halim had already got rid of the goods. In his mind the only things that might be found at Halim's home were the computer and the sheepskin coat. He still found that puzzling. Why would someone who had successfully stolen thousands of pounds worth of small, easily transportable items suddenly burden himself with a computer and a sheepskin coat? Overconfidence? Or not the same burglar? No. He'd already decided that was too much of a stretch. He'd seen medals in the stockroom, and both jewellery and medals had been taken from Ed Grayson. Halim must have taken the computer and the coat on a whim when he was on one of his burgling sprees.

'Catch him in the act, you mean.' His father's voice brought him back to the moment.

'That's the idea, yes.'

'You've told the police what you suspect, you say?'

Quentin answered warily. 'Yes.' It wasn't a lie. He just hadn't mentioned the circumstances of how and why he'd been forced to speak to the police.

'It's their job to trap him, then, not yours. Mind you, they couldn't do much tonight, with everything going on.'

'What's going on?' Quentin recalled the lines of people with banners he'd seen. 'You mean that demonstration? Has there been some trouble?'

He couldn't remember seeing any police with the marchers, but knew there was usually a police presence on such occasions.

'Not that. The explosion.'

'Explosion?'

'On the news just before you came in. Big explosion in the business centre. Two people confirmed dead, one shot, apparently, a guard they think, so a deliberate attack for some reason or other. That's all they know at the moment.'

So that's what all the sirens they'd heard had been about. An explosion, possibly deliberate, and somebody shot. A horrific scene. And one that would keep a large part of the city's police force tied up for quite a while. And if *he* realized that, so would Halim.

'Look, Fath– Dad, I know it's a lot to ask, but if the police are busy with this explosion there's far more chance of Halim trying his luck here tonight. I only told the police what I know this afternoon, so the chances are they haven't had time to do anything about it yet.'

He stopped, remembering the man he had chased. Wanda was right – he had probably told Halim what had happened by now. But even if he had, could Halim resist the temptation to get one last haul while police resources were elsewhere?

'After all, it's us and people like us that he's stolen from,' he said. 'You might have been done if you'd been away anywhere. Wouldn't you like to catch him red-handed?'

Herbert's pale blue eyes bulged in his florid face. He gulped so hard that Quentin could see his Adam's apple vibrate in his throat.

'He'll be more than red when I've finished with him,' he spluttered. 'Bad enough stealing people's precious things, making them frightened to leave their homes, but involving one of my family–'

'So you agree, then?' Quentin asked, banking on his father's outrage.

'If it gives me a chance to catch this blighter, then yes, we'll give it a go. Can't lose anything by trying. Had to take risks in the army. Don't want your mother here, though.'

Quentin shook his head. 'I wouldn't dream of putting her in danger, or you. Shelagh says you can sleep there tonight.'

'And miss a chance of seeing this bastard face-to-face? I'll do no such thing. Your mother can go. I'm staying right here.'

'Won't it be dangerous?' Rosemary asked, looking at each of them in turn. 'They might be armed.'

'There's nothing to suggest any sort of violence in any of the robberies,' Quentin told her, anxious to allay her fears. 'They've never needed to be armed. They've only ever targeted empty properties, so they've never encountered any resistance or opposition.'

'Except at Shelagh's, when you were there,' his mother reminded him.

'No arguing, Rosemary,' Herbert blustered. 'Got a chance to nail this bloke and we're going to take it. You and Wanda will go to Shelagh's. Not putting women in danger.'

Quentin put a finger to his lips as Wanda opened her mouth to protest. He knew she hated to be left out, but she took his meaning and kept silent. His mother pressed her lips together and continued fingering her wedding ring.

Once again Quentin questioned his plan, and once again he came up with the same answers.

What the hell, he thought, tired of trying to rationalize things. Either he'll come or he won't. It's as simple as that.

* * *

A few hours later, Wanda drove herself and Rosemary to Shelagh's in the hired Micra, leaving the family car parked further along Hibiscus Crescent so that the driveway and garage were empty. After they'd gone, Quentin poured himself and his father a beer and switched on the TV. They watched the end of a comedy programme and then the local news bulletin.

The explosion dominated the news and showed footage of the building, taken minutes after the explosion on a mobile phone. The front of the building sported a yawning hole where it had partly collapsed, and people

145

were running out in confusion and panic. Later media footage showed the area cordoned off with police tape and several bystanders being interviewed. Police swarmed everywhere, Quentin noted with satisfaction, then chided himself. People being hurt was not how he would have liked the police to be kept busy.

Three hours later they sat, TV off, lights out, Quentin staring straight ahead, fingering the mole by his ear, while his father clamped headphones to his ears and made a pretence of listening to music. Every now and then he held the headphones away from his head as if trying to pick up any audible signs of an impending break-in.

Eventually he threw down the earphones and grunted. 'Wasting our time. Hare-brained idea.'

'Why don't you go to sleep?' Quentin suggested. 'I'll wake you if I hear anything.'

His father harrumphed his best *if you can do it so can I* harrumph and pulled himself up straighter. After a few minutes, though, he leaned back, resting his head against the back of the chair and closing his eyes. Quentin could see the shape of him in the semi-darkness. The night was lightened by a full moon whose brightness penetrated the thin summer curtains, and Quentin touched the torch wedged by his side, doubting that it would be needed. He was tempted to close his own eyes, but resisted. He checked the time on his phone. Two o'clock. About the same time as the attempted break-in at Shelagh's. If Halim was running true to form, he'd put in an appearance soon.

In his mind he ran over the arrangements they'd put in place in case Halim showed. The back door, where Quentin guessed Halim would break in, was locked but not bolted, and they'd taken out the bulbs from the security lamps so as not to spook the intruder. If anyone bothered to stop and think about it, they might query the fact that both back and front lamps were non-operational at the same time, but Quentin doubted that this would deter or even occur to any burglar once they were here and about to embark on a job. Plenty of outside lights didn't work, just as many security cameras didn't actually record anything; they just acted as a deterrent.

If Halim showed up and gained entry, the plan was to let him find the jewellery – a necklace and earrings that Quentin's mother had inherited from her sister – along with some other, less valuable pieces. Quentin's father had carefully hidden his precious coin collection, insisting that it was just as valuable as the jewellery and ignoring the fact that if all went to plan the burglar would be caught and his collection therefore safe.

The jewellery alone was enough for any burglar, Quentin decided, and once they had it in their possession, Quentin would tackle them while his father called the police. A length of rope, obtained from the garage and previously used for keeping a tarpaulin over the barbecue, hung on the back of Quentin's chair, along with a pillowcase. Pictures of Halim trussed up like a chicken, with a pillowcase over his head, paraded themselves in front of Quentin's eyes.

He yawned, tiredness overcoming him. It had been a long day. He must have dozed for a while because a noise woke him. Not the intermittent hum of the fridge from the kitchen or his father's soft snores, but something else. He jerked himself upright and listened. There it was again. A scraping sound at the back door. Worried that his father might wake and make a noise, Quentin stood up and shook him gently, placing his hand over his mouth.

'Don't make a sound. I think I heard something,' he whispered. When his father had nodded his understanding, Quentin removed his hand and whispered again. 'You know what to do.'

Herbert rose and, as arranged, went silently into the hall to wait behind the coat stand near the front door. Quentin positioned himself behind the settee, crouching down but ready to spring up at any moment. The scraping noises had become louder, then there was a loud click and the scraping noises stopped. Quentin held his breath, his thoughts racing. What if it wasn't Halim, and if it was, what if he wasn't alone? What if–

His thoughts stopped and his body tensed. Whoever it was, they were inside.

Chapter Twenty-four

Quentin was relieved when he realized that whoever the intruder was, they were alone. From the shape that appeared he could see it was a man. The figure moved forward, seeing his way with a slim torch beam angled away from the windows, taking no chance of being seen from outside. The air in the lounge was disturbed when the intruder passed through it. Quentin held his position, not moving a muscle until the burglar started up the stairs. Most jewellery was kept in bedrooms, Quentin knew, as it had been at Ed Grayson's. He'd expected the burglar to make straight for the bedrooms, and he'd been proved right.

Standing up, he crept to the bottom of the stairs, then crouched down again, ready to launch himself at their uninvited guest when he came down. Anger stirred in him as he heard the person above move from room to room. There was a few minutes' stillness, when Quentin guessed that the jewellery had been found. The minutes lengthened. What was he up to? Looking for more? Then he remembered the coins. Perhaps he'd found them too and was trying to decide whether they were worth taking.

The movements started again. Quentin could feel, rather than hear, feet approaching the top of the staircase. He slunk back as a torch beam was shone downwards and the intruder began to descend. Muscles tensing, he prepared himself for the fray as each tread on the stairs brought the intruder nearer. Then he was there, on the bottom step.

Quentin gasped when, before he had time to spring at the descending figure, a whooshing and a bear-like growl reached his ears and something flung itself at the figure as it turned from the bottom step towards the lounge. There was a clunking sound, like something had hit the wooden floor. The attack knocked the burglar sideways, sending him sprawling onto Quentin, who buckled under his weight. The weight grew heavier as Herbert fell on top of the intruder.

His father's venomous snarl filled Quentin's ears. 'Gotcha, you bastard. I'll teach you to break into people's houses.'

Quentin squirmed under the weight of two bodies crushing his. His free arm flailed, encountering the torch the intruder had dropped. Grabbing it, he shone it into the face of the man on top of him.

Halim! A sense of victory swept through him. His theory was right, and the bait he had laid had been taken. He wriggled free as his father pulled Halim to his knees. When Quentin was on his feet, he leapt the few feet to the light switch and flicked it on. It took seconds, but it was long enough for Halim to wrench himself away from his captor and shove him backwards, making the older man slump against the stair rail. The telephone handset lay on the floor, dropped by Herbert in the attack, and Quentin saw Halim swoop it up and raise his arm to bring it down on his father's head. His breath coming in ragged gasps, Quentin hurtled into Halim, sending him off course and causing his arm to swing round, still holding the handset. It struck Quentin in the face, smashing against his cheekbone and sending a searing pain through his head. Momentarily dazed, Quentin loosened his grip on his adversary. Halim tore himself away, and in a whirlwind of air, ran through the lounge and out the way he had come in.

'Bloody hell!' Quentin yelled, putting his hand to his cheek as he ran after the fleeing man.

Halim was round the side of the house and through the front garden before Quentin realized his mistake – he should have gone out through the front door. Then he could have stopped Halim before he got away. As it was, by the time he'd rounded the side of the house Halim was wrenching open the door of a car. Quentin reached the car and pulled desperately and unsuccessfully at the door handle as the engine roared into life. With a screech the car shot forward, almost pulling Quentin's arm out of its socket as it sped away.

Still clutching Halim's torch in his other hand, Quentin shone it onto the car's number plate, and with the help of a streetlight was able to make out the first three digits. Then the car was gone, along with Halim. And Quentin's chance to catch him.

* * *

'At least he didn't get Mum's jewellery,' Quentin said when he was back inside and had helped his father to his feet. A leather pouch lay on the floor, the top open and part of a diamond necklace spilling out. Picking it up, Quentin tipped it upside down and let the necklace and two earrings fall into his palm, along with a couple of brooches and a bangle.

His father put a hand to the back of his head and winced. Blood smeared his fingers when he brought them away. He must have hit his head on the banister when Halim shoved him backwards, Quentin realized.

'Let me look at that,' Quentin offered, stretching out his arm. His father pulled back, turned and marched up the stairs.

'Better not have found my coins,' Quentin heard him say.

Quentin couldn't believe what he was hearing.

'Your coins?' he shouted. 'You've just lost us the chance to catch a burglar in the act, caused me to get my face smashed in, and you're worried about some stupid coins? Your job was to call the police, not tackle him and me at the same time!'

His father seemed not to hear. He carried on up the stairs, muttering to himself. He's in shock, Quentin thought. Serves him right. What a stupid, stupid… Shaking his head, he hovered in the hallway wondering what to do. If only he'd made his father go to Shelagh's, if only–

His chaotic thoughts stopped when he heard a pathetic howl. And he knew. Not only had Halim escaped, he'd got his father's coins as well.

Chapter Twenty-five

Wanda had made Quentin promise to ring her if anything happened, no matter what time it was. 'I won't be able to sleep anyway,' she'd said before going to Shelagh's.

Knowing she would be cross if he didn't let her know about the burglary, he rang her mobile. When he'd gabbled out what had happened, that his father had foiled their attempt to catch Halim, she said in a hushed voice, 'Calm down, Quentin. I'm coming over.'

Too agitated to try to stop her, Quentin ended the call. He should have told her not to come, that there was nothing she could do, but at this moment he needed her calming influence. Or perhaps he just needed a sounding board. Either way he knew she would be there as soon as she could, and he blessed her for it.

His father was still upstairs, lamenting the loss of his beloved collection. Serves him right, Quentin thought savagely, pacing the floor from the lounge to the front door and back. Stupid bloody fool, pushing Halim on top of me like that. What the bloody hell were they supposed to do now?

He stopped at the bottom of the stairs as his father's voice filtered down from the bedroom. It took him several seconds to realize he was on the upstairs telephone.

'Yes, 7 Hibiscus Crescent. A burglary. Valuable things stolen. Saw the burglar, nearly caught the bastard but he got away … As quick as you can … What? What's wrong with now? … I know it's the middle of the night – would you say that if there was a bomb about to go off? … What? … Oh. All right, when you can.'

Quentin sank onto the bottom step, his head in his hands. Bloody hell. Not only had his attempt to catch Halim red-handed failed, now he had to explain the whole thing to the police. It didn't fail, he reasoned with himself. We did catch him red-handed, but we let him get away. That's worse.

He got up as his father came down the stairs. 'Called the police,' he said, his usual bluster reduced almost to a whisper.

'I wish you hadn't.'

'What? That's what you told me to do in the first place.'

'Yes, but the plan was to have someone here for them to arrest.' Quentin groaned. And it's all your fault, he wanted to shout, but the slump of his father's shoulders told him he was just as disappointed as he was himself.

'Got to report a theft. Why wouldn't you want to?'

Quentin closed his eyes and put his hands over his ears, trying to block out the voice that answered this question: Because instead of the conquering hero I'm now the victim. And what sort of detective lets a criminal slip through his fingers like that? What will Ed Grayson say? And what would the police, especially DI Jackson, say if they thought I'd set the burglary up?

He found the whisky bottle and poured generous measures into two glasses.

'Right,' he said, handing one to his father, 'here's what we do, or rather, here's what we don't do. We don't tell the police that we enticed this bloke here tonight – it's just coincidence that he happened to pick on your house.'

Herbert stared at his son, then plumped down in an armchair and took a slurp of whisky.

'You mean they'd take a dim view of it, getting the bloke here and then him getting away?'

Still too agitated to sit down, Quentin shuffled from one foot to the other, the glass clasped tightly in his hand.

'Just getting him here. They'll say we should have taken our suspicions directly to them.'

'We should have. Told you so.'

Quentin quashed the hackles that threatened to rise in him. 'You agreed to my plan readily enough.'

He was surprised to see his father looking slightly abashed. 'Couldn't resist the temptation,' he admitted. 'Wanted to see the bastard face-to-face.'

Quentin wondered whether bastard was the only swear word his father knew. Certainly "bastard" and "blighter" were the only words he'd heard him use as expletives.

'Well, you did that all right,' he said tersely. 'I suppose that's one good thing. We can both give the police his description.'

'When they get here,' his father snorted, something of his old belligerence resurfacing. 'Not supposed to touch anything. Said we'd have to wait till morning. Some big job on.'

'That explosion, probably,' Quentin reminded him. 'And there's nothing they can do here that can't wait till morning.'

'Huh. Should get the army in – they'd soon sort things out.'

Quentin was saved from having to give his opinion on the merits of the military when he heard the purr of a car engine outside.

'There's Wanda,' he said, and went to let her in.

'He's buggered up the whole thing!' Quentin exploded as soon as he opened the door.

'Shh,' she whispered, hugging him. 'I'm sure he didn't mean to. As long as you're all right.'

'He was just supposed to call the police, not play James Bond.'

'Hush, Quentin. It's no good worrying about it now. It's happened and that's that. We need to sit down and think what to do next.'

'He's reported it. The break-in. The police'll be here.'

'Ok, we'll talk it through. Are you going to let me in or have I got to stand on the threshold all night?'

Quentin stood aside while she went past him, then shut the door and followed her into the lounge. His father was still sitting in the chair, an empty glass his hand and a vacant look on his face. It was the first time Quentin had ever seen him look vulnerable, uncertain, like a child who'd had his sweets confiscated and didn't understand why. He looked up when Wanda went towards him.

'Herbert! What an ordeal for you both. Are you OK?'

Herbert raised a hand and touched the back of his head. 'Blighter pushed me over. Hit my head.'

'Let me see.' She bent over and pulled the crown of his head down towards her. 'You poor thing. It's not too deep. I'll get something to clean it up.'

Quentin's hand went to the gash on his cheek. She hasn't even noticed, he thought, then felt a pinprick of regret when she returned with two clean, dampened cloths. Motioning him to sit down she handed him one.

'Hold this on your cheek while I look at your dad's head.'

Ten minutes later the three of them sat, each with a glass of whisky, Quentin with a wodge of gauze taped across his cheek and his father holding a medicated pad in place through his thinning hair.

'We're not telling the police that we set the robbery up,' Quentin told Wanda. 'It wouldn't look good.'

For a few moments Wanda was quiet. 'Yes,' she said, nodding slowly, 'that might be best. There's no need for them to know. As far as they're concerned it's just another burglary, a house picked at random. And you can both identify Halim. That'll be quite a breakthrough for them. Nobody else has seen him.'

'Except all the other robberies have been at empty properties,' Quentin pointed out.

'That doesn't necessarily mean anything. Halim's thinking of moving, Linda said. He might have got careless, taken a chance to finish off his time here in Sydney for all the police know.'

'Let's hope they think that,' Quentin mumbled, thinking that if DI Jackson believed that, then he wasn't as bright as he'd judged him to be.

'Don't worry,' Wanda soothed. 'We'll play the innocents. After all, you told them about Halim yesterday. It's not your fault they didn't nab him straight away. If they find out we set the whole thing up, we'll cross that bridge then. All right with you, Herbert?'

Herbert looked confused for a moment. Then, as if Wanda's words had just sunk in, he said, 'Huh, I suppose it's all right. Shouldn't lie to the police really, but–'

'We're not lying, just not telling them everything.' Quentin sounded more positive than he felt.

'That's settled, then,' Wanda said. 'We'll check in with your mum, Shelagh and Howard in the morning.'

'It's nearly morning now,' Quentin said, glancing at his watch.

'Yes, but… Herbert, why don't you go and try to get a few hours' sleep. You'll feel better for it.'

'Might as well. Police won't be here yet anyway. They said not to touch anything, so I'll go down to the rec room. There's a pull-out bed down there.'

Quentin had almost forgotten about the recreation room in the basement. An image of his father marching up to his bedroom to check if his coins were safe flashed into his head, but he said nothing.

'Goodnight, my dear,' Herbert went on. 'Sorry to drag you out in the middle of the night.'

'Think nothing of it, Herbert. You're the one who tackled a criminal while I was tucked up in bed. You need some rest.'

Wanda looked at Quentin, defying him to contradict her.

Quentin bit back his scathing retort and watched as his father lumbered from the room. He waited until the door closed before turning to Wanda.

'You're the one who tackled a criminal!' he mimicked. 'You're treating him like a bloody hero instead of the one who let the criminal get away.'

'Of course I am. You're both heroes, the pair of you, staying here and waiting for him like that. So Halim got away. How do think your dad feels about that?'

'He's more worried about his stupid coins than anything else,' Quentin said darkly.

'Well, he's had them a long time. They're precious to him.'

'Which is more than I am,' Quentin said pointedly. 'I don't think he'd have cared if Halim had killed me.'

He heard Wanda's exasperated sigh.

'Now, Quentin, don't be so dramatic and stop feeling sorry for yourself. It can't only be his fault Halim got away, surely? It doesn't matter, I don't want to know. Why don't you try to get some sleep, too?'

'Sleep? Are you kidding?'

'No. At least lie down for a bit. You might doze off for a couple of hours. We'll talk again when you wake up.'

'I can't sleep.'

'Don't, then. Just lie here.' She shifted up to the end of the settee and put a cushion on her lap. What the hell, Quentin thought, lying down with his head in her lap. What a mess. What a bloody mess.

Chapter Twenty-six

When he awoke his head was still on the cushion but the cushion was no longer on Wanda's lap. She'd obviously managed to get up without disturbing him. He struggled to sit up, massaging the crick in his neck and sniffing the air at the smell of coffee that came from the kitchen.

'Hello, sleepyhead.' Wanda appeared with two steaming mugs. 'I was going to wake you. I've been thinking.'

'Sounds ominous,' Quentin said, taking a mug from her. He took a sip of coffee, then ran his hand through his hair. His mouth felt dry and his eyes were heavy from lack of sleep. 'What time is it?'

'Six-fifteen. Listen, when you were wrestling with Halim, did he recognize you, do you think?'

Quentin shrugged. 'I've no idea. Probably not. If he did it would only be as a customer – he may remember that he gave me a haircut, but he's done loads since then. I don't think he noticed me when you pretended to faint at his shop the other day. There were too many people milling about. Does it matter?'

Wanda looked pensive. Her usually sleek hair was tousled, which somehow made her look more attractive. It reminded Quentin of how she looked after their lovemaking.

'It might,' she said, putting down her coffee cup. 'If he did, then he might guess that last night was a set-up.'

Quentin considered this. 'Hmm. It could just be a coincidence. His customers have to live somewhere. As far as we know he doesn't know my connection to Shelagh or the salon. Oh! You're thinking of Linda and Suzy.'

'Yes. If he thinks it was a set-up, he'll contact whichever one it is to warn her. I would, if it was me.'

'So what are you thinking? They'll do a runner, too?'

'Maybe, or at least they'll be prepared to lie their way out of trouble. Still, even if he did recognize you, there's no reason for him to connect you to the salon, as you say. When you went in for a haircut you didn't mention being related to Shelagh or having anything to do with the salon, did you?'

Quentin shook his head. 'No. Halim wasn't in a chatty mood – he hasn't exactly got a bedside manner.'

'OK.' Wanda was quiet for a moment. 'So, you think he won't make the connection? I mean, he'll go on the run anyway I should think, whether he recognized you or not. After all, you can identify him.'

'He didn't give any sign that he recognized me. We only saw each other for a few moments. If he did, and realized I'd been in his shop, then he'll have to run. He won't risk being caught at his business address. If he didn't, well, he might stay put.'

'All right, let's go over this again.' Wanda paused before carrying on. 'The police will come here to investigate the robbery. Like we said last night, we'll tell them what happened but nothing about what we know. If Linda or Suzy don't know about last night yet, then–'

Quentin jerked himself upright. 'Then we could get to them first,' he said, excitement starting to bubble. 'Yes, we'll say we know everything, that we nearly caught Halim and that the police are on the lookout for him. We'll make them tell us whether they've heard from him, and if they know where he is we'll go after him–'

'Whoa! Not so fast. I was thinking more on the lines of persuading them to go to the police and owning up. We could take them in.'

'We could do both.' Quentin was standing now, ticking off the possibilities on his fingers. 'We wait till they're both at the salon, take them out the back, get them to spill the beans, then you can take whoever it is to Jackson while I go after Halim.'

Wanda frowned. 'I don't think you should go after Halim. We'll just take them to Jackson. What if they don't spill the beans? What if they deny the whole thing? And should we wait until they get to the salon? Halim might have warned them by then.'

'Yeah.' Quentin hovered, wondering what to do. 'I'll ring Shelagh, find out their home addresses. I'll need to tell her and Mum about last night anyway.'

'You can't go barging into their houses.'

'Why not? The police would soon barge in if they thought it was necessary. I wouldn't barge anyway. I'd be discreet. I'm ringing Shelagh. We all need to agree not to let on that last night was a set-up.'

Minutes later he was talking to Shelagh. As briefly as possible he explained about the previous night's events and went through their concerns.

'It would be better if Mum stayed at yours today,' he said when he'd finished. 'Dad can collect her when the local coppers have been. He can stay here and deal with them when they come. He won't say anything about what we know – we'll keep it simple just in case, in case…' In case of what he couldn't put into words. 'Well, I think we should get to Linda and Suzy now, see if we can get one of them to confess. If Halim's done a runner, they'll know the game's up anyway. Can you tell Mum and Howard?'

'Yes, of course, but…' Shelagh sounded doubtful. 'Suppose neither of them confesses?'

'We'll play it by ear.' Despite his earlier assertions to Wanda, Quentin didn't really know what they would do when they questioned the two women. 'What time would they have to leave home to get to you?'

'Why? You're not thinking of going to their home addresses?'

'I was.'

'Well, it's nearly seven now. Wait till they get to the salon. If you leave by seven-thirty you'll be here when they arrive. I'll make sure I'm there too. Our first client's not till eight forty-five, but you must keep them in the staff room. I don't want a scene. Shouldn't you go straight to that policeman you spoke to yesterday? The one who's investigating the robberies?'

'I will, as soon as we get something out of one of them.'

'Um, I'm not sure about it really. I still can't believe… Well, if it is one of them, I'll give them a piece of my mind.'

'Don't say anything until we get there if you're there before us,' Quentin said, anxious that his sister might spook the culprit and send her running.

'Don't worry, I won't. I'll tell Howard and Mum what's going on before I go. Howard'll be off to work soon and I'll ask Mum if she'll look after Michael instead of him going to pre-school. That'll keep her occupied, take her mind off the break-in.'

'OK, bye, sis.' Ending the call, Quentin turned to Wanda.

'I heard,' she said. 'We'd better get going if we're going to be there on time.'

'Where are you going?' Herbert came into the room, still in last night's clothes and with his sparse hair sticking out above his ears like wings.

Wanda smiled at him. 'Morning, Herbert. Quentin and I have decided to follow up this lead on the girls at the salon. I know we can trust you to deal with the local police when they get here. You haven't forgotten what we agreed last night?'

'No, but now I think about it I don't see why we can't tell them that we know who the burglar is without telling them we got him here purposely.'

'It'll make it complicated,' Quentin told him. 'Just say we had a break-in, surprised the burglar, had a tussle with him and he got away. Give his description and say I had to take Wanda to work. It's the truth anyway. Say I'll speak to them later in the day if they need me to. I'll tell the whole story to the detective I saw yesterday later on.'

Not waiting for a reply, Quentin went to the bathroom, had a quick shower and put on fresh clothes. Wanda did the same and within twenty minutes they were on the road.

'Your poor dad,' Wanda said. 'I feel like we've deserted him, leaving him to face the police on his own.'

'He'll cope. He's always saying what difficult situations he had to face in the forces. By the time he's given them a hard time for taking so long to get there, and for not catching the burglars yet, they'll be glad to get out of there.'

'So,' Wanda said, giving him a sideways glance, 'if we manage to get a confession, we're taking them in?'

'Of course. What else would we do?'

'I know what you're like. You might come up with some hare-brained scheme. We could just tell the police and let them pull them in.'

Quentin pursed his lips. 'Better if we take them.'

'You mean presenting them with a fait accompli will make up for letting Halim get away?'

Quentin felt Wanda's sarcasm. 'No! Well, maybe.' Bugger it, he thought. Why does she have to be right all the time?

'It doesn't make any difference,' he insisted. 'The police will still get them as an accomplice whether it's us or the police that take them in.'

'Well, we're nearly there. If we're going to change our minds we need to do it now.'

Quentin didn't need to answer. He knew she knew very well that he wouldn't change his mind.

Chapter Twenty-seven

Shelagh was at the salon when they got there. 'What if one of them doesn't turn up?' she asked when she let them in.

'Then we'll know Halim's warned whichever one it is,' Quentin said. 'And we'll go to their home address. If they've scarpered from there, then we're sunk.'

'Surely he'd have to contact them, even if it was only to tell them to keep their mouth shut if anyone asked questions,' Shelagh said.

'Not if he didn't recognize Quentin,' Wanda told her. 'Because he was seen doesn't mean the game's up, as far as he sees it. It just means the police will have his description so he'll have to lie low. He could even brazen it out and carry on working at the barber's, though if he's got any sense he won't. It all depends on whether he makes the connection.'

'Dina's usually in first,' Shelagh said, peering through the window ten minutes later. 'Ah, here she is.'

'This is cozy,' Dina said, seeing them standing together. Then, as if noticing Shelagh's worried look and the tension that hung in the air she continued, 'Anything wrong?'

'Yes, but I'll explain later,' Shelagh said. 'I'm trusting you to keep the place running as usual. When Linda and Suzy come in tell them I want to see them in the staff room. Don't tell them Quentin and Wanda are here. Act normally, and tell my first client I'll be with her as soon as I can, then ring my ten o'clock and see if she can come in later. We may have to juggle things between us.'

Quentin could see Dina was burning to ask what was going on, but after depositing her bag in the staff room, she went to her workstation and began rearranging her trolley.

When Quentin and Wanda followed Shelagh to the staff room, the first thing Shelagh did was to put the kettle on.

'I need a caffeine fix to get me through this,' she said grimly.

Ten minutes slipped by, during which coffee was made and they stood around, cups in hands, Shelagh practically dancing round the room in agitation.

'Suzy's usually here by now,' she said, glancing at the wall clock. 'Suppose she's not coming? Suppose she's—'

'She might just be late,' Wanda said. 'Whoever comes in first, don't tackle them straight away about the break-ins. Ask why they're late – they might give something away.'

At that moment the staff room door opened and Suzy came in.

'Morning,' she said, looking surprised to see Quentin and Wanda. 'I thought I wasn't going to make it before opening time. The bus was late. Dina said you wanted to see me, Shelagh.'

Shelagh folded her arms across her bump and spoke quietly. 'Yes, Suzy. It's about the words you had with Linda last night.'

'Words?'

'Call it what you like. It's my place to tell her what she should or shouldn't be doing at work, not yours.'

Suzy shifted from foot to foot, apparently uncomfortable with being taken to task in front of Quentin and Wanda, something Quentin guessed Shelagh wouldn't normally do.

'Well, she's always nipping out or going early.'

'So did you the other evening. Why did you leave early – just because Wanda was here and I wasn't?'

Suzy reddened but said nothing. Her hand went to her chest, where an oval shape showed through her T-shirt.

'Is that the locket you had on yesterday?' Wanda asked, stepping forward. 'It looks like one I had years ago. Can I see it?'

Suzy hesitated. Then, with three pairs of eyes on her, she pulled on the chain around her neck and raised the locket. 'It was my grandmother's,' she said. 'I don't usually wear it to work, but...'

Moving closer to Suzy, Wanda took the locket between her forefinger and thumb. 'It's lovely. It looks old. Does it still open?'

Without waiting for a reply, Wanda squeezed the catch on the side and the locket sprung open. Suzy gasped and pulled back, yanking it from Wanda's grasp. Hurriedly she snapped it shut, but not before the photo inside was exposed. A man's face. Halim's.

Before anyone could say anything, the door opened and Linda appeared, looking harassed.

'Sorry, I'm late,' she said to Shelagh. Her red hair looked uncombed and she'd forgone her usual eye make-up. Her eyes were red-rimmed, as though she'd been crying.

'What happened?' Shelagh asked.

Linda turned and looked at each of them in turn, then lowered her eyes. 'I had an early phone call,' she admitted breathily. 'It put me all behind.'

Shelagh's back stiffened. 'Oh? What was so important they couldn't ring you after work?'

Quentin grimaced. Shelagh's normal response would have been to ask if anything was wrong, not to bite Linda's head off.

Linda hesitated, staring at Quentin and Wanda as though wondering why they were there, then casting a questioning look at Shelagh.

Shelagh tossed her head, impatient to get to the bottom of things. 'Go on, Linda,' she said. 'Who was this phone call from?'

'It– why do you want to know?'

Wanda intervened. 'It's important that we know, Linda.'

Tears shimmered in Linda's eyes. 'It was Halim. He's going away.'

'Does that mean you'll be going with him?' Shelagh asked.

'I– I can't.'

'Why not?' Shelagh demanded.

'Because... Why are you asking me this, and what's it got to do with them?' Linda asked, her gaze sweeping from Quentin to Wanda, then settling on Suzy.

'He's told you, hasn't he?' Suzy said, a tiny note of triumph in her voice.

'He hasn't told me anything. He won't tell me where he's going. I don't even know where he is now. His father said he doesn't know where he is. He said Halim had some things to sort out and needed time to think.'

Shelagh turned to Suzy. 'What is it you think Halim's told her, Suzy?'

Suzy flushed and sent a pitying look to Linda. 'It's between me and Linda,' she murmured.

While Linda looked confused, Shelagh exploded. 'If you value your job, if you both value your jobs, we'll get this out in the open – now!'

'All right,' Suzy conceded. 'If you must know I saw Halim and he said... he said he still loves me.'

'Liar!' Linda spat the word out. 'He couldn't have said that. It's me he wants. I don't believe you.'

They faced each other like sparring partners, each ready to attack the other.

Quentin stepped between them. 'I saw Halim kissing Suzy in the churchyard.'

Linda gasped and Suzy recoiled.

'When?' Linda croaked after a few painful seconds.

'The day before yesterday, just after five o'clock. So, if what he told Linda is true and he's going away, it looks like he's leaving you both in the lurch.'

Quentin looked from one to the other. Both girls seemed devastated at what he'd said.

'I've had enough of this,' Shelagh said through gritted teeth. 'I'm not interested in your love lives. Your precious Halim is a thief.'

'W– what?'

Quentin took in Suzy's apparent shock at this, while Linda's earlier aggression seemed to wilt. Shelagh, evidently tired of talking around the subject that filled her mind, rounded on them.

She was stopped by Wanda's restraining hand.

'What Shelagh means,' Wanda said, 'is we know Halim is involved with these burglaries that are going on.'

There was a stunned silence.

'I don't believe it,' Suzy choked out. 'How do you know?'

'We know someone who was burgled, and they took his service medals,' Quentin revealed, not wanting to accuse either Suzy or Linda directly.

'That's right,' Wanda agreed. 'And Quentin found a stash of medals in Halim's stockroom.'

Suzy's big eyes grew bigger and she paled. 'You– you found stolen goods in Halim's stockroom?'

'Yes. Suzy, did Halim give you that locket?'

'No!' Suzy's tone was vehement. 'I told you, it was my gran's. Ask Dina. I brought it in to show her when gran died. That was before I even met Halim.'

Quentin looked at his sister. He guessed she was thinking that this had to be true. It was pointless Suzy lying about something that could be disproved in minutes.

As if reading their thoughts Suzy stammered on. 'I– I only started wearing it because– because–'

'Because you put a photo of Halim in it?' Wanda suggested.

Suzy gulped. 'Yes. He said he'd made a mistake going with Linda, and if I waited until he'd sorted a few things out, he'd tell her, then we'd be together.'

'Liar!' Linda spat again. 'You're just bitter because he dumped you!'

'You took him from me!'

'Shut up, both of you,' Shelagh said, looking as though she wanted to bang their heads together.

Quentin tried to get back to the main thrust of the conversation. 'Suzy,' he said. 'What did you say to Halim in the churchyard?'

Linda snorted. 'It's obvious. She begged him to go back with her.'

From what Quentin had seen, he thought this could be true. Suzy had seemed to be pleading with him. He could have said anything to placate her, it wouldn't have mattered if he was planning to leave anyway.

'You're delusional if you think he'll leave me for you,' Linda said. 'He can't leave me.'

'Why can't he?' Shelagh asked.

Linda stared at her. Her gaze flickered to Quentin and Wanda, then back to Shelagh.

'You said you weren't interested in our love lives,' she said, as though something had just dawned on her.

Shelagh brought her hand down on the worktop. 'I am when someone who works for me finds out when my customers' houses are going to be empty, then tells Halim so he can burgle them!'

A gasp came from Suzy. 'No!' she cried, shrinking back. 'You can't think I'd– I'd never do that, never in a million years!'

'Nor would I,' Linda said.

After a tense silence, Quentin decided it was time to get to the nub of the matter. 'The thing is, Linda, the burglaries didn't start till after you started working here.'

Linda's head jerked up. 'Wh– what do you mean?' she stammered uncertainly. 'I've never done anything–'

'Well, somebody has,' Shelagh snapped. 'Somebody's found out from customers when they're going to be away, told Halim and he's burgled them.'

Another gasp from Suzy. 'It wasn't me. I swear on my life.'

Wanda stepped forward. 'Linda. Quentin saw you with Halim and heard you telling him.' Not quite true, but Linda didn't know that.

Linda stared at Quentin in disbelief. 'Wh– when?'

'I was in the barber's, with my face covered,' Quentin told her. 'I heard what you said, and I saw some stolen items in Halim's stockroom.'

Linda's face turned bright red, but she said nothing. It was as though she'd suddenly been struck dumb.

'You were always popping off, going to see him,' Shelagh reminded her. 'He even tried to rob me.'

Linda paled, but still said nothing.

'How else would he have known we were going to be away overnight?' Shelagh continued, her voice harder than Quentin had ever heard it. 'I only knew myself that day. Someone told him, and he tried to break into *my* house, with *my* son asleep upstairs–'

'Stop!' Linda clapped her hands over her ears. She took a moment to compose herself, then straightened up and looked at each of them in turn. 'I'm not saying anything,' she croaked.

Quentin exchanged a look with Wanda. So, they'd been right to suspect Linda. If she wasn't involved, surely she'd be declaring her innocence?

Wanda moved forward and laid a hand on her arm. 'Linda. It's pointless trying to defend Halim. He broke into Quentin's parents' house last night. Quentin and his father both saw him. That's why he's on the run.'

Linda's reaction told Quentin what he wanted to know – that Halim hadn't made the connection between him and the salon. Eyes widening, Linda stared at Wanda as though she'd said Halim had stolen a rocket and flown into space. Then her gaze switched to Quentin, a strangled gasp coming from her.

'Y– your house?'

'Yes. I can identify Halim as the burglar. What did he say when he rang you?'

Linda shook her head dumbly.

Wanda, her hand still on Linda's arm, said gently, 'Tell us, Linda. The police will be asking you anyway.'

At the mention of the police Linda wrenched her arm from Wanda's hand. She looked round the room wildly, as though seeking an escape from this nightmare. Shelagh lurched forward and gripped the door handle.

'Don't even think about it,' she hissed.

Seeing escape was impossible, Linda said slowly, 'He said something had happened, and it would be better if he went away for a bit, but he wouldn't tell me where.'

'Something happened? What happened?' Quentin demanded.

'He didn't tell me.'

'Linda.' Shelagh spoke as though she was trying to rein in her anger. 'You knew he was going to that house last night because you heard Wanda give the address here yesterday.'

Quentin half expected Linda to say that Suzy had heard as well, but the fight seemed to have deserted Linda.

'How could you?' Shelagh went on when Linda didn't answer. 'And how could you let him break into my house after I took you on and always treated you fairly?'

'I didn't! I told him to stay away from yours. I told him not to—' Linda stopped, as though realizing she had just given herself away.

'If it's any consolation, I think that's true, Shelagh,' Quentin said. 'When I heard her speaking to Halim she did say she'd told him not to go to yours.'

'So you admit it, then, you deceitful little bitch! You, you…' Shelagh ran out of words.

'Think about what you've done, Linda,' Quentin said. 'You've taken advantage of your employer, put her clients' properties and belongings at risk and aided and abetted a criminal. You could be looking at quite a stretch in prison.'

Linda's face crumpled. 'Prison?'

'Tell us what he said,' Quentin persisted. 'Then if we go to the police we might be able to strike a bargain.'

'Linda.' Wanda's voice was soft. 'Why cover for him? He's used you, he's two-timed you, and now he's run off without you. He won't hesitate to implicate you if he has to.'

'No, he wouldn't, he…' Linda gulped. Then, taking a deep breath, she said resignedly, 'All right, I'll tell you what he said, but it won't do you much good. He went on at me because this was the second time he'd gone to a property and it wasn't empty. He said he'd have to lie low because he'd been seen. It would be safer if I didn't know where he was, and he'd send for me when he decided what to do.'

This brought another gasp from Suzy, and she covered her face with her hands.

'I said I'd go with him,' Linda went on, 'but he wouldn't have it. He said there was no reason for me to disrupt my life because of him, and he promised to contact me when he could.'

'But you don't think he will?' Quentin asked. 'You think he was trying to finish with you?'

Linda tilted her chin up. 'I thought maybe… but he can't, can he?'

'Of course not,' Wanda said. 'You know too much. He'll either have to keep you in with him or…'

'Or what?' Linda asked, suddenly turning to Wanda. 'Go on, he'll have to keep in with me or what?'

Quentin answered before Wanda had a chance. 'I think what Wanda means is that he'll have to be certain you won't shop him.'

Linda's mouth tightened. 'He wouldn't hurt me. He's not like that. We're going to get a place together. He promised we'd have some money after he'd got enough for what he needed it for.'

Quentin exchanged glances with Wanda. She shrugged, obviously as mystified as he was. 'What did he need it for?'

Linda shook her head. 'I don't know, but it's something to do with his father.'

Quentin frowned. Something to do with his father. He pictured Ahmed as he'd seen him in the barber's. He'd seemed affable and anxious to please. He was certainly kind enough to Wanda when her fainting act had taken her into his shop.

There was a tap on the door and Dina appeared.

'Mrs Shergold's in, Shelagh,' she said tentatively. 'There are already two people waiting.'

'All right, Dina. I shouldn't be much longer.'

'OK.' Dina cast an inquisitive look at Linda, who refused to meet her eyes, then at Suzy.

'Hold on Dina,' Quentin said. 'Just for the record, have you seen this before?' He gestured for Suzy to show Dina the locket.

'It's the one you brought in that time, isn't it?' Dina asked Suzy. 'Your gran's?'

'OK,' Quentin said, convinced that Suzy had nothing to do with the robberies. 'I think Suzy can start work now, Shelagh.'

Shelagh nodded. 'I'm sorry about this, Suzy, but please don't say anything, especially in the salon, or we'll have no clients left.'

Suzy started towards the door. She looked ashen. She stopped by Linda as if to say something, then shook her head and walked on.

'So,' Quentin said when Suzy and Dina had gone, 'Halim's father needs money. Why?'

'I've told you, I don't know,' Linda said. 'All I know is he needs money. We've had rows about it. Apparently his father is sending money back to Turkey.'

'What for?' Shelagh asked.

'How should I know? To support his family, I suppose. His mother's still there.'

'His mother? You mean Ahmed's mother?' Quentin demanded.

'Yes. I've nearly asked Ahmed a few times, but I chickened out.'

'OK,' Quentin said. 'So he's getting the money for his father. Does Ahmed know how he's getting it? Are they in it together?'

Linda sniffed, and reached into her pocket for a tissue. 'Ahmed found out a month or so ago and said Halim had to stop. There was an almighty row and Halim threatened to leave. I wasn't there but Halim said his father was very upset.'

'Well,' Quentin said thoughtfully, 'it doesn't matter why he needs the money, it still makes Halim a thief.'

Shelagh glared at Linda. 'And you an accessory,' she blurted.

'So what you need to do, Linda,' Wanda said quietly, 'is to tell the police everything you've told us.'

A whimpering sound escaped Linda. 'I can't. I can't turn him in.'

'I'm sorry,' Wanda went on, 'but you'll have to.'

Squaring her shoulders and looking at each of them in turn, Linda said, 'I don't have to and you can't make me.'

'I think we can.' Quentin's voice was calm and measured. 'Because we've recorded everything you've said.' He slid his mobile phone from his pocket, looking at it as if to ensure it was recording. Tempted to turn the record facility on now, he decided it would be too obvious. Instead he nodded and returned the phone to his pocket. Praying that Linda wouldn't demand to hear what he had supposedly recorded, he didn't flinch when he felt Wanda and Shelagh's surprised eyes on him, knowing they would go along with his lie.

Linda's whimper turned to a howl. 'You set me up – you set *Halim* up last night, didn't you? He'll never forgive me.'

'Neither will I,' Shelagh told her.

Wanda put a comforting arm around Linda. 'Come on,' she said. 'We'll take you to the police station. If you tell them what you told us voluntarily, they'll go easier on you.'

'But I'm not going voluntarily,' she choked.

'The police don't know that,' Quentin pointed out. 'We won't tell them we've recorded you. We'll just say we told you we were broken into and that we saw Halim, and you decided that enough was enough.'

Linda stared at them, the fingers of one hand clutched tightly round the tissue she'd been using. The other hand clawed at her face, leaving angry red streaks down her cheek. Then, slowly, resignedly, her shoulders sagged and she whispered, 'It looks like I haven't got much choice.'

'No, you haven't,' Shelagh huffed. 'I still can't believe what you've done.'

'It's all right, Shelagh,' Quentin said. 'Why don't you get on now? We'll go with Linda. We'll go out the back way.'

'All right,' Shelagh said through tight lips. 'Make sure she gets there.'

Quentin took a step towards Linda. 'Don't worry, we will.'

Chapter Twenty-eight

'Of course,' Quentin said when Shelagh had left the room, 'there is a way we could avoid going to the police, at least for now.'

'Is there?' Linda eyed him suspiciously.

Wanda merely looked at Quentin and raised a well-shaped eyebrow.

'Yes. If you help us get to Halim we could make sure the police know that, say we only found him because of you. They'd definitely go easier on you then.'

Stiff-lipped, Linda said, 'How can I do that? I don't know where he is.'

'No, but you could find out.'

'How?'

Quentin read the same question on Wanda's face. 'You must have his mobile number. Ring him, try to find out where he is.'

'He won't tell me.'

'He might, if you give him a good enough reason to.'

'Yes,' said Wanda slowly, warming to the idea. 'Think of something that will make him tell you where he is. Even if he doesn't, we might pick up on something in the background. Has your phone got a loudspeaker facility?'

Linda sniffed. 'Yes. But why should I tell you anything? You'll only use it against me.' She pointed towards Quentin's pocket.

'I think I can turn the recorder off now,' Quentin said, wondering if his timely invention might turn out to be an impediment. 'We've got enough to take to the police, and I'm sure we can trust you to do the right thing, Linda.'

Reaching for his mobile, he jabbed his finger at it as if to switch the recording facility off. He was actually switching it on, cursing silently that he hadn't thought to have it on in the first place. In order to distract Linda's attention away from his actions, he coughed several times and swung away from her, his elbow knocking over two of the coffee cups on the worktop. The dregs spilled out, forming a brown pool on the counter, and one of the cups rolled onto the floor with a shattering crash.

'Oops! Looks like I'll be buying Shelagh another cup,' he said, slipping the phone back into his pocket.

He grabbed a cloth and mopped up the spillage, then kicked the broken pieces into a corner.

'Come on. We've disrupted Shelagh's work enough for one day. We'll go to the car and talk there. And no funny business. If you try to run we'll take the recording straight to the police. They'll have the evidence they need to arrest you and Halim, and they'll soon track you down.'

* * *

The Micra was parked in the adjoining street, in the first space from the corner. Quentin and Wanda sat in the back with Linda sitting rigidly between them staring straight ahead, her face pale and her hands shaking in her lap.

'OK,' Quentin said. 'So, what do you think would make Halim tell you where he is, or even better, make him come back?' When Linda just shrugged he went on. 'Well, what does he care enough about to make him come back?'

'You?' Wanda asked gently. 'If you were ill, or his father?'

'Maybe.'

Quentin could see Linda didn't want to give them any information that would lead to her boyfriend's whereabouts. She seemed bent on protecting Halim, despite what Suzy had said.

'Right,' Quentin said after a moment. 'What if you ring him and say you've got some vital information, something you can only tell him face-to-face?'

'It wouldn't make any difference,' Linda said stubbornly. 'He doesn't want to implicate me.'

Wanda raised her eyes heavenwards. 'Doesn't want to implicate you! You can't be any more implicated than you are already. Come on, Linda, have some sense.'

Linda huffed and shifted on the seat.

'What about something more personal, like, I don't know, you could say…' Wanda paused, thinking carefully before she spoke. 'You could say… you were pregnant or something.'

A howl came from Linda. Her hands covered her face and she sobbed, deep, noisy sobs. And Quentin knew. Bloody hell, he thought, she is pregnant. That's why she's defending him.

Wanda obviously guessed at this too, because she put a comforting hand on Linda's and said softly, 'You are pregnant, aren't you, Linda?'

'Y– yes. I only found out a few days ago.'

'Does Halim know?' Quentin asked.

'I told him this morning on the phone. I was going to wait till– till I thought the time was right, but when he said he was going away… Well, I told him.'

'Before or after he said he wouldn't take you with him?' Quentin's voice was sharp.

Another howl, another bout of tears. Wanda felt in her bag and found a tissue. 'Here, dry your eyes and calm down. So you told him you were pregnant – how did he react?'

'He… well, he wasn't exactly jumping for joy.'

'I don't suppose he was,' Wanda said. 'He probably didn't want to hear that after what happened last night. Do you… want the baby, Linda? What will you do if Halim deserts you?'

'He won't desert me. He's not like that.'

'What about what he said to Suzy?' Quentin looked sideways at Linda then went on ruthlessly, 'He wouldn't take you with him and he won't tell you where he is. Sounds like desertion to me.'

'Quentin.' Wanda glared at him, then swivelled her gaze to Linda. 'Look, Linda, you've already done more than you should for him. You've risked being caught as an accessory to burglary, you've betrayed the trust of Shelagh and her clients. If he thought anything of you, he wouldn't put you in that position. If he was getting money to help his father, and if he hasn't got a previous record, they might go easier on him, and you, if you cooperate. But if they've got to spend more time and manpower tracking him down they won't be too happy. And what about your family? Your parents will have enough to cope with when they find out you're pregnant without being told the father of their grandchild is a burglar on the run.'

Linda made a scrunched-up ball of the new tissue. 'My dad will kill him,' she admitted. 'He's never liked Halim. And he'll be so disappointed in me, so will Mum.'

Wanda nodded. 'There we are, then. Better if they think you've seen sense and helped put him away. Better for him, too, before he gets into even more trouble.'

'I can't put the father of my baby in prison,' Linda said, her voice steadier now.

'Yes, you can,' Quentin told her. 'If he behaves, he'll be out before long. The longer he's on the run the harder it will be for him. And what kind of life would you have if he isn't caught? You'd either be with him, running from place to place, or be on your own with the baby wondering if and when he was going to show up. You couldn't go on like that. Still, I suppose you don't have to have the baby.'

This earned him a look from Wanda that he couldn't identify.

'Well, anyway,' he continued hastily, 'that's up to you. Halim used to go away at weekends sometimes, didn't he? Could he have gone to one of those places? He was thinking of moving to Melbourne, wasn't he?'

'Yes, but there's nowhere specific that I know about.'

A short silence ensued. Linda sat stock still, a frown creasing her forehead, as though mulling over her options.

'All right, I'll ring him,' she said at last, 'but I don't think it will help.'

'We can but try,' Wanda said, fanning her face with her hand as the sun streamed in the window.

As she wound down the window Linda produced her phone. Quentin laid his hand on her arm. 'Hold on. We need to think about what you should say. What—'

He stopped as a loud, shattering noise carried through the still air and filtered through the open window. The unmistakable sound of glass breaking. Then there was a shout, and the screech of brakes as a car squealed round the corner and passed them at breakneck speed, smashing the rear outside wing of their car as it did so.

'Bloody hell!' Quentin groaned. 'He's just hit us. What the devil was he doing, driving like he was on a racetrack?'

Climbing out of the car he examined the wing of the Micra. 'That'll cost me,' he muttered. 'Lucky I took the insurance out.'

Wanda put her head through the back window. 'Perhaps he hit something and ran,' she suggested. 'I definitely heard glass breaking.'

'I'll go and find out,' Quentin said, realizing they might have just witnessed the escape of someone running from an accident. 'You stay here. And don't move,' he added pointedly to Linda. '*And* I'll take your phone.' He held out his hand as Wanda took the phone from Linda and handed it to him.

Quentin put the phone in the glove compartment. That phone was important. It held the only means of contacting Halim, and he wasn't prepared to take any chances. Linda might suddenly decide to throw it out and smash it on the road while he wasn't there.

Leaving Linda in the back of the car with Wanda, he jogged to the corner and looked in the direction the noise had come from. A knot of people was gathered on the pavement a little way up – right near Shelagh's salon, he realized. Alarmed, he hurried along to where they stood staring towards a shop – not Shelagh's, he could see now, but the barber's. Then he saw why. The barber's front window was gone. Shards of glass lay on the pavement, though it looked as though most of the glass had been propelled inwards. Something had hit the window with quite a force.

'What happened?' he asked a bystander.

The man he'd asked puffed up as though he was preparing to give a television interview. 'I was on the other side of the road,' he said. 'Then this car drove up and some man got out. Next thing I heard this almighty smashing sound, and the man got back in the car and drove off.'

'I saw it,' a woman chipped in. 'He threw something at the window and then scarpered.'

Ahmed was in the shop doorway. He looked grey and upset, but there was an air about him that suggested to Quentin that the attack wasn't entirely a surprise. He looked resigned somehow, as though this was just another thing he had to deal with.

Quentin elbowed his way nearer the barber's.

'I've called the police,' a woman was saying to Ahmed.

'Police no good,' Ahmed told her. 'They won't get them. It happens before.'

The woman looked shocked. 'But you must tell the police. Look what they've done to your shop. They're on their way.'

Ahmed raised his hands in a conciliatory gesture. 'Thank you for thought. I will talk to them. Go away now please. Everyone, go away. I will take care of things.'

'You shouldn't touch anything,' a man from the crowd said. 'Not till the police get here.'

Ahmed nodded, paused to take a lingering look at his destroyed shop front, then walked slowly back inside.

A familiar voice hailed Quentin. 'Quentin! What are you doing?' He turned to see Shelagh behind him. 'Why are you here?' she hissed. 'You're supposed to be taking Linda to the police.'

'I am,' he said. 'She's in the car with Wanda. Don't worry, she's safe enough. We were just about to drive off when we heard the smash. Whoever did this' – he indicated towards the broken window – 'drove off round the corner and hit our car in the process.'

'What?' Shelagh's anger gave way to concern. 'Are you all right?'

'Yes, we're OK. There's no major damage, but he was going like a bat out of hell. He was gone before I knew what was happening. Anyway,' – he leaned in so no one else could hear – 'it seems very strange that this should happen right after Halim's disappearance. Someone's got it in for our Turkish friend.'

'Good,' Shelagh said. 'Serves him right, making a dishonest living from my customers.'

'We don't know that he was, only that Halim was,' Quentin reminded her. He was surprised at her vehemence, but then her livelihood had been threatened. If her clients knew that the burglaries they'd suffered had been made possible by information from her salon she could lose a lot of trade. 'Ahmed said this had happened before. Do you know anything about that?'

Shelagh screwed up her face. 'Yes, I think it did happen once, when we first opened. That was at night, though, not in broad daylight.'

'Right. OK, go back to work, sis. Leave the detecting to me. We'll get to the bottom of this, and Linda will get her comeuppance. Trust me.'

Shelagh sighed. 'It looks like I'll have to. I'll have to tell Dina what's been going on, but she won't say anything to the clients, nor will Suzy. I don't want our customers finding out about our link to the robberies. I'll say Linda left for personal reasons.'

'OK, we'll go with that. O-oh, here come the boys in blue.'

Shelagh went back to the salon and Quentin edged away. Most of the crowd had dispersed, leaving only a few stragglers, including the woman and man he had spoken to and a man with traces of foam on his chin, presumably Ahmed's customer.

Quentin stood well back as a police car drew up and two officers got out. After a cursory inspection of the scene outside, one went into the barber's and the other began to ask questions of the bystanders. Quentin stepped into the doorway of a nearby ironmonger's shop and watched as a second car, this time an unmarked one, arrived. He gave an involuntary gasp as he recognized the second of the two men who climbed out. Detective Sergeant Wilson.

Chapter Twenty-nine

Shrinking back into the shadow of the ironmonger's doorway, Quentin checked his watch: 9.45. Was Wilson here in response to his report the previous day? Had he finally come to check on Halim? Surely they should have taken action before this. He'd given them the information on Halim at about three-thirty. At that time, a lot of the force had been policing the demonstration. The explosion had taken place at around five. He recalled hearing the sirens and his father telling him it had been on the news at teatime. So, as he'd gambled, they'd been too busy to follow up the intelligence on Halim last night.

Quentin hovered, wondering what to do. Should he stick around, see if anything developed? Go in and tell Wilson that he had the link to the robberies sitting in a car not a hundred yards away? Tempting, after the scorn Wilson had shown him at the police station. But no, getting one over on DS Wilson wasn't as important as finding Halim.

A car pulled up in the middle of the road and a police officer went to speak to the driver. Taking his chance, Quentin darted along the pavement, stopped outside the barber's, then bent down and fiddled with his shoelace. Voices filtered through the open door and the gap where the window had been.

'The longer you keep quiet about these people the longer they'll keep harassing you, and not just you.' It sounded like DS Wilson.

The next voice was unmistakably Ahmed's. 'What can I do? You know I can do nothing.'

Seeing the police officer returning Quentin stood up and moved away, wishing he had heard more. Deciding not to push his luck, he made his way back to the car.

* * *

'It's your boyfriend's shop,' Quentin said to Linda when he was seated in the Micra. 'Someone's smashed the window. The police are there.'

A gasp escaped Linda, and she put her hand to her mouth.

Wanda caught his eye and followed his thinking. 'You think it was the bloke in the car? The one that was in such a hurry?'

'Yes. Why would anyone want to smash his window in? Linda, do you know?'

'No. Why should I? I don't know anything except what I've told you.'

Quentin almost believed her. 'Well, we need to find out,' he murmured. 'It might have something to do with Halim.'

'Did you see Ahmed?' Wanda asked.

'Yes, but he didn't see me.'

Wanda nodded, immediately picking up on the implication. Ahmed didn't know of Quentin's connection to the salon, and if they were going to try to trace Halim themselves it might be useful if it stayed that way.

'That detective's there,' Quentin said, 'the sergeant we saw at the police station. I heard him talking to Ahmed.' Quickly he repeated what he'd heard.

'Who do you think he means, these people who keep harassing Ahmed?' Wanda asked Linda.

'I don't know. I don't,' Linda insisted.

'OK,' said Wanda. 'So who would be harassing a middle-aged barber?'

Who indeed? Quentin thought, turning this over in his mind. As far as he could see there was only one answer. Halim must be working for an organisation, stealing things

182

then passing them up the line. The smashed window was a warning, or even retribution. Perhaps Halim had displeased them in some way, hadn't towed the line. The barber's shop belonged to Ahmed, not Halim, yet it had still come under attack. Did that mean that Ahmed was in on the robberies? Whatever the answer, the smashed window wasn't a random attack. The barber's had been targeted, and not for the first time.

Linda stirred, jolting Quentin out of his thoughts. 'Are you sure you can't think of anywhere Halim might have gone?' he said. 'Think, Linda.'

Pressing her lips together, Linda shook her head. Quentin felt a sudden surge of sympathy for her. He didn't believe she was a criminal at heart. She obviously loved Halim, enough to be persuaded to give him the information he asked for, and her reward was to be left high and dry. Unless it was all an act. Perhaps *she'd* suggested passing on details of empty properties. She certainly hadn't had any qualms about deceiving Shelagh, or had any regard for the clients who were robbed. His sympathy waning, he tried again.

'Is there anyone, anyone who would take Halim in?' He waited for a response that never came. 'All right, let's go through this again. He rang you early this morning to say he had to go away because something had happened. Did anything he said give you a clue as to where he might be? He must have friends, relations, apart from you and his father. What about his mother?'

'His mother's dead. There's a sister but I've never met her. She married a guy over in Perth. Ahmed doesn't approve – they don't communicate much. Halim wouldn't go there.'

'No one closer?'

Linda looked about to speak, but seemed stuck in hesitation. Quentin seized on it.

'Listen, Linda, if I thought there was any way we could leave you out of this I would. But the police suspect

Halim, and they'll get him, and when they do they'll know someone gave him information on empty properties. They'll suss it, even if Halim doesn't tell them.'

'He won't.' Linda's voice was fierce. 'He won't tell them.'

'Won't he? You'd be surprised how many people crack under pressure. And he's already gone against your wishes – he went to Shelagh's when you told him not to. He's been a bit careless lately, banking on a place being empty for only one night. He must have been desperate to take that risk, or too complacent. He's had a good run. He thought he could take more chances and look where it's got him. And you.'

Linda clapped her hands over her ears. 'Stop it!'

Quentin could almost feel her weakening. 'Come on, Linda. There must be someone, someone he could go to in a hurry.'

'There's a cousin,' she blurted. 'Bora.'

'Bora? A man?' When Linda nodded Quentin went on, 'Where does he live? In Sydney?'

'Yes, and that's all I'm saying.'

'Have you been there? To his house?'

'I'm not taking you there, if that's what you think.'

'You don't have to. Just tell me where it is.'

'I don't know the address. I only went there once and it was dark.'

'What district?' Quentin persisted. He was getting somewhere at last. 'What district? In town or outside?'

Wanda put her hand on Linda's arm, and spoke softly. 'Come on, Linda. Think of yourself, and the baby.'

Linda flinched and folded her arms across her stomach. 'An apartment in Parramatta somewhere,' she whispered. 'Near the mosque. That's all I know.'

'That's all we need to know,' Quentin said. Not much to go on, but it was a starting point. Unless Linda had just told him this to shut him up, knowing that Halim wouldn't

be there. Or perhaps she'd invented this cousin. Perhaps…
A thought came to him, and his heart bumped.

'This cousin,' he said, anticipation rising in his stomach, 'does he look like Halim?'

Linda's eyebrow's shot up and Quentin knew he'd guessed right. The cousin, Bora, was the man he'd chased the day before, the one who'd had the cloth bag. Halim had passed the bag and its contents on to him, either at the quayside or before, presumably for Bora to pass the goods to a fence or sell direct. It was all beginning to make sense now. And if they found the cousin, he might lead them to Halim.

'How much longer are you going to keep me here?' Linda asked. 'I've told you all I know. Can't you let me go?'

'Not an option, I'm afraid,' Quentin told her.

Linda seemed to have lost her resigned demeanour. 'Why not?' she demanded. 'You know as much as I do. You'll report me to the police and they'll come for me. At least I'll have time to go home and tell my parents.'

'And warn Halim,' Quentin said drily. 'I don't think so.'

Slumping back in her seat, Linda's face resumed its defeated expression. 'So the police will knock on my parents' door and tell them their daughter's been arrested. Thanks very much.'

'Don't you think you should have thought of that before?' Quentin asked. 'For goodness' sake, Linda, how long did you think you'd get away with it? You didn't worry about your family when you were helping Halim steal.'

A fresh bout of tears convulsed Linda, making her plump shoulders shake. 'I didn't think it would go on this long,' she snivelled. 'Halim said it would only be for a few months, until he had enough money.'

'Perhaps he did,' Wanda said, handing her a clean tissue. 'Perhaps he only meant it to last a few months. All the same, Halim may have been taking you for a ride.'

'No! He loves me. At least he said he did,' she added, as if remembering what Suzy had said.

Quentin voiced something he'd been thinking about earlier. 'Maybe he does now. But maybe he only got to know you so that you could get the information he needed. Unless… unless you offered to pass the details of empty properties on yourself.'

Linda's snivelling stopped and she turned frightened eyes on Quentin. 'Why would you think that?'

'I don't know. You fell for him, were desperate to keep him? Offered him a way to make some money quickly so you could get enough to set up house together?'

'No. I didn't do that.'

'So, it was his idea, then? He persuaded you to go along with it?' Quentin scrutinized Linda's face, trying to read it. It was no good, though, and suddenly he didn't care. The important thing now was to get Halim.

'I need the loo,' Linda said, pulling him back to the moment.

'Right. Give us a minute. Wanda?' Quentin motioned her out of the car. She got out and so did he, locking the car doors and watching Linda through the windows.

'What shall we do?' he spoke softly so that his words wouldn't penetrate through to Linda. 'I'd like to take her with us to find this cousin Bora, but–'

'I know what you're thinking,' Wanda cut in. 'She could claim we're holding her against her will and forcing her to do what we want.'

'Yes. Still, the police would do that if they needed to.'

'We're not the police. I wonder… Why don't you take her to the station, tell that inspector you saw yesterday, Johnson was it?'

'Jackson.'

'Jackson, then. Tell him what happened last night, what we know about Linda and make some excuse to get away. Then we go after Halim. As far as we know we're still one step ahead of the police. By the time they've got everything out of Linda we could have found this cousin and even Halim, if he's there.'

Quentin mulled this over. 'Sounds like a plan. But I could be in there all day.'

'That's why it's better if you go in without me. There's no point in both of us getting tied up with the police when one of us could be finding out something useful. If you say you've got an important appointment or something, I can't see why they would keep you there once you've delivered Linda. They've got all your details and they know how to contact you.'

'Yes, I suppose. What will you do?'

'I'll wait for you, but if you're too long I'll try to suss out something about the place where this cousin lives.'

Something stirred in Quentin's memory. 'Haven't we forgotten something?'

Wanda looked at him. 'I'm not a mind reader. What have we forgotten?'

'What we said we'd do earlier. Get Linda to ring Halim, see if he gives anything away.'

'Oh. Yes, we did say that, but what's to stop her warning him? It only takes a few words. Anyway–' Wanda stopped, and chewed at her lip.

'Anyway what?'

Dropping her voice to a whisper Wanda said, 'I've got a better idea. *I'll* ring him.'

'What?'

'Well, why not? We'll keep Linda's phone – his number's bound to be on it. I put on a pretty good Aussie accent when I rang the salon yesterday. I think I could imitate Linda's voice. It's quite distinctive, very breathy, but I bet I could do it.'

Quentin pulled a face. It was risky, and it might warn Halim that they were onto him, but...

'All right, it's worth a try, but wait until I'm with you. I'll be as quick as I can with Jackson – that's if he'll see me. If not, I'll say my piece to whoever and get out as fast as I can.'

He checked his watch. 'It's ten-thirty. We'd better not leave it too much longer before taking Linda in or we'll be charged with withholding information. I don't think we're going to learn any more from her anyway. Right, we'll drive to the station and park up. I'll take Linda in, and you can wait in the car. Don't do anything major without me.'

Wanda shot him an *as if I would* look, then said, 'Hold on, though. Now we've decided to take Linda in, why are we driving to the station when DS Wilson's just round the corner?'

Quentin paused. There was so much going on in his head that for a moment he couldn't think of a logical answer.

'Because,' he said at last, 'she's supposed to be going in voluntarily, and because I'd rather see Jackson than Wilson if I can, and because… because at the moment Ahmed's with Wilson and he doesn't know my connection to the salon. We'll keep it that way for as long as possible, just in case.'

'OK,' Wanda said doubtfully.

Giving her a half smile, Quentin said, 'Good. Let's do it.'

Chapter Thirty

'All right, tell me what's going on.'

Quentin gazed over the desk in the interview room at DI Jackson, who was eyeing him warily. After an hour's wait and his insistence on seeing the inspector, Quentin was trying to work out exactly what to say. Linda had played her part, agreeing sullenly when Quentin told the officer in reception that she had something to confess, and that it was connected to the burglaries. She was taken to a separate room, and Quentin had no idea whether she had been questioned yet or not.

Jackson tapped his fingers on the desktop while he waited for Quentin to speak.

'Right,' Quentin began. 'Did they give you the report of a break-in last night? I asked them to pass it to you.'

Shuffling some papers on the desk and glancing at them Jackson said, 'Yes, a break in at Hibiscus Crescent, Roseville, last night, reported by Mr Herbert Cadbury.'

Alleluia, Quentin thought, at least we're on the same page. 'That's my father. He and I were woken up when we heard something. We caught a man stealing my mother's jewellery and my father's coin collection. It was Halim, the Turkish guy I told you about yesterday.'

The door opened and a head with a coconut thatch appeared round it.

'Sorry, sir,' DS Wilson said. 'I heard he was here,' he nodded towards Quentin. 'I thought you might want to know what I found out before you go any further.'

Quentin straightened his back. What had he found out? Had Ahmed cracked, told him where Halim was? Bugger it, he thought savagely. If that's what's happened we've got no chance of finding Halim first. We should have taken Linda with us and followed our lead.

Jackson left the room. Five minutes later he was back, DS Wilson in his wake.

'Go on, Mr Cadbury,' Jackson said.

'Well, as you know, this Halim broke in but we caught him at it. There was a scuffle and he dropped the jewellery but got away with the coins.'

'Why was that? Weren't the coins with the jewellery?'

Quentin shook his head. 'They were in a sort of wallet, one that folds over three times. My dad had it made specially. Anyway, he must have had that in his pocket or something. It wasn't in the pouch with the jewellery and it's not in the house.'

'And you saw the man? Clearly?'

'Yes. It was Halim.'

'And who was in the house at the time?'

'Just me and my father. My partner and my mother were babysitting my nephew at my sister's house, and stayed the night.' Quentin's voice didn't falter. It was only a half lie, after all.

Jackson glanced down at the papers on his desk. 'No fingerprints found at the scene, apparently.'

'He wore gloves.' Quentin closed his eyes, picturing Halim's hand as he picked up the telephone handset that he'd intended to hit his father with but which had smashed into his cheek instead. 'White latex things, like doctors use.'

'Why do you think he picked on your house? OK, I know it's your parents' house, not yours. Why did he pick that house? How did he know there was anything worth stealing?'

'Through Linda, the girl who came in with me,' Quentin said reluctantly, realizing he couldn't keep Shelagh and the salon out of it any longer. 'She works at the hairdresser's salon next door to the barber's where Halim works. My sister owns the salon, and she had an attempted break-in at home not long ago – that should be on your records – and two of her clients had break-ins as well.'

'Your sister?' DS Wilson spoke for the first time. 'Your sister owns the salon next door to where this Halim works and she's had an attempted break-in? And two of her clients?'

Jackson cut in. 'And now your parents?'

'Yep.

Jackson and Wilson exchanged glances.

'And you've only just thought to tell us this?' Wilson glared at Quentin accusingly.

'I didn't find out until after I spoke to you yesterday. I only made the connection this morning.'

There was a short silence, then Jackson asked, 'What do you know about this girl at the salon?'

'Her name is Linda, I don't know her surname. I can't tell you much about her except she's Halim's girlfriend. She's been with my sister for about six months.'

Quentin felt a little beat of triumph. He knew the robberies had started sometime in the last six months. He was sure now that Jackson had known nothing about Halim before yesterday.

Once again Jackson tapped his fingers on the desktop. Quentin noticed the shadow on his chin and thought how tired he looked. His shoulders sagged, accentuating his stoop, and there were dark smudges under his eyes. Perhaps he'd been up half the night working on another case, the explosion, possibly. He stopped tapping his fingers and leaned back in his chair, regarding Quentin as though he couldn't make his mind up whether to believe him or not.

'So, you think Linda may have been hearing things from clients and then passing them on to Halim?'

'Yes. She has admitted to it.'

'Bit funny if you ask me,' DS Wilson snapped. He seemed more short-tempered than the previous day, and his face looked pale under his coconut matting. 'You told us about this Halim yesterday when you were here, and about the bloke you chased, the one you thought had the stolen medals. Why would Halim suddenly decide to rob your parents last night?'

Quentin shrugged. 'How should I know? If you'd acted on what I said yesterday he wouldn't have been able to rob us.'

Wilson answered through gritted teeth.

'It may have escaped your notice, but we have more than just one case to deal with. If you haven't heard, a bomb went off yesterday, and there was a shooting. People died.'

'I know. That was awful.'

'Convenient, though, for this Halim,' Jackson said. 'Maybe he was banking on us being tied up. Maybe you were.'

'What do you mean?' Quentin said, feigning shock.

'I mean, perhaps you deliberately lured him into robbing your parents' house last night.'

'Why on earth would I do that?'

Jackson picked up a pen and pointed it at Quentin. 'You're the one who urged us not to rush in and arrest him. Set a trap, you said. You wanted to be involved in catching him. You like to be in on things. I spoke to DCI Philmore at Scotland Yard.'

Quentin's spirits rose. They would have to take notice of a detective chief inspector in the Metropolitan police.

'Really? There you are, then – you know I've helped him in the past. What did he say?'

'He said you were a pain in the–' DS Wilson stopped as Jackson banged his fist on the desk.

'He said you had been helpful,' Jackson said, shooting Wilson a warning look, 'but that you had a tendency to take things into your own hands.'

Quentin stared at him defiantly. 'I wouldn't say that. It's just that sometimes I'm at liberty to do things the police can't, you know, with your heavy workload and limited resources. A member of the public can blend in, find out things, sometimes accidentally, sometimes by making a conscious effort. I'm a detective. Surely we're on the same side?'

Jackson sighed wearily. 'All right, Mr Cadbury, we accept the fact that you're trying to help. But all that's happened is this man's got away, and by now he'll be long gone.'

That told Quentin one thing – Ahmed didn't know where Halim was, or if he did, he hadn't told DS Wilson this morning.

'We'll circulate a description of him and the bloke you chased,' Jackson went on. 'You said you saw Halim's car when he drove off last night. That's not much help without the full registration and the make or colour the car.'

'It was a dark colour,' Quentin told him. 'It wasn't white, or any light colour, I know that much. If it wasn't his it could have been his father's. Or he could have stolen it, I suppose.'

'Right,' was all Jackson said, and Quentin cursed silently. He'd hoped they would mention what had happened with Ahmed earlier, but it seemed Jackson wasn't going to share this information with him.

'OK,' Jackson went on. 'Well, we've searched the shop and Halim's home address. We didn't find anything.'

'You wouldn't, would you, if he's passed the stuff on?'

Wilson huffed, but after a glance at his boss said nothing.

Unable to resist, Quentin asked, 'You haven't arrested him, then? Ahmed?'

Jackson shook his head. 'Not yet. There's no proof he was involved, but we'll be watching him very closely.'

Choosing his words carefully, Quentin said, 'Em, when I was speaking to Linda earlier, she said that Halim needed money for his father. She didn't seem to know what for.'

He deliberately said when *I*, not when *we* spoke to Linda. He didn't want to mention Wanda in case they asked where she was. He needed to get back to her soon if they were to have any chance of tracing Halim.

If he'd thought Jackson was going to tell him why Ahmed needed money, though, he was mistaken. Jackson merely nodded and said, 'It seems Ahmed's got problems of his own.'

'Really?' Quentin looked at him questioningly, but no answer came.

DS Wilson unlaced his fingers and pointed to Quentin. 'This robbery of yours doesn't exactly fit the same pattern as the others. The other properties were empty, but this bloke broke into your parents' house while you were there. I wonder why.'

'It would have been empty,' Quentin said, scrabbling for something credible to say. 'We were all going out together but our plans got changed. My father and I ended up staying at home.'

The detective sergeant clearly didn't believe him, but after another warning look from Jackson he let it go. Ignoring Wilson's hostile glare, Quentin turned to Jackson.

'Have you spoken to Linda yet?'

'We thought we'd get your side of the story first,' Jackson told him. He twirled his pen around in his fingers. 'So tell me, how come Linda suddenly decided to come here and confess?'

Quentin answered carefully. He didn't want to admit that he *had* taken things into his own hands.

'Well, like I said, after last night I made the connection between Linda and the robberies. I'd seen the stolen goods in Halim's stockroom, then yesterday I found out that Linda was his girlfriend and I put two and two together. It occurred to me that someone in the salon was getting the info about when their customers' houses would be empty and passing it on. It had to be Linda.'

He paused. Should he tell them Linda was pregnant? No. She could do that herself, when she was ready.

'I see,' Jackson said. 'So, you had this idea and then what?'

'Em, I went to the salon first thing and told my sister. We… spoke to Linda and she confessed to telling Halim when people's houses would be empty.'

'Spoke to her?' Wilson barked. 'You coerced her into coming here?'

'Wilson.' Jackson held his hand up. 'So, you spoke to her and she agreed to give herself up?'

'That's about it, yes.'

There was a silence, filled only by the ticking of a wall clock and a cracking noise from Wilson, who sat with his fingers interlocked, cracking his knuckles.

'Is there anything else?' Quentin asked. 'Only I've got an urgent appointment I need to get to. I can come in again if you need me to.'

Wilson eyed him suspiciously. 'An urgent appointment?'

Quentin dredged his brain cells for something plausible. 'The dentist,' he said. 'I've had this toothache since I arrived in Oz. They're fitting me in as an emergency. If I miss it, I'll have to wait ages. You've got my details, my phone number and my parents' address. I'll come in again whenever you want.'

'I don't know,' Wilson began, but stopped when Jackson raised his hand again.

Bloody hell, Quentin thought. You've got a key suspect, thanks to me. What more do you want?

'All right, Mr Cadbury, you can go,' Jackson said.

'Thanks, and my name's Quentin.' Quentin stood up, a surge of anger filling him as he noticed the smirk on Wilson's face. Supercilious sod, he thought. He turned to leave, then stopped.

'About my sister. I know you'll have to question her about Linda, but do you have to go to the salon? She's more than willing to come here, or to see you at her home address, but if what's been going on gets out she could lose a lot of custom. She took Linda on in good faith and she's devastated about all this. Surely there's no need for the salon to be dragged through the mill?'

Jackson seemed to be mulling this over.

'Please,' Quentin added. 'It's not much to ask, is it?'

'I expect we can arrange that,' Jackson agreed.

Wilson snorted.

'Wilson,' Jackson said, quietly but with authority, 'go and see if there's any more news on the bloke that was seen running from the explosion site.'

His mouth set in a grim line, DS Wilson left the room. Quentin could only guess at his thoughts – indulging this bloody interfering pomme just because he knows a big noise in Scotland Yard.

'Thanks,' Quentin said when he'd gone.

'Let's get one thing straight,' Jackson said, standing and rounding on Quentin. 'If you do one more thing without telling me–'

'I haven't–'

'Don't give me all that bullshit, and for what it's worth I thought of more or less the same plan when you were here yesterday. I didn't have a chance, because of that damned bomb.

'And I don't think the bloke you chased through town could have got the medals from Halim – if he did, why didn't he get onto Halim straight away and let him know about what happened? Halim can't have known or there's no way he would have gone out burgling last night. He would have laid low until the heat was off.'

Quentin had been wondering about that himself. For some reason the Halim lookalike – Halim's cousin if Quentin had got it right – hadn't told Halim about being chased. Why ever not? Was he too scared to admit to being caught and narrowly missing the goods being found on him? Or had something happened to stop him from contacting Halim? He shrugged the thought away. Whatever the reason, it had at least enabled him to confirm that Halim was definitely the burglar.

'You're right,' he said. 'But perhaps there was a reason he didn't let Halim know.'

'It would have to be a pretty good reason, wouldn't you say?' Jackson looked intently at Quentin, and Quentin cringed inwardly. He had no idea why the man he'd chased hadn't contacted Halim, but he did know that the man was probably Halim's cousin, something he hadn't shared with Jackson. It doesn't matter, he thought, trying to justify his reasons. If we can't find Halim, I can tell him about the cousin later. That's if Linda doesn't tell him first.

'I'd better go now or I'll be late,' he mumbled. 'I hope I've been helpful.'

'That remains to be seen. And don't forget what I said,' Jackson warned as Quentin left the room.

Quentin gave a conciliatory nod. How could he forget what Jackson had said just a few minutes ago – that he shouldn't do anything without letting him know? Yet he knew that, when the circumstances were right, his memory had an unfortunate habit of letting him down.

Chapter Thirty-one

He was pleased to emerge into the open air, away from the confines of the police building and DS Wilson's scathing comments. He hurried to the car park, anxious to tell Wanda everything that had been said.

Wrapped in his thoughts, he was deep into the car park before he realized he'd passed the place where he'd left the car. He stood, disorientated for a moment, his eyes searching the rows of cars. He walked up and down, but neither the car nor Wanda were anywhere to be seen.

Groaning, Quentin fished out his mobile and rang her number. The call went straight to voicemail and he cursed. What was she thinking, going off without him? Surely he hadn't been that long? An hour and three quarters, he calculated.

A horrible thought came to him, and he jolted himself upright. What if she'd used Linda's phone, called Halim, pretended to be Linda and arranged to meet him? Anything could happen to Wanda if Halim realized she was onto him.

He rang her again, but still the voicemail clicked in.

'Bloody hell,' he muttered, frustration filling him. 'What am I supposed to do now?'

He weaved his way through the lines of cars to the exit, then walked a short distance along the pavement. He was reluctant to go too far in case Wanda came back.

He was still in a state of indecision when the toot of a horn startled him. The Micra pulled up on the opposite side of the street and Wanda waved at him. Relief swamped him, and he dashed across the road, causing an oncoming car to swerve and sound its horn.

'Sorry,' he mouthed to the driver, then tumbled gratefully in the Micra's passenger seat.

'Been waiting long?' Wanda asked.

'Long enough. Where have you been?'

'On a wild goose chase.' Wanda checked the rear-view mirror and indicated to pull out. She waited until they were safely in the stream of traffic before continuing.

'I called Halim's number but it didn't even ring.'

'What? You called him? What were you going to say?'

'Nothing – I wasn't going to do anything until you were here.'

'Well, that's something, I suppose. But what was the point of ringing him if you weren't going to say anything? He'd have known it was Linda's number and he might have called back.'

Wanda gave him a sideways glance. 'It wouldn't have done him any good, would it? We've got her phone.'

Quentin stared at her. 'OK, now I'm totally confused. You rang him on Linda's phone–'

'No, I got the number from Linda's phone and rang from my phone. He doesn't know my number from Adam's. I just wanted to know if he'd pick up, and if he did whether I could suss out anything in the background to give us a clue as to where he is.'

Quentin gave a low whistle. While he'd been giving explanations to Jackson and enduring Wilson's barely concealed scorn, Wanda had been doing real detective work.

'Good thinking, Batman. So where did you go?'

'Well, I guessed you'd be ages and I didn't want to sit there like a lemon. I remembered what Linda told us about the cousin, the district he lived in, so I thought I'd drive out there and have a look round. It was a waste of time, though. She said an apartment, didn't she? Anyway, there were lots of apartment blocks and lots of houses divided into flats. We need something more specific, at least a road name.'

'Yeah, but Linda said she didn't know.'

Quentin slumped back in his seat and stifled a yawn. Now he was in the safety and comfort of the car without having to think about driving, he suddenly felt exhausted. He'd been up half the night, he realized, and so much had happened in the last twenty-four hours that he felt as though he'd been awake for days.

'Where are we going?' he mumbled, struggling to keep his eyes open.

'Back to your parents' house. There's nothing we can do at the moment – I can't ring Halim and pretend to be Linda if his phone is turned off or out of battery, and it's pointless just hanging around the area on the off chance of seeing him. We've done our bit for now – we've got a confession from Linda and we've taken her in. Anyway, you look worn out. I am, even if you're not. We'll go back, have a sleep and then we'll be able to think more clearly.'

By then, though, Quentin realized, Linda might have told the police everything and they could be well on the way to finding Halim. They had more resources at their disposal, although he guessed finding the perpetrators of the explosion would take priority. Fatigue overcoming him, he pushed these thoughts away. 'Sleep?' he said drowsily. 'Sounds wonderful.'

* * *

'You nearly had him, then?' Ed Grayson said that teatime when Quentin and his father went to see him.

After three hours sleep during the afternoon Quentin was feeling much better. He was relieved at Grayson's tone. Instead of being full of disappointment and accusation, it held sympathy and understanding.

'Had him right there,' Herbert blustered. 'Got my coins, the bastard. Shouldn't have got away.'

Go on, then, Quentin urged silently. Admit it was your fault he got away.

'Still,' Grayson went on, 'it was a good, brave plan, and at least now they know who to look for. And they've got an accomplice. Not that I can see the connection between all the robberies. I still don't understand how my robbery can be connected to the others – how did they know my place was empty?'

'I don't know,' Quentin said, baffled, 'but your robbery fits the pattern – empty private residence, only small items taken. He must have found out somehow.'

'What about the club?' his father asked. 'That's not a private residence. How did they know it was empty, or that the medals were there?'

'Anyone could see it was empty,' Grayson pointed out. 'There was a notice in the window telling people it was closed for refurbishment.'

'But how would they know the medals were still there? It must be down to one of the workmen,' Herbert insisted.

'Not necessarily,' Grayson said. 'The police have checked them all out, anyway. As far as I know there's no evidence against any of them.'

Quentin frowned. The more thought he gave the case, the more he was convinced that Halim was responsible for all the robberies. He'd found medals in the stockroom – too many for them just to be the ones stolen from Grayson. All the crimes had to be committed by the same perpetrator.

When they were back at Hibiscus Crescent, he shared these thoughts with Wanda.

'I think you're right,' she said. 'It can't be two lots of people operating in the same area. We may not find a connection at the moment, but there must be one, unless Halim just happened to find out that those properties were empty by chance. Anyway, with Linda being questioned now, she's bound to tell them what she knows. She told us, didn't she?'

'Yes,' Quentin agreed, 'but she wasn't going to give Halim up – she only went to the police because of my non-existent recording. She could take days to tell the police everything she knows. She might string it out, give Halim more time to get away.'

He pictured Linda sitting in the same interview room where he had seen Jackson, her plump face as red as her hair, her voice breathy as she stammered out her involvement.

Wanda interrupted his musing. 'She will talk, you know, in the end, recording or no recording. She's not the type to defend him faced with all the evidence.'

'Yeah, maybe.' Quentin recalled how angry Linda had sounded in the barber's when she'd confronted Halim about trying to break into Shelagh's, and how she'd said she might not accompany him to Melbourne. Perhaps she'd been tired of being used, afraid of being caught as an accessory. But all that was before she'd found out she was pregnant. She may feel obligated to stick by him now. Or would she crumble as soon as the police questioned her, plead coercion and pour out her remorse? After all, she thought he had recorded her confession. Even though they'd agreed not to use it if she gave herself up, she might think it could be used against her. Whatever she said to the police could give them a lead. She might even know where Halim was. Had she been lying? No, he reasoned, I don't think she was. It sounded as though Halim didn't want her to know where he was. Not her, not anyone, not even his father.

'What about Ahmed?' he said. 'Do you think he knows where Halim went? I know Linda says he doesn't, but he might want her to think he doesn't know.'

Wanda shrugged. 'I don't know. Linda said he only found out what Halim was up to recently. Seems funny –

him and Halim live and work together. How could he not know what was going on?'

Quentin remembered the discord he'd sensed between Halim and Ahmed. According to Linda, Ahmed's discovery of his son's activities had caused a row, so it was apparent that Ahmed didn't approve. Regardless of what Ahmed needed the money for, he obviously didn't like Halim stealing to get it. Whatever their differences, though, Quentin was willing to bet that Ahmed would defend Halim through thick and thin, no matter what he'd done. Which is more than my father would do for me, he thought, then pushed it away, annoyed that he'd made the comparison. Harping on personal differences wouldn't do anything to catch Halim.

'I mean,' Wanda was saying, 'where did Ahmed think Halim was when he went on his burgling sprees?'

'Perhaps Halim said he was with Linda,' Quentin suggested. 'She could have covered for him. Now I think about it, that's quite likely. And this idea that Halim could be with his cousin…'

Wanda looked at him. 'Well?'

'We might be barking totally up the wrong tree. Halim was moving to Melbourne. Perhaps he's hiding out there somewhere.'

'Hmm.' Wanda didn't sound convinced. 'He'll still be travelling, then. It's a heck of a drive from here. He'd have to stop to sleep and eat.' She sat cross-legged on the settee next to Quentin, twirling a lock of blonde hair round her fingers. 'Do you think he's still driving the same car?'

Quentin shrugged. 'Could be, might have hired one, borrowed or stolen someone else's, or he could be halfway across the country by coach or train.'

'Or plane,' Wanda added. 'He might have left the country by now.'

'Only if he went home to collect his passport. It depends if he did or if he just went straight on the run. I can't believe he'd take off without going back to get some things and explain to his father. Still, he might have panicked, and if he didn't get his passport he'll still be in the country somewhere.'

Wanda pursed her lips. 'Yes, that would be something, I suppose.'

Would it? Quentin didn't think so. Australia is huge. Anyone could disappear for years if they wanted to. Somehow, though, Quentin didn't see Halim as a hardened bushman. He would want to be in a town somewhere or other. Not that that narrowed the field much. The words "needle" and "haystack" came to mind, and he felt dispirited. He might have been instrumental in stopping the burglaries in Sydney but he'd let the perpetrator get away. He had blamed his father, but was it his fault? He had jumped the gun, yes, and prevented Quentin from tackling Halim as planned, but Quentin had had his chance – he had wrestled with Halim and lost.

Failure by joint effort, then, he admitted to himself. Stupid. Bloody, bloody stupid.

Chapter Thirty-two

While the family were discussing the burglaries over dinner that evening, Shelagh called in.

'One of my own girls passing information to a thief,' she said, shaking her head. 'I still can't believe it. No wonder she was always going in there. I'll be giving her a piece of my mind when I see her.'

'You already have,' Quentin reminded her.

Shelagh squared her shoulders. 'Huh! Not as much as I wanted to. Do you think she'll be kept at the police station overnight?'

'Don't know,' Quentin said. 'Depends what she tells them. If she spills the beans straight away she'll probably be charged with aiding and abetting then let go on bail. They might want her outside to see if he contacts her.'

'That makes sense,' Shelagh said. 'Though if he's got any sense he won't.'

'No,' Quentin agreed, 'and Halim's got a lot of sense or he'd have been caught by now.'

'Slippery character,' Herbert growled, with a purposeful glare at Quentin.

'What about Suzy?' Wanda asked. 'Will she stay with you?'

Shelagh made a face. 'She says she will. Silly girl. If it didn't work out with Halim the first time, why did she think he'd change his mind now? Still, she is a good hairdresser.'

'Well,' Rosemary chirped brightly, 'thanks to Quentin's idea he's on the run, so at least the burglaries will stop. We can all sleep easily again.'

Bless you, Mum, Quentin thought, sending her a grateful look. Fighting my corner again.

'Anyway,' Shelagh said, 'the police have asked me to go in tomorrow and make a statement. I need to see a Detective Sergeant Wilson, apparently.'

Good luck with that, then, Quentin thought, but he said nothing. There was a small silence, as though everyone was searching for something appropriate to say. Rosemary was first to speak.

'So that's it, then? As far as you're concerned, Quentin, the case is over? There's nothing else you can do, is there, now the police have everything in hand. I don't suppose poor Ed will see Joan's jewellery again, or his medals. Or your coins, dear,' she added to her husband, as if by afterthought.

Herbert grunted and Quentin felt more disheartened than ever. The case over. Nothing else he could do. There was Wanda's idea about using Linda's phone to call Halim, but he didn't hold out much hope for that. If Halim was trying to distance himself from Linda, he may not accept any calls from her. Bugger it, he thought, bringing his fist down on the arm of the chair and sending a newspaper flying. There must be something we can do to track Halim down. There's got to be.

* * *

'I don't see what we can do,' Wanda said later when they were alone. 'After all, we've done our bit.'

Quentin pushed his hands into his shorts pockets. What had started as a brisk walk to the park had become a slow trudge as he tried to come up with something to keep him on the case. He didn't feel fulfilled enough to give up on it. Halim had to be caught and he wanted to be the one to catch him.

'Come on,' he said, turning and starting briskly back the way they had come.

'Come on where?'

'To see Halim's father. We might get something out of him.'

'But he won't be at the shop,' Wanda said, jogging to keep up with him. 'And we don't know where he lives.'

'Shelagh does. She gave Linda a lift there once. She was telling me about it earlier.'

'How do you know he'll be there?'

Grimacing Quentin said, 'If he's not, we'll go to the pub. I've got to do something, not just hang around waiting for the police to get Halim.'

Half an hour later, after ringing Shelagh to confirm where Ahmed lived, they were driving to the address she gave them, although she couldn't remember the number of the house.

'I still think we're wasting our time,' Wanda said as they entered the area. 'He could have scarpered, and we don't even know what number he lives at.'

'No, but apparently it's got a very tall hedge at the front. Shelagh remembers because she thought it must

205

make the front room very dark. And I don't think he'll run. There's something not right, but I don't think he's in with Halim's burglaries.'

'Why not?'

Why not indeed? Quentin thought. He didn't know why, but something told him Ahmed was an honest man who'd come to Australia seeking a better life for his family.

'It's just a feeling,' he said, shrugging. 'I think he found out, like Linda said, but I don't think he's in on it. It's just the way they interacted with each other that day when I was there.'

'OK, Freud, so now you've done your psychological character assessment we can work with that. I must admit he didn't strike me as a criminal type. He was so nice when I fainted – well, pretended to faint – and he's got kind eyes.'

Quentin laughed. 'Now who's being Freudian? Still, as I said, he found out – after all, the goods were in his stockroom. He could easily have missed the small items if they were well hidden. I wouldn't have found them if I hadn't been looking for them, but the computer and coat were in plain view.'

'Halim could have got those anywhere. Ahmed needn't have known they were stolen.'

'Yeah, I guess.' Quentin swung the car round a corner. 'This is the road,' he said, peering at the street name. He noticed the narrow, terraced houses with small front yards on either side of the street. 'Hmm. If they made any money from crime they didn't spend it on their living accommodation. These places don't look very salubrious.'

Halfway down the road he spotted a house with its lower front almost concealed by a brown-leafed hedge. So this was where Ahmed and Halim lived. Did this look like the residence of someone raking in profits from illegal dealings? Surely such profits would warrant a more upmarket area than this? He pulled up outside and tapped his fingers on the steering wheel while the engine idled. Now he was here, he had no idea what he was going to do.

'What are you waiting for?' Wanda said. 'It was your suggestion to come, so we might as well get on with it.'

Quentin switched off the engine. 'Right. He might not even be here. Still, there's only one way to find out.' Unbuckling his seat belt, he reached for the door handle.

'Hold on.' Wanda laid a hand on his arm. 'Let me go.'

'What, on your own?'

'Yes. I mean he doesn't know you're connected to me – OK, so he's seen you, but I doubt he'll remember, whereas I fainted in his doorway and he fussed over me. I don't think he'd have forgotten me.'

As if anyone could, Quentin thought. No man, anyway. 'So what difference does that make?'

'Well, I could say I've lost something – my reading glasses, say – all right, I know I don't wear glasses, but he won't know that – and I wondered if they'd fallen out of my handbag when I fainted that time. And I'll say I wanted to thank him for letting me recover in his shop. I'll say Linda told me where he lived – she could have told me before Halim did his disappearing trick, he won't know any different. I'll have to admit to knowing that she works in the salon and that I know her, but it won't matter now. If you keep out of it, he won't know your connection. I'll say I was going to see him at work, but it was closed.'

'That's pretty thin. He'll be daft to fall for that.'

'He'll be upset. He may not be thinking straight. I won't say anything about Linda going to the police.'

Fingering the mole by his ear, Quentin said, 'What if the police have let Linda go, or if she's managed to contact him somehow and told him she's had to confess?'

'Why would she? From what she said there's no love lost between them. Ahmed must know she's involved with the burglaries. We took her in about ten-thirty, and the police were busy today. I bet she's still there.'

Quentin pursed his lips, mulling this over. 'Well, they can only hold her for so long. So when you've asked him about these imaginary glasses, what then?'

Wanda smiled a beguiling smile. 'I'll use my feminine charms of course. Look, what have we got to lose? He might let something slip. He'll be more inclined to talk to me rather than both of us. He'll feel less intimidated. Don't look so worried. The worst that can happen is he'll shut the door in my face.'

Reluctantly Quentin agreed. 'OK, it's worth a try, though I don't see how you'll get him to tell you anything about Halim.'

'Leave it to me. Keep your phone handy just in case, and stay in calling distance.'

Winding the window all the way down, Quentin said, 'I'll stay here. It might look odd if I hang about on the pavement.' He caught Wanda's hand as she opened the passenger door. 'And be careful.'

'Don't worry,' Wanda quipped. 'I don't suppose he takes his cut-throat razor home with him.'

'Not funny,' Quentin snapped.

He saw Wanda's eyes turn heavenwards, and watched her climb out of the car and walk through the gate. Oh well, he thought, if Wanda can't get anything out of him, nobody will. A few minutes later he heard voices. Ahmed was there.

And then the voices faded as the two of them went inside and the door closed behind them.

Chapter Thirty-three

For twenty minutes Quentin sat in the car with the windows open, his ears straining to pick up any sound from the house. Unable to stand the waiting any longer, he got out, walked the few paces to the gate and peered sideways, trying to see into the front window, but it was no good. He needed to get closer. Quietly he pushed open the gate and, side-stepping the front door, flattened himself against the wall and slid along to the edge of the window. He could only see the far side of the room. Ahmed was out of sight, but there was Wanda, sitting on a dining chair, talking, then nodding, then talking again. She didn't look alarmed or worried. It seemed she had the situation in hand.

Heaving a relieved sigh, Quentin crept away. He was concentrating so hard on being quiet that he didn't notice the broken paving slab, miraculously missed on his entry, until the front of his foot caught on it and sent him toppling into the hedge. Sharp twigs pierced his arms as he spread them out to save himself, and a vicious thorn tore at his cheek. Cursing silently, he righted himself and hurried to the car, hoping nothing had been heard inside the house. Once inside the car he waited anxiously for any reaction, but none came. Feeling blood trickle down his face, he rifled through the glove compartment, found a tissue and dabbed at his cheek.

Slumping back in the seat, he tried to analyse the facts as he knew them. Halim was responsible for the burglaries, then passing the goods on, sometimes going away to do so but sometimes to Bora, his cousin. So at least two members of the same family were involved. If they couldn't find a way to catch Halim soon, he'd have to tell Jackson about the cousin. Of course, he thought despondently, Linda may have told him already. Bloody hell! If she admits to telling me about him, I'll be in the doghouse. I'll just have to say I forgot. It's this toothache, Inspector – it's affected my memory…

He jerked upright as he heard a door open and close. Wanda appeared and slid into the passenger seat.

'Well?' he demanded. 'Did you learn anything?'

'Nothing useful, that is nothing to lead us to Halim, but I know why Ahmed needs money.'

'Really? Why? Not to send back to his old mother in Turkey, I bet.'

Wanda's face took on a triumphant expression. 'Protectionism.'

'Protectionism? You mean – like the mafia, or something?'

'More or less. He has to pay money to certain people on a regular basis. In return they very kindly refrain from ruining his business. If he defaults on the payments they give him a little reminder.'

'Like a smashed window?'

'Got it in one.'

'And he told you all this in the short time you were in there? What are you, an agony aunt?'

'I had a little trick up my sleeve. I brought the conversation round to the broken window. He said it was vandals at first, but then I told him that my late husband had suffered the same treatment in London at the hands of a gang of extortionists.'

Drawing in a sharp breath, Quentin stared at her. All he knew of Gerry, Wanda's late husband, was what she'd told him when they'd first met two years before – that he was an antiques dealer who'd been involved in a crime. But extortion?

'That's not true is it?' he asked uncertainly.

'Of course not, but Ahmed doesn't know that. And it's not just him – apparently his brother is being forced to pay them, and probably other people too. They're all too scared to blow the whistle.'

'So that's what DS Wilson meant when he said "these people" I suppose. Did Ahmed own up to it?'

Wanda nodded. 'It took some coaxing, but yes. I said I was sorry, and that he should tell the police who they were, but he said he couldn't. If he lost his business he wouldn't know what else to do. I said at least he had his son to support him. I was hoping he might break down, say something about Halim, but no luck, although he did say –

what was it? Yes, he said, "Whatever my son does he does it for me." He looked sad when he said that.'

'So, Ahmed's not in on the robberies, then, but he hasn't put a stop to them either?'

'No.'

'And you don't think he knows where Halim is?'

'I didn't say that. He might know, but there's no way he was going to tell me. He didn't even mention that Halim wasn't around.'

'Did he know Linda was with the police?'

'He didn't seem to. Why are you bleeding?'

Quentin pulled a face. 'I had a fight with a hedge.'

Wanda stifled a giggle. 'The hedge won by the looks of it. They'll be calling you Scarface soon.'

'Ha ha. Did he say anything else?'

When Wanda shook her head Quentin started the engine and pulled away.

'We'll go for a drink before we go back, shall we? Down on the waterfront? Or shall we stop somewhere on the way home?'

'I don't mind.' Wanda suddenly sounded downcast.

'What's up?'

'Oh, nothing really. It's just, well, I feel sorry for him. He's got all that trouble, he's told me about it in good faith and now his son is going to get caught for trying to help him, thanks to us.'

'Come on, Wanda. Whatever the motive for Halim becoming a burglar, it doesn't alter the fact that he's broken into people's houses and stolen from them.'

And got away with it for a long time, he added to himself. If he was honest he rather admired the way Halim had gone about his illicit business. Except for the last couple of times, he'd made sure that the properties he'd targeted would be empty, dealt with any alarms or cameras, broken in and got clean away without leaving any fingerprints or clues behind. He had managed to dispose of the goods without them being traced back to him as well. All in all, a successful operation. If, as now seemed possible, Halim wasn't part of a gang but just working with his cousin, then he was quite clever, too. It must take quite a lot of planning to organise everything himself.

A loud toot made him start, and he swerved to avoid a car that was reversing into a parking space.

'Concentrate, Quentin,' Wanda said.

'Sorry. Look, I agree Ahmed's had a hard time of it, but that's not our fault. We're just doing our jobs. We're detectives, and it's our duty to uphold the law.'

'Yes, but when he finds out I was only there to get information to use against his son, well, now I know he's not involved I feel awful about it. Everyone we've helped catch before has been a criminal, you know, a proper criminal.'

'So is Ahmed, technically. He's harbouring a criminal.'

Wanda's eyes blazed. 'What do you expect him to do? Would you give your son up to the police?'

Quentin pursed his lips and said nothing. He understood exactly how Wanda felt, but crime was crime whatever shape or form it took. He was surprised at her outburst. Perhaps she was thinking of Gerry. She hadn't known her late husband had been involved in dodgy dealings until a week before his death, and hadn't given him away even after he had died. And when it came down to it, who was whiter than white, realistically? Him? Hardly.

'Well, there's nothing we can do about it now,' he said. 'It's our job to find Halim.'

'No, it's not. It's a job for the police. Are we nearly there? I could use a drink.'

Quentin's hopes of several large whiskies faded. When they went for a drink Wanda usually drove, but it sounded as though she didn't want to today. Oh well, he thought, touching the fresh cut on his cheek, it won't hurt me to forego a drink for once.

Chapter Thirty-four

The next morning, Wanda seemed to have recovered her sense of purpose.

'Ring Jackson,' she said as soon as they'd finished breakfast and were alone. 'See if you can find out if Linda's still in custody or whether they've found Halim yet.'

'I can't just demand that he tells me,' Quentin pointed out. 'Still, I'll try. If he's there, and if he'll talk to me. He's under no obligation to tell me anything, and if I get Wilson, he'll tell me to get stuffed.'

Wanda put on a patient face. 'Just ask if they need you to go in, to add any more to the statement you made about Linda. You could ask if they'll be talking to Shelagh. I know they've asked her to go in today, but you wouldn't necessarily know that.'

'OK, I'll ring, see what happens.'

It took him twenty-five minutes to get through to Jackson's office. He was passed on to various people, each insisting that DI Jackson wasn't available and that someone would take a message. Determined not to be fobbed off, Quentin asked if Jackson would call him back and said it was important. Within ten minutes Jackson rang. Alleluia, Quentin thought when he heard Jackson's voice. It's not what you know it's who you know, and a DCI in Scotland Yard was worth knowing.

'Thanks for calling back, Inspector. I was wondering if you needed me to come in again, or if there's anything else you need to ask me.'

'Not just yet, but at some point, yes. I'll call you when I need you.'

'What about my sister?'

'She's agreed to come in today sometime and make a statement.'

'Has she? About Linda, I presume. Has Linda confessed?'

'We're getting there.' Jackson obviously wasn't going to volunteer any information.

Sod it, Quentin thought. I don't see why he can't tell me what I want to know. I'm going for it.

'So has she told you where Halim is? Have you got him?'

A sigh sounded in Quentin's ear. 'Not yet, Mr Cadbury.'

'Quentin,' Quentin corrected.

'Quentin, then. Not yet. A lot of my officers are tied up.'

There was a pause. Quentin heard an indistinct voice in the background, then Jackson's response.

'What's that? OK. Quentin? Apparently Miss Hodges – Linda – says you've got her phone.'

'Does she? I don't think I have.'

'She's says she left it in your car.'

'Oh. All right, Inspector, I'll check.'

'We'll need it. Can you bring it in?'

'Yes, of course. My partner or I will come down as soon as we can.'

Jackson grunted. 'Right. You can leave it at the front desk. Tell them I'm waiting for it.'

'Bugger it,' Quentin said when he rang off. 'They haven't got Halim, so either Linda doesn't know where he is, and I don't think she does, or they haven't got it out of her yet. Anyway, they want Linda's phone.'

'Of course they do,' Wanda said. 'They'll know as well as we do that Halim's number is on it. We'll have to give it to them, but not before we've had a go at it ourselves. Maybe Halim's switched his on today. Where is it?'

Quentin located Linda's phone and passed it to Wanda. She brought up Halim's number but he stopped her from pushing the call button.

'Hold on. What are you going to say if he answers? We don't want to spook him into running even further away.'

Wanda frowned. 'I'll think of something,' she said, pressing the call button. 'It's ringing.' She switched on the loudspeaker facility and Quentin held his breath. If Halim answered, then a single word could blow the whole thing.

The ringing stopped and for a few seconds all they could hear was what sounded like traffic, and a noise Quentin couldn't identify. Then a voice said, 'Linda, I can't talk right now. I'll call you soon, I promise, but don't call me again, OK?' The line went dead.

'He cut me off!' Wanda groaned. 'And I didn't even get to do my impression of Linda.'

'Never mind. What was that noise? Traffic? A crowd of people? And that loud noise, like a hooter?'

Wanda's head jerked up. 'A hooter! That's exactly what it was. A ship's hooter. He's down at the quay, or on a ferry. Come on.' She jumped up and went to get her bag and a jacket.

'If that noise was traffic or crowds he can't be on a ferry, he's waiting for one,' Quentin gabbled, excitement rising.

He snatched the car keys, his wallet and mobile, shouted to his parents that they'd see them later and sprinted out to the car. He'd reversed onto the road by the time Wanda joined him. Within seconds he was taking the corner at breakneck speed, the tyres screeching in protest.

'Not too fast,' Wanda told him. 'If we get stopped for speeding we'll never get there.'

Slowing a little but keeping his foot down as much as he dared, Quentin took the quickest route he knew to Circular Quay, overtaking and weaving in and out of the morning traffic.

'I'll stop as close as I can,' he said. 'You go and park and come when you can. If I need you urgently, I'll call you and you'll just have to leave the car anywhere and risk getting a ticket.'

'OK, but where will you look first? It's a big area and ferries dock on different wharves. He could be on any one of them, or he could be gone by now.'

'It'll depend where he's going and how often the ferry runs there,' Quentin reasoned. 'Some run every hour or less, some only four times a day. I don't know where he'll be, but I've got to give it a go. If I spot him I'll ring you and you can ring Jackson, or anyone if you can't get him.'

They made Circular Quay in record time. When the car had squealed to a halt Quentin jumped out, leaving Wanda to slide into the driver's seat and find a parking place. Deciding to take each wharf in order, he walked up and down the lines of waiting people on the quayside, his eyes scanning the queues and surrounding areas. There were so many destinations. He knew from his day out to Manley Cove that they ran there frequently. If that's where Halim was headed, he'd be gone by now. Hurrying on, he reached the last embarkation point and felt a sense of disappointment. It was useless trying to find someone in such a busy, spread-out place, someone who might not even be here. He checked his watch: forty minutes since they'd made the call. It was feasible that Halim was still here, but finding him?

We're clutching at straws, he thought as his mobile rang. Wanda, he saw when he looked at the display.

'Can't see him,' he blurted before she had a chance to speak.

'I can.'

Thinking he'd misheard, Quentin said, 'What?'

'He's in the café in at the train station round in Alfred Street, probably filling in time before his ferry or train is due to leave. He keeps looking at his watch. Oh, he's on the move. Where are you?'

'By the cruise ship terminal.'

'OK, you come up towards the station and we'll follow him from here. Wait a mo… He's gone into the toilets. Now's our chance. Get a move on.'

Heart thumping and feet pounding the ground, Quentin wound his way through the crowds towards the train station. Please let me get there in time, he prayed silently, hoping Halim would have the longest toilet break in history. I can't let him get away again.

Blessing his running skills he raced towards where he knew Wanda would be. In his desperation to get to Halim the noise and bustle of the quay went over his head, though as he ran he was vaguely aware of the wail of a siren. When the toilets came into view he saw Wanda outside, her gaze fixed on the entrance. He'd nearly reached her when she jumped sideways, hurtling into an emerging figure. Halim.

'Bloody hell,' he muttered, spurting forward and reaching Halim just as he was regaining his balance.

Head down, Quentin bulldozed into Halim, knocking him backwards against the wall. Winded, Halim slumped halfway down the wall before hitting out at Quentin, landing a hefty blow to his stomach. Quentin gasped but stood his ground. He made a grab for Halim's arms, caught one and pinned it to the wall.

'Call the police,' he yelled as he dodged a second blow from Halim's free hand.

As if by magic a large hand came from behind him and caught Halim's flailing fist. An arm and then the whole body of a man appeared beside Quentin. A man in the blue uniform of the Sydney police force.

'We'll take it from here, sir.'

A second policeman approached, waited until Quentin had relinquished his position and, with Halim still struggling, grasped Halim's other arm.

'Quieten down there now,' he said. 'Are you Halim Akan?' When Halim didn't reply he repeated his question.

Halim stopped struggling. He looked from one to the other of the two policemen, then at Quentin, recognition showing on his face.

Quentin felt a beat of triumph. 'Yes, his name is Halim,' he said, watching Halim's face. 'This man broke into my house and stole some valuable items. He's the man who's been burgling homes in Sydney in the last six months.'

As if realizing it was useless to deny it, Halim muttered, 'Yes, I am Halim Akan.'

'Well, well, well, who'd have thought we'd find *you* here.' The sarcastic voice belonged to DS Wilson, who strolled towards them with an air of nonchalance.

Quentin was speechless. How could Wilson have arrived so quickly? He saw Wilson cast a glance at Wanda, and he knew. Of course. Wanda must have rung them when she'd rung him. Or before, as soon as she'd spotted Halim. He looked around for DI Jackson, but couldn't see him.

Wilson took a long look at Halim, then turned to Quentin. 'Can you identify this man as the one who broke into your house?'

'Yes,' Quentin said. 'That's him.'

Wilson nodded, then turned to the uniformed officers. 'OK boys, arrest this man on suspicion of breaking and entering.'

Despite Wilson's disparaging attitude towards him, Quentin was gloating as Halim was told he was under arrest, then led away, his hands cuffed and his shoulders sagging. As he disappeared from sight Quentin caught Wanda's eye and smiled. She smiled back, a smile that told him she was thinking exactly the same as him.

They'd done it.

Chapter Thirty-five

'Well done, Quentin,' Ed Grayson said, giving Quentin a hearty slap on the back. 'Quite a boy you've got here, Herbert.'

It was the next evening, and the family had invited Grayson round to celebrate Halim's arrest. Quentin, whilst revelling in the afterglow of success, was quick to acknowledge that he hadn't acted single-handedly.

'It was just as much Wanda as me,' he said, placing an arm round Wanda's shoulders. 'Go on, tell them how you got the police to the quay so quickly.'

Wanda laughed. 'It was easy. As soon as I saw Halim I called the inspector in charge of the case, DI Jackson. He wasn't there so I told the person who answered what was going on. I didn't want to rely on them being able to get to us in time so I rang the emergency police number and told them that a criminal they'd been looking for was at the quay and that if they didn't move quickly they'd risk losing him. They put me through to someone and I told them where Halim was headed as I followed him.'

Shelagh looked confused. 'But I thought you were on the phone to Quentin the whole time, telling him where to go.'

'I was. I used Linda's phone to call the police. As it happened, Linda had told them her number and they were arranging to put a track on it in case Halim called it, so they would have found me anyway sooner or later.'

'Lucky it wasn't later,' Howard put in. He sat beside Shelagh with little Michael on his lap, looking tired but less strained now his brother was recovering after his accident.

'And they've got his accomplice now, haven't they?' Rosemary asked. 'This cousin you told us about?'

Quentin nodded. 'Yes, Bora his name is. They went to his flat. He wasn't there but they found a packed suitcase. They couldn't find any stolen goods, but they waited and when he came back they nabbed him, searched his car and found something.'

'Not my coins, apparently,' Herbert growled. 'Bastard got rid of them pretty quickly.'

'So, what did they find?' Shelagh demanded.

Quentin gave her an amused look before answering. 'Em, a computer. And a coat.'

'A coat?'

'Huh-huh, a sheepskin coat.'

'Oh my God!' Shelagh gasped. 'You mean the one stolen from my client? But why would he keep that and the computer when he'd got rid of everything else?'

Quentin shrugged. 'Who knows? My guess is Halim broke his own rule and took those when he saw them. Perhaps he intended to keep them for himself then changed his mind and gave them to Bora. Different market to jewellery and medals, so they'd probably need different contacts if they decided to sell them. Anyway, it was enough to charge Bora with handling stolen goods.'

Shelagh looked puzzled. 'But you said earlier that this Bora was the man you cornered when you thought he had the medals. If he knew you suspected him, why didn't he warn Halim?'

'There was a big demonstration in town that day,' Quentin explained.

'Apparently, when Bora did a runner he got tangled up with the crowd. He was pushed over, his phone got damaged and he cracked his head. One of the demonstrators took him to hospital. Jackson says now they've got him as well as Halim they stand a fair chance of finding out who the goods were passed on to. They may even recover some of the items, if they haven't already been sold.'

'Let's hope so,' Rosemary said. 'What I can't understand is how they knew Ed's house and the club would be empty. Ed doesn't go to the salon, nor does anyone at the ex-servicemen's club, so how did they know? What's the connection?'

'There isn't one as far as I can see,' Quentin admitted. 'They must have found out about those another way. Maybe–' He stopped when he saw Ed Grayson's face change suddenly, as though he'd just remembered something. 'Anything wrong, Ed?'

Grayson's expression was a mixture of understanding and embarrassment.

'Betty,' he choked. 'Betty Barker, the cleaner at the club. Since Jean died, she cleans for me at home as well. She knew when I'd be away, and that the medals were being left at the club. And she has her hair done once a fortnight.'

'At my salon?' Shelagh asked.

'I don't know, but I can soon find out.'

'So can I,' Shelagh said. 'The name doesn't ring a bell, but I wouldn't necessarily remember it if she goes to one of the girls. I'll check the appointment book. I can't believe *all* the robberies came through my salon. There's been too many.'

'I don't suppose they all did,' Howard said. 'This bloke may have started on his spree before he teamed up with Linda. She just made it easier for him.'

'I don't know why I didn't think of it before,' Grayson said. 'You asked me about Betty that day at the club. I didn't think–'

'No reason why you should, old chap,' Herbert said, looking at his friend with something Quentin took to be sympathy.

'Of course there isn't,' Wanda said soothingly. 'Don't worry about it, Ed. Ladies often chat and talk about things when they're at the hairdresser's. It's not Betty's fault Linda passed the information on.'

There was a chinking sound as Rosemary tapped a spoon against her glass. 'Quiet everyone,' she said, her face red from the wine she'd drunk. 'A toast, and our thanks to Quentin and Wanda for everything they've done.'

'Hear, hear,' said Grayson, and Quentin felt the familiar glow that praise for a job well done always brought him.

'There's more,' Wanda said when the toast was over. 'Tell them what you found out this morning, Quentin.'

Quentin couldn't help feeling smug when he recalled the telephone conversation he'd had with DI Jackson, and how elated he'd felt at the end of it. He imagined how DS Wilson must have cringed when he heard his boss admitting to Quentin that the information he'd given them had been invaluable.

He grinned now. 'Well,' he said, 'now that Halim's been caught and likely to go to prison, Ahmed's decided enough is enough. He's agreed to tell the police everything he knows about the people who are squeezing money out of him and testify against them in court. So the extortionists could soon be rounded up and their nasty little game stopped once and for all.'

'Thank goodness,' Shelagh said. 'I might have been targeted next.'

'So, you've solved two cases at once.' Rosemary beamed, her pride brimming over. 'Congratulations, Quentin, and you, Wanda.'

'Thank you,' Wanda said, casting a meaningful look at Quentin. 'Now perhaps we can get on with our holiday. I want to go up to Cairns and see the Barrier Reef.'

'Oh, you must do that,' Shelagh urged.

Quentin felt his mother's anxious gaze. 'But you'll be here for Christmas, won't you, dear?'

'Don't press him, Rosemary,' Herbert said. 'He might need to go home. He's got a business to run. Got to earn his living.'

He would say that, Quentin thought. Probably can't wait to get rid of me. He exchanged glances with Wanda, who nodded.

'I think we'll be all right for a while longer,' he said, trying to recall when the last time the whole family had been together at Christmas. 'We'll do a bit of sightseeing and come back for Christmas. After that...'

His words trailed off. After that what? Go back to Greenwich, risk being murdered by a criminal he'd aggrieved not once, but twice?

'After that, we'll see,' Wanda said, picking up on his thoughts. 'I love it here, but I miss my dog and... well, I miss London.'

Quentin pressed his lips together. We'll see. Not exactly a positive statement, but then what else could they say?

Chapter Thirty-six

23 December 2006

After four weeks of travelling around Australia, Quentin and Wanda had returned to Hibiscus Crescent. Wanda was helping Shelagh in the salon, and even Quentin went in on the busiest days to help out. A new girl had been taken on but couldn't start until January, so Shelagh was still short-staffed. Linda's departure had been explained to her clients as being for personal reasons, and unless anyone saw her name in the paper when the court case came up nobody would be any the wiser. So far, there had been no adverse consequences to the business, and the Christmas season was as busy as ever.

On the penultimate day before they closed for the Christmas holiday, Quentin was there helping as much as he could. Making tea and sweeping up wasn't much, but it saved the girls some time. Towards the end of the day, when things were quietening down, Wanda cornered him, took his elbow and steered him out through the front door.

'Where are we going?'

'To see Ahmed. I want to make sure he's all right.'

Somehow Ahmed's business was still open, though he worked alone now, with just the meet-and-greet man to help him. The window had been replaced, and they peered through it to ensure there were no customers inside. They got to the door just as Ahmed was turning the sign round to closed. Ahmed pulled the door open, then frowned when he realized who they were.

'Ahmed,' Wanda said as they hovered on the threshold. 'I'm so glad to see you're still in business. I– I'm sorry about– about the last time we met, about your son.'

The barber gazed at Wanda, then gestured them inside. 'You just do what you had to,' he said heavily. 'I knew he be caught some day. He does it for me.'

Wanda laid her hand on his arm. 'I know, and we're sorry, aren't we Quentin? Still, I'm so glad you've agreed to testify against the people who've been terrorising you.'

Ahmed's brown eyes flickered. 'I can't pay them with the money I earn here without Halim. I take my chance. They are powerful people. They can get to me even if they are in prison. But I do my best. If they kill me–' He shrugged. 'I take my chance.'

'You're a brave man,' Quentin said, feeling humbled. He'd been right about Ahmed – he *was* honest and hard-working. He'd come to Australia to give his family a better life, and although Halim had seemed to dislike working with his father, he obviously thought enough of him to get money for him, albeit illicitly.

'You will testify, too, against Halim?' Ahmed asked.

'I hope not,' Wanda said. 'He's pleading guilty, so is Linda, so they probably won't need to call on us.'

Ahmed nodded. Then he spread his hands and sighed.

'Come on,' Quentin said to Wanda. He felt uncomfortable in the presence of the man whose son he had helped apprehend. 'Best of luck, Ahmed.' Hesitantly he held out his hand. Ahmed looked at it, then took it for a brief moment before letting it go.

In a swift movement Wanda reached up and planted a kiss on Ahmed's cheek, then whirled towards the door. Ahmed looked startled, then a trace of a smile touched his lips.

As they walked back to the salon Quentin's mobile trilled. He went through to the staffroom, looking at the display as he went. Colin, calling from England. He was surprised. Colin usually rang Wanda.

'Hello, Colin,' he said, hoping he wasn't going to be told that anything had happened to either Magpie, his cat, or Wanda's dog, Mozart. 'Anything wrong?'

'No, quite the opposite. I thought you might like some good news.'

'I'm always up for good news, Colin. What, have you won the lottery?'

'Not that good, unfortunately, but I've had a call from DCI Philmore. Apparently, your criminal friend who threatened you has been caught.'

Quentin gasped. 'What? When, where, what happened?'

'Don't know exactly, but someone was killed.'

Quentin gulped, his thoughts racing. He'd killed someone? So the threat against him hadn't been empty – not that there had been any doubt of that.

'Quentin? You still there?'

'Yes, Colin, go on.'

'I don't know the ins and outs but he's banged up and so are the people he was working with. He's been refused bail, so you can come home whenever you like.'

A whirlwind of thoughts flowed through Quentin's brain. His arch enemy caught. It was the best news he'd had since leaving England.

'Quentin? You are coming back, aren't you?'

'I am now,' he said. 'Thanks, Colin. Why didn't Philmore call me himself?'

'He said he tried to ring a couple of times but couldn't get you. Maybe you were out of signal or something. He was going on leave, so he asked me to tell you. You gave him my number before you left, remember, in case anything urgent came up? Anyway, he remembered me from that last case, and he knew I'd be in touch with you.'

'OK, Colin, I expect we'll be back before the New Year. How are Magpie and Mozart?'

'Fine. How's Wanda?'

'She's fine too. I expect she'll ring you later.'

'That'll be nice. OK, bye then, Quentin.'

'Bye, Colin. Merry Christmas.'

'Merry Christmas,' he repeated to himself. 'And now it will be.'

Chapter Thirty-seven

27 December 2006

The argument Quentin had had with his father that morning still rankled. It was a stupid argument, brought about by his father's reaction when Quentin had implied that his stolen coins weren't as valuable as Rosemary's jewellery. Since then, Herbert had hardly spoken a word to him. Determined not to end his visit on a bad note, and to appease his mother, Quentin had waited until his father had gone to his bedroom to get something and followed him in.

'Dad. Look, I didn't mean your coins weren't important. Of course they're important. I just meant that

Mum's jewellery is probably worth more on the open market, that's all. And, you know, Aunt Josie left it to her. It's got sentimental value.'

Herbert's face turned puce, and his mouth twitched as it always did when he was angry about something. Quentin braced himself against the tirade he thought was coming and stood his ground. He strained his ears when his father looked away, mumbling something he couldn't make out.

'What was that?' he asked, wondering if he really wanted to know and tempted to walk out of the room, away from this man who never seemed satisfied with anything he did. Despite all that had happened, despite the success he had achieved, he obviously didn't measure up to his father's expectations. Before Quentin could call on his usual comforting assurance that it didn't matter and he didn't care, Herbert spoke again, more clearly this time.

'I said, you look like him.'

'Who?'

Herbert sighed. 'John. You look like him.'

Quentin's breath caught in his throat and the blood thundered in his ears. What was he saying? Lots of people resembled other members of their family more than their parents. But he hadn't said "Your Uncle John", he'd said simply "John". John, who'd been married to Quentin's aunt, his mother's sister; John, who'd bought the jewellery his mother now owned.

'What do you mean?' he asked, feigning ignorance.

'I think you know.'

Quentin gazed at the man before him, the man he'd called father for twenty-five years. What should he say? That his mother and he had shared a secret for the last two years? He had only found out accidentally, and his mother had sworn him to secrecy. For her sake he had agreed to keep it to himself. Nobody knew – he hadn't even told Wanda.

But Herbert knew.

'How long have you known?' Quentin whispered, sensing that denial was useless.

'Since John married your Aunt Josie.'

Quentin gasped. His father – no, not his father – this man, had known for years that the boy he'd raised was not his son. And he'd said nothing. Nothing, in twenty-five years, either to Quentin or his mother. It was beyond belief.

'I don't blame your mother,' the older man was saying. 'I was away a lot. Seen marriages fall apart when wives are left alone, tied to the house if they've got a child, like she was with Shelagh. Didn't want our marriage to break up. Rosemary had her punishment, seeing John marry her sister. No point in causing a song and dance.'

Quentin's mind was in chaos. This man had suspected his wife of having an affair and that Quentin was the result of that union – a love child, because he knew his mother had loved John.

'But– but–' Quentin's voice failed him. He had so many questions he didn't know where to start. 'Why did you think– I mean, why did you think I would know?'

Herbert shrugged. 'Don't know really. Just… there's been something different between the two of you since the last time we saw you. You've always been her golden boy, couldn't do anything wrong, though God knows you did enough wrong. Still…' He paused and, totally out of character, looked embarrassed. 'Suppose I might have had something to do with that. Always been hard on you.'

For the first time in his life Quentin understood this man's treatment of him, and why he favoured Shelagh. Of course he would. She was his daughter.

'Does… does Mum…'

'Don't see why she should. Never said anything to her, but sometimes I think she thinks I know. Shan't say anything. You neither, nor to Shelagh. No need to rock the boat, especially now John and Josie are both dead.'

Why me, then? Quentin wanted to say. Instead, he stared at this man, who for all intents and purposes, was his father. His name, Quentin knew, was on his birth certificate. So why should his father suddenly blurt out that he'd known for years that Quentin wasn't his son? Just to explain his harsh treatment of him?

'I– I won't say anything, of course, if you don't want me to, but if we both know and you think Mum suspects you know, why not get it all out in the open?'

'No!' his father sounded adamant. 'I don't want any unpleasantness.' He lapsed into silence, a faraway look in his eyes.

Quentin frowned. What was he thinking about and why had he chosen this moment for his revelation? An idea was forming in Quentin's mind. Had his father had an affair when he was abroad? Had he forgiven his wife's indiscretion because he had done the same himself?

His father's voice shattered this theory. 'Truth is, I had a bit of a scare earlier in the year. Thought I had cancer. Gave me a turn, and your mother, but we decided not to tell you or Shelagh unless we had to. As it happens everything is fine, but… makes you think, when you might not have long to live. Just wanted you to know why– well, why things are the way they are.'

A hundred ways that his father could have changed the way things were rushed into Quentin's head. He could have accepted Quentin as adoptive parents accepted their children, or he could have flung it in his mother's face every time there was an argument or when Quentin caused disruption. At worst he could have left her to struggle on alone. He'd done none of these things. He'd suspected, but said nothing to anyone. The opinion that Quentin had held of this man for twenty-five years changed in twenty-five seconds. Underneath that blustering, holier-than-thou attitude was a heart, not made of stone as Quentin had often thought, but a beating heart made of flesh and blood and full of understanding and love. Not love for him, he realized, but love for his wife. And anyone who loved a woman that much couldn't be all bad.

'So…' Quentin stopped, at a loss as to what to say. At last he said, 'You're all right, then, now?'

'So they say, but you never know. Not getting any younger.' Herbert cleared his throat noisily. 'Anyway, my boy, I hope… well, I hope that's cleared the air a bit between us. Not your fault, any of it.'

Not your fault. Of course it wasn't. But, Quentin realized in a rush of clarity, he'd always harboured a sense of guilt, always wondered if somehow he was responsible for his father's treatment of him. And now he knew he was.

'When you came to Australia,' Quentin said, 'I– I knew you wanted to be with Shelagh, but I thought it was to get away from me as well.'

Herbert's eyebrows lifted, creasing his florid forehead. 'Can't say that wasn't part of it. Knew if you had to stand on your own feet you'd get on better, and I was right.'

Quentin grimaced. 'Were you?'

'Yes. Been a rocky road but look at you now. Good detective, own business, contacts in Scotland Yard, decent woman on your arm. Not that I know what she sees in you, woman of the world like that, but there you are. Quite an achievement, all of it.'

Quentin couldn't help a smile. He still wasn't sure whether his father was incredulous of his relationship with Wanda, or envious. Both, probably, he decided, but let it go.

'Thanks,' he muttered.

'Don't thank me, thank your mother. She's the one who's kept the family together, put up with me all this time. Wouldn't be anything without her, that's a fact.'

Quentin couldn't believe what he was hearing. He gaped at his father, this man he'd forced himself to call "Dad". He was actually admitting that he wasn't God's gift to man or even the army.

Herbert looked at him. 'What are you gawking at?'

'Er, nothing.'

'Well, stop gawking and get us a beer.'

Niceties over, Quentin mused. Perhaps I'm dreaming. I'll wake up in a minute. But as he turned to go out his father's voice stopped him.

'By the way, my boy.'

Quentin swung back and waited.

'Thanks for what you've done here, especially for trying to help Ed Grayson and not taking anything for it. Proud of you.'

A lump rose in Quentin's throat and he tried to swallow it. 'Thanks, Dad,' he choked, and fled from the room.

Chapter Thirty-eight

'There you are,' Wanda said when Quentin told her what had passed between him and his father. 'I told you he wasn't as bad as you made out.'

Quentin detected a note of surprise in her voice, but no hint of reproach at being kept in the dark. He had thought long and hard about telling her the truth about his parentage. Honouring his father's wish not to tell his mother or Shelagh, he'd said nothing to them, and wouldn't without his father's permission. But he knew he could trust Wanda with any secret, and he wanted to share his new understanding of his father with someone. He felt a measure of chagrin at not having told her about his mother and John before.

'I don't see that it excuses his treatment of me,' he said, 'but at least he's admitted that he *has* treated me badly. I don't know why he didn't have it out with her, clear everything up from the start and just tell Mum that he knew about John and understood. That would have helped their marriage, I think, saved Mum from having to hide it and saved him from having to stop himself blurting it out whenever he lost his temper.'

'Or your mother could have told him,' Wanda said gently.

Quentin shrugged, guessing that his mother had judged silence as the best and quickest way to overcome the situation.

'When did you find out?' Wanda asked.

'Just after I met you, when she was in London that time. It came out accidentally.'

'That must have been a shock.'

Frowning, Quentin recalled his feelings on that day. 'It was, but the funny thing is when I got used to the idea I was pleased. It explained so much, and I was really glad that I had no chance of turning out like him. Still, he stood by her, and me. I still think things might have been better if they'd had it out at the time.'

'But you know, Quentin—' Wanda paused, as though wondering whether to carry on. As if choosing her words carefully she went on, 'Some people can't talk about things that are painful to them. Some like to thrash it out, but others can't face it. Everyone deals with it differently. Even me.'

'You?'

'Especially me.'

Quentin stared at her. Her cheeks were flushed and there was a faraway look in her eyes, as though she was remembering something from long ago. Ignoring the questions that chased themselves round in his head, he kept quiet.

After a lengthy silence, Wanda said, 'I've haven't told you much about myself before I married Gerry.'

'No, but– Well, I've picked up on a couple of hints recently. You mentioned that someone had hurt you, but that's all. I guessed you'd tell me when you were ready.'

This earned him an appreciative look from Wanda. 'Yes, you've been very good, and I will tell you, but not today. You've already had more than enough to take in this week.'

Quentin took her hand. 'That's fine. It doesn't matter what happened in your past. I'm only interested in our future.' All he knew was that he wanted to be with Wanda, that no other woman compared with her and that he dreaded the thought of another man taking his place.

As if reading his thoughts, she leaned forward and kissed him. 'Good,' she murmured. 'So am I.' Then she drew back and said, 'I'm going to the loo,' and the moment was broken.

* * *

'Goodbye, Quentin dear.' Rosemary's voice quavered a little, and she blinked back her tears as she looked up at her son in the departure hall. It was New Year's Day, though Quentin knew that back in the UK the New Year was only just beginning.

'It's been so lovely having you here,' his mother continued. 'You'll come again, won't you?'

'Try and stop me.' Quentin grinned. Sad though he was to leave his family, he was glad to be going home, and he knew Wanda was, too.

'Goodbye, Rosemary,' Wanda said, hugging her. 'Come over and see us soon. Goodbye, Herbert. Thanks for having me. I've had a wonderful time.'

Quentin's father turned beetroot when she hugged him, then kissed him on the cheek.

'Goodbye, my dear. You're welcome anytime. Both of you,' he added, turning to Quentin. 'Goodbye, my boy. Look after this fine woman.'

'I will, Dad,' he said, taking his father's outstretched hand and shaking it longer and harder than usual. 'And I nearly forgot. I got these for you.' Rummaging in his flight bag he took out a leatherette box and opened it. Coins of various colours, shapes and sizes nestled inside. 'I know they're not as good as the ones you lost, but I thought they might make a start for a new collection.' Practically pushing the box into his father's hand, he turned away, not giving himself time to register his reaction.

A startled, 'Thank you, my boy. Good of you,' reached him, and he knew he had done something right at last.

'Don't forget me, brother dear,' Shelagh said with a mock pout.

Quentin turned to his sister. 'As if I could. Bye, Shelagh. Say goodbye to Howard and Michael for us, and send us a photo when the new baby comes.'

Shelagh hugged him affectionately. 'I will, but I don't want it to be five years before you see him or her. Start saving for your next visit now.'

'OK. We'll set up a special fund.' Quentin checked his watch. 'I think we need to go now, Wanda.'

An hour later he sat on the plane thinking over everything that had happened since their arrival in Sydney. That he had solved another case pleased and satisfied him; but his father's revelation had amazed him. He knew that although things between them might still be strained they would be better. He guessed his father felt the same. Nothing approaching love, but mutual respect was a great step forward.

At the instruction to switch off mobile phones and turn all electronic appliances to flight mode, he reached for his phone. He was about to switch it off when he noticed that he'd missed a call. After pressing the voicemail button he lifted the phone to his ear.

'Hello, Quentin,' said a familiar voice. 'Steve Philmore here. Colin Ward told me you're on the way back to the UK. I believe he's told you about our mutual friend being

in custody, so there's nothing to worry about, but I
wonder if you could give me a ring when you're home and
got over your jet lag. There's something I need to talk to
you about. OK. Safe journey.'

Quentin switched off the phone. So, DCI Philmore
wanted to speak to him? Intrigued, he sat back and gripped
the armrest as the plane began to taxi. His hand brushed
Wanda's, and he wondered whether to tell her about the
message. No. Better leave it until he'd spoken to Philmore.

He would wait. Wait and see.

THE END

235

If you enjoyed this book, please let others know by leaving a quick review on Amazon. Also, if you spot anything untoward in the paperback, get in touch. We strive for the best quality and appreciate reader feedback.

editor@thebookfolks.com

www.thebookfolks.com

More fiction by the author

THE MYSTERY OF THE HIDDEN FORTUNE

Book #1 in the Quentin Cadbury Investigations

Quentin Cadbury, a useless twenty-something, is left to look after his late aunt's London house when his parents head to Australia. But burglars seem determined to break in, and not even the stray cat he befriends can help him. As the thieves are after something pretty valuable, and illegal, he must grow up pretty fast to get out of a sticky situation.

THE MYSTERY OF THE LUCKY CAT

Book #2 in the Quentin Cadbury Investigations

Private detective Quentin Cadbury has his neighbour's recently demised cat in a holdall. Quite why, will be explained. But when he tackles a mugger, his bag gets mixed up with another. This has different contents – some very suspicious goods. Seeing an opportunity to catch a criminal, he blunders into a dangerous situation.

THE MYSTERY ON THE CORNISH COAST

Book #4 in the Quentin Cadbury Investigations

Most people relish going to sunny Cornwall. Not so private investigator Quentin Cadbury, who is forced on a fool's errand by a career criminal who has his teeth into him. Tasked with delivering a package on pain of death, the hapless private eye is sent on a wild goose chase. Can he wrong-foot a master villain?

FREE with Kindle Unlimited and available in paperback and hardback from Amazon.

Other titles of interest

MURDER ON A COUNTRY LANE
by Jon Harris

After the shock of discovering a murder victim, young barmaid Julia isn't too perturbed because local garden centre owner Audrey White was a horrible so-and-so. But when her fingerprints are found all over a death threat, Julia becomes the police's prime suspect. Equipped with an unfetching ankle tag she must solve the crime to prove her innocence.

FREE with Kindle Unlimited and available in paperback!

BRIGHT SPARKS
by Traude Ailinger

The death of a local businesswoman in a house fire has grumpy detective Russell McCord running around in circles looking for the culprit. Sassy journalist Amy Thornton has some ideas of her own. But when the smoke has cleared, can the two crime-solvers put their differences aside and their heads together to work out the truth?

FREE with Kindle Unlimited and available in paperback!

Sign up to our mailing list to find out about new releases and special offers!

www.thebookfolks.com